Honeysuckle Dreams

Center Point
Large Print

Also by Denise Hunter and available from Center Point Large Print:

Just a Kiss
Married 'til Monday
The Goodbye Bride

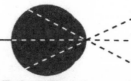

This Large Print Book carries the Seal of Approval of N.A.V.H.

Honeysuckle Dreams

A BLUE RIDGE ROMANCE

Denise Hunter

CENTER POINT LARGE PRINT
THORNDIKE, MAINE

This Center Point Large Print edition
is published in the year 2018 by arrangement with
Thomas Nelson.

The text of this Large Print edition is unabridged.
In other aspects, this book may vary
from the original edition.
Printed in the United States of America
on permanent paper.
Set in 16-point Times New Roman type.

ISBN: 978-1-68324-850-7

Library of Congress Cataloging-in-Publication Data

Names: Hunter, Denise, 1968- author.
Title: Honeysuckle dreams / Denise Hunter.
Description: Center Point Large Print edition. | Thorndike, Maine :
    Center Point Large Print, 2018. | Series: A Blue Ridge romance
Identifiers: LCCN 2018014375 | ISBN 9781683248507
    (hardcover : alk. paper)
Subjects: LCSH: Domestic fiction. | Large type books. |
    GSAFD: Christian fiction. | Love stories.
Classification: LCC PS3608.U5925 H66 2018b | DDC 813/.6—dc23
LC record available at https://lccn.loc.gov/2018014375

Honeysuckle Dreams

CHAPTER ONE

Playing house was just a little too easy for Hope Daniels. Her special chicken casserole waited in the oven, covered with foil; butter beans were simmering on the stovetop; and the yeasty smell of baked rolls hung in the air. Over by the living room window, six-month-old Sam cooed happily from his Pack 'n Play.

She walked over to him, smiling, as her friend's baby kicked happily on his back, making the monkeys on his mobile dance.

"Whatcha doing, sugar? Oh, you're so cute. Yes, you are. Yes, you are! Your daddy sure hit the jackpot with you."

Sam gave a toothless grin, his pudgy cheeks bunching up, his blue eyes sparkling, and she couldn't resist a second longer. She scooped him up and buried her nose in his fresh, clean baby smell.

"Where's that daddy of yours, huh? He's just so late! He's a hard worker, isn't he? Oh, yes, he is!"

She treated Sammy to a session of rapid-fire neck kisses until he was belly-laughing. Oh, this baby! Brady had offered over and again to pay her for watching the little darling, but she'd be darned if he shouldn't be charging *her*.

7

A text dinged in.

Sorry! Customer running late. Be in soon.

She one-handed a text, assuring him all was well, and pocketed her phone. "Daddy'll be home soon for some snuggles, won't he, little Sam."

"Ma, ma, ma!"

Hope's smile drooped a little as she pressed a kiss to Sammy's forehead. It was just babbling, she knew. Probably meaningless. But the idea that he might be missing his mama made her chest ache.

Audrey, Brady's ex-wife, had passed suddenly in a car accident just shy of four weeks ago. Hope—and most of Copper Creek—had no love lost for the woman. Audrey hadn't been a very kind soul, but by all appearances she'd been a decent mother.

Now Brady was juggling full-time fatherhood along with his booming auto repair business, which he ran out of his old barn.

Hope was happy to watch Sam when she wasn't filling a shift at WKPC in Atlanta. Other ladies about town had pitched in too, for a morning or an afternoon. But that couldn't go on indefinitely. Brady really needed to find full-time care for the little guy. Sammy needed stability. Routine.

The baby tugged on her ear, fondling it for comfort the way he did sometimes.

"Where's Boo Bear, huh? Where's your little

lovey?" Hope wandered back over to the crib and bent for the blue stuffed bear that wore a fraying woven hat.

"Here he is."

Sam clutched Boo Bear, and Hope settled in Brady's recliner, a comfy leather thing that all but swallowed her up. She set Sam on her lap, supporting his weight with her crossed leg—he wasn't quite sitting up by himself.

She played pat-a-cake with him, chuckling when he did. She couldn't help it. He had the most infectious laugh. "Wheels on the Bus" was next. He liked the *swish, swish, swish* and the *beep, beep, beep* parts best, so she did those twice.

"Oh, you are just such a happy guy, aren't you?" He was faring much better the past couple of days. She smoothed down his freshly shampooed hair. It was light and fine and baby soft. His skin like a rose petal.

He stared at her with wide, blue eyes that melted her heart. Then he felt for his pacifier, hanging from a ribbon attached to his sleeper, and plopped it into his mouth.

"Getting sleepy, little guy?" It was only eight o'clock, but he'd awakened early from his after-noon nap, and she knew he hadn't been sleeping well at night. All she had to do was look into his daddy's tired eyes.

Sam laid his head on Hope's shoulder, setting

his chubby little hand over her heart. Her womb gave a heavy sigh. Oh yeah, this was just a little too easy.

⊰╫⊱

Brady Collins closed up his barn as Mr. Lewis started his candy-apple red Ferrari 488 GTB. The businessman regularly put the twin-turbo engine to the test at the track in Dawsonville, and the engine had been in need of general maintenance.

Brady gave the man a wave as the car turned down the gravel drive, letting his ears fill with the hum of a perfectly tuned engine. Music to his ears.

He snapped the padlock and started toward his house, checking his watch. Shoot. He felt bad running late like this. Hated taking advantage of a good friend, being dependent on Hope and everyone else. He had to find a nanny or something.

It had been a month now. He should be doing better than this. Single moms did it all the time and made it look easy as pie. But when he was at work he felt guilty he wasn't with Sam, guilty he was putting out one of his neighbors. And when he was at home he worried about shirking his job. He'd worked long and hard to build a reputation with the local sports car enthusiasts. He didn't want to blow it now.

But his heart broke for his son. Sammy had regressed when Audrey died. He'd been fussy and restless the first couple weeks and was no longer sleeping through the night. The pediatrician had assured him nothing was physically wrong. It was just so hard to watch his boy go through this and feel so helpless to comfort him.

Brady reached the walk that led to his two-story farmhouse. The sun was only now sinking behind the north Georgia mountains, offering a reprieve from the sweltering June heat. He swiped his palm across his forehead, probably greasing himself up good. He needed a shower and food, but that would have to wait till Sammy was down for the night.

His pace picked up at the thought of his boy. Hard as this full-time father gig was, it was his son he longed for at the end of a busy day.

The kitchen light was on, shining through the window over the sink, beckoning. He liked it best when Hope tended to the baby. Not only did she come to the house, making it much easier on him, but she clearly enjoyed taking care of Sammy.

Brady opened the back door and pulled off his boots. Heavenly smells wafted his way, making his stomach growl. Something savory, a hint of garlic and yeast. Whatever it was, it was sure to beat the Hot Pocket he'd been fixing to zap in the microwave.

"Hope?" He padded across the kitchen, the wood

floor squeaking in predictable spots. He stopped on the threshold of the living room and took in the sight.

Hope was curled in his recliner, sleeping. Sam was out like a light, his little hand holding a fistful of Hope's dark locks. The lamplight cast a golden glow over them, and heaven's bells if it wasn't the most beautiful sight he'd seen in months.

Hope's hand rested on the baby's back protectively, and her long eyelashes swept over the tops of her cheeks. Sam was tucked under her chin, his mouth slightly parted, the pacifier dangling precariously.

Brady approached quietly, not wanting to give her a fright. "Hope?"

The floor squeaked again, this time louder, and her eyes opened. They darted around before lighting on him, awareness settling in her green eyes.

"I fell asleep," she said quietly. "What time is it?"

"Eight thirty. Sorry I'm so late."

"You're fine." She shifted, glancing down at Sam. "I should wake him, or he'll be up in the night."

"Let's not. He didn't sleep well last night. Probably needs the extra z's."

Brady reached for Sam, and his heart skipped a beat as the back of his hand grazed her inappropriately. "Sorry." He shifted his hands, his face heating, but there wasn't a better way to pick up the baby.

She gave an awkward laugh as she lifted Sammy, placing him in Brady's arms. Color bloomed in her cheeks, but her gaze was fixed on the sleeping baby.

Sam's eyes remained closed, but he'd latched onto his pacifier and was sucking away as Brady tucked him against his body.

"Thanks again for watching him."

"Trust me, it's my pleasure. He ate at seven thirty. And your dinner's in the oven."

"You didn't have to do that, Hope."

Her eyes sparkled as she stood. "But aren't you glad I did?"

"You have no idea."

She leaned close, brushing a knuckle over Sammy's cheek, gazing adoringly at the baby. "Bye, little guy."

She pressed a kiss to Sam's forehead, coming close enough for Brady to notice the golden flecks in her green eyes, the feminine scent of her.

She stepped away and started gathering her purse and some work she'd brought along, her dark-brown hair spilling over her shoulder. "Same time tomorrow?"

He gave a pained look. "I hate to ask two days in a row."

"Then don't." Hope smiled saucily and waved over her shoulder as she left.

Brady took Sam upstairs and held him for an extra minute before setting a kiss on his forehead and laying him in his crib.

His stomach gave a sharp growl, making him decide on supper before shower. He headed back downstairs, made sure the baby monitor was on, and dug into the casserole. He moaned aloud at the juicy chunks of chicken, smothered in gravy and topped with something crispy.

He ate until he was uncomfortably full and was just rinsing his plate when a knock sounded at the front door. He dried his hands on a towel and went to answer it.

His eyes widened at the sight of the woman on his front porch. "Heather."

His former sister-in-law couldn't look any more different from Audrey, with her mousy brown hair and petite frame.

She had a warm smile, though, and she employed it now. "Hi, Brady." Her eyes flickered over his dirty coveralls, and her face fell a little. "Sorry, I should've called."

"Not at all." He opened the door wider and stepped aside. "Come on in. It's good to see you." He'd seen her at Audrey's funeral, of course, but that had been a strained event, everyone still in shock, little time to talk.

"Can I get you something? Tea? Coffee?"

"Decaf?"

"Coming right up." He slipped into the kitchen, and Heather followed. "Jeff's not with you?"

"He's home with the kids. Where's Sammy?"

Shoot. That was probably why she'd come. "I just put him down, but I can get him up—"

"No, no. Don't wake him. Maybe I can just peek in on him?"

"Of course. Up the stairs, second door on the right."

The stairs squeaked as she went up. Brady started the coffee brewing and got out two mugs and milk and sugar.

Heather lived a couple towns over in Dalton, where Audrey had moved after the divorce. His ex-wife had been a late-in-life baby, making Heather ten years her senior. Heather had always been kind to Brady even through the divorce, and though she'd never said as much, he sensed she'd understood her sister's flaws better than most.

He wondered why she was here, if not to spend time with Sam. An uncomfortable foreboding filled his chest, but he shook the feeling away.

Once the coffee was poured, he brought the mugs into the living room and sat in his recliner. The smells of motor oil and brake dust filled his nostrils, making him wish he'd taken the time to shower earlier.

He could hear Heather murmuring softly to Sam through the baby monitor, though he

15

couldn't make out the words. His eyes burned at her tenderness. Apparently she'd exhausted that particular trait in the Parker gene pool, leaving nothing for Audrey. He had no idea how Heather had turned out to be such a wonderful person, but he was glad she'd found a good match in Jeff.

He heard her on the stairs and looked up in time to see her pressing a knuckle to the corner of her eye.

"He's so precious," she said as she took a seat on the end of the sofa closest to him. Her feet barely reached the floor. "I could just stare at him all night. Is he doing any better?"

"I think so. He's not fussy like he was. And he slept through the night a few days ago."

"I hate that he'll grow up without Audrey. I know she had her . . . faults. But she did love that little guy."

"I know she did. And I'll make sure he knows that. And so can you. We should set up a schedule for visits. I want him to know his family, Heather."

She averted her eyes, reaching for her coffee. "I'd like that."

"Do you need milk or sugar?"

"No, this is just fine."

"How are Jeff and the kids?"

"They're faring well. The kids are keeping me busy with baseball and swimming lessons, and Jeff's business is thriving."

"Glad to hear that. How are your parents? They seemed pretty grief-stricken at the funeral, understandably. I hardly knew what to say." The Parkers had never seemed to like him much, though he hadn't a clue why. But they weren't the warmest people, so maybe it wasn't him at all.

Something passed over Heather's features that made the foreboding unfurl in his gut again.

"Well. That's what I wanted to talk to you about." She set her coffee on the coaster and laced her fingers tightly in her lap. Her brown eyes were filled with pity.

"What's wrong? Do they want visitation rights or something? I don't have a problem with that. Like I said, I want Sam to know his family."

According to Audrey, the Parkers had been distant and unaffectionate parents, but visitation was only fair. He wanted his son to know his grandparents, and they did love him in their own way. Plus, Audrey's death had hit them hard, and the baby was the only piece of her they had left.

But judging by the dread rolling off Heather in waves, this wasn't about visitation rights. "You're scaring me, Heather. What's going on?"

"Brady . . ." She closed her eyes and gave her head a shake. "I've been round and round with myself about coming to you with this, but I just couldn't keep it to myself another day. They've hired a lawyer. They want custody of Sam."

Brady reared back, his thoughts scrambling. A useless cloud of fear spread like poison through him.

"They've already filed the petition. You'll be getting served in a day or two, and I just felt you deserved to be forewarned."

"That's ridiculous, Heather. I'm his father. They can't take him away."

She gave him a troubled look, her fingers twisting in her lap. "That's just it, Brady . . . They're saying you're not Sam's biological father."

His lips parted as his heart kicked into high gear. He shook his head, his thoughts in a whirlwind. He and Audrey hadn't been married when she'd conceived. They'd gone to the same high school, but that was years ago, and he'd barely known her before that night. She'd pursued him hard, and he'd been too filled with grief—and alcohol—to resist. The one night that steadfast, reliable Brady loses his mind and of course this happens.

He'd woken the next morning alone and full of regret. He'd been taught better, and he was deeply ashamed of himself. Never again, he promised himself, promised God. But five weeks later a phone call had assured him that once was all it took.

Audrey hadn't been with anyone else since she'd broken up with her boyfriend almost a

18

year before, she told him. The baby was his. She couldn't bear to give it up.

Brady didn't want that either. Audrey had seemed nice enough. They got to know each other over the next couple months, and he felt compelled to make this work. He proposed on her birthday, and she seemed truly happy as she threw her arms around him, saying yes over and over again.

"That's absurd." His voice sounded thready and strained. His heart raced, and his mind was spinning. Spinning out other scenarios. Scenarios where she might've lied to him. She'd been capable, he knew that now. But she wouldn't have lied about this.

Would she?

Heather shifted on the sofa. "Mom said Audrey told her some things one night when she'd had too much to drink—that she was already pregnant when she met you."

"That's not true." If he said it, maybe it would chase away this fog of doubt enclosing him. "He has my eyes. My chin. Everyone says so." He had the insane urge to run upstairs and scoop Sammy into his arms. But that wouldn't protect either of them from this nightmare.

"Listen, Brady . . . I don't know if it's true or not. Maybe it was just drunken rambling. But I thought you had a right to know what's going on. A little forewarning before they . . ."

19

Her words hung in the space between them, the pity in her eyes doing nothing to ease his fears.

"What? Before they what?" His tone was a little sharp, but he didn't have the capacity to feel guilty about it.

"As part of the custody complaint, my parents made a motion requesting a paternity test." She gentled her voice. "I'm afraid the judge is ordering it."

He blinked. How could they make him do this? "My name's on the birth certificate! I'm his father! I've been taking care of him. I'm all he has now. Your parents have only seen him a dozen times in his whole life."

"I'm sure you'll have legal recourse even if the paternity test is negative. Surely."

"It won't be negative. I'm his father."

But what if he wasn't?

Fear took full-fledged flight. He let himself go there for just a second. Finding out he wasn't Sam's father. Being forced to turn him over to the Parkers. Having no legal rights to see his boy again. The feeling of devastation left him drained. A knot tightened his throat, and his eye sockets stung.

Heather's eyes had filled with tears. "I'm so sorry, Brady. You don't deserve this. My sister, God love her, had a way of leaving messes everywhere she went. But this one surely takes the cake."

He remembered something then. Something that hadn't seemed important at the time but now seemed critical. "He was almost four weeks premature."

She tilted her head sympathetically. "But he did have a low birth weight. It's possible he was truly early."

He allowed that thought to comfort him for a long moment. Audrey hadn't eaten enough during pregnancy, no matter how much he'd encouraged her. She'd been so worried about losing her figure, she'd only gained fifteen pounds. That could've attributed to Sammy's low birth weight too.

He swallowed hard. "Who are your parents saying is the biological father?"

"Audrey never told them. Just said he was no good and definitely not father material."

As opposed to Brady? Everyone knew he was the reliable sort. He made a good living, and hadn't Audrey reminded him time and again that he always did the right thing? At first she'd said it as a compliment. But soon after the wedding she'd flung it in his face like an insult. Had she only been using him all along?

His friends believed she'd gotten pregnant on purpose, tricked him into marriage. Sometimes he'd half believed it himself. But he'd never suspected this. Not for a second.

He couldn't let himself believe, though, that

21

Sammy wasn't his. He'd take the test. He had no choice anyway, apparently. But no matter the results, Sammy was his son. Brady knew how it felt to have a parent give up on you. No way was he doing that to Sammy. He'd lay down his life for the kid. Fight for him till his last breath.

He looked at Heather, strength and energy pulsing through him at the decision. "Forewarned is forearmed. Thanks for letting me know."

CHAPTER TWO

Hope pointed her red Civic toward Atlanta, set her cruise control for sixty-five, and eased back for the hour and a half drive. She'd been filling a shift the past six weeks at Oldies 102.4, one of the state's biggest stations, while their regular DJ was on maternity leave.

It was a great opportunity. Her dream had always been to land at a major station, and she hadn't expected to have the opportunity so early in her career, even temporarily. But her regionally popular call-in show, *Living with Hope*, had caught the attention of WKPC.

Her home station, however, had recently been bought out, and a change in direction had cost her a full-time job. Fingers crossed, the exposure from this temporary gig would net her another opportunity—perhaps something bigger.

Her phone rang, and she took it on her Bluetooth.

"Are you headed to Atlanta?" her best friend—and Brady's sister—Zoe said by way of greeting.

"Well, good morning to you too."

"Sorry, I'm calling between deliveries so I have to make it fast." Zoe owned a peach orchard, and her new market, the Peach Barn, was a huge success. "So, are you? On your way to Atlanta? Did you remember the claim ticket?"

"Yes, ma'am, I surely did."

"Oh, thank you. You're a lifesaver."

Hope had agreed to pick up Zoe's engagement ring, which had been resized. Twice. The jeweler had botched it the first time. Zoe was engaged to Brady's best friend, Cruz. High school sweethearts, true love, soul mates, blah, blah, blah.

"I'll pick it up after my shift. Then I'm headed to Brady's to watch Sam for a few hours."

"That's a lot of running around. You're such a doll to help him out. You have no idea how much he appreciates it. I feel bad I can't babysit more."

"Your hours are crazy at the Peach Barn, and you've got a daughter, a fiancé, and a wedding to plan. What have I got but my work?" Well, didn't that just sound bitter. "Any word yet about the paternity test? I've been praying my heart out."

Brady had taken the test almost a week ago after consulting a family lawyer his dad had put him in touch with. He'd also responded to the Parkers' custody petition with a counter complaint claiming that he should have custody of Sam. The hearing for temporary custody was next week.

"Not yet. He hasn't said much, but I know the wait is killing him. I don't know what he'll do if he's not Sammy's father. He loves that kid so much. We all do. I can't believe even Audrey would do something so cruel and selfish."

"What if it's true?" Hope said. "Surely it would

weaken Brady's chance at permanent custody."

"I'd have to think so. And the final hearing would be several months away yet."

If that happened, Brady should at least get visitation rights during those months. But Hope was getting ahead of herself. The test results weren't even back, and surely the judge wouldn't give the Parkers temporary custody.

"I don't understand why the Parkers are so set on this anyway. From what I hear they didn't do such a great job the first time around. And they've got to be getting up there in years. They'll be eighty by the time Sam graduates. How could that be in his best interest?"

"I don't get it either. Hopefully the test will show Brady's the father, and all this will go away."

"Here's hoping."

"Oh—I've got a customer coming in," Zoe said. "Hey, you know we're the same ring size. Would you just slip it on and make positively sure it fits? I don't want to make another trip down there."

"Sure thing. See ya."

"I'll stop by Brady's house and pick it up after I close."

"Sounds good."

When Hope arrived at the station she fussed with the collar of her blouse and straightened her skirt, then stepped out into the carpeted hall. The place took up an entire three-story building and made the station in Dalton look like the rinky-dink operation it was. Her time here was almost over, and she hated to see it end. She had no idea what she was going to do next.

She was grabbing a water bottle from the vending machine in the break room when Diana Mayhew, the operations director who'd hired her, passed by.

The woman backtracked, peeking around the doorframe. "Everything going all right?"

"Just terrific."

Diana gave a warm smile. "We should catch up. Stop by my office before you leave."

"Of course."

Eight hours later Hope pulled off the headphones as "Addicted to Love" came on the air. It amazed her how quickly time passed when she was working. She loved her job. She'd been a little nervous here at first, unaccustomed to such a large listening audience. But big or small, it was all the same, really. She loved being able to touch people in all walks of life. Maybe make them laugh, think twice about something, or just keep them company. Brighten their day. It was a pleasure.

She said good-bye to the producer and announcer. Then she stopped in to chat with the gals in the front office before heading over to see Diana.

The director was on the phone when Hope

peeked in. Diana waved her in, and Hope took a seat in the chair opposite the desk as her boss wrapped up a phone call—to one of the salespeople, sounded like.

Her eyes drifted over the professionally appointed office. Natural daylight poured in from the wall of windows. A large desk of dark, glossy wood dominated the room and matched the tall credenza behind it. The shelves were laden with hardcover books, family photos, and beautiful, real plants that made Hope wish her thumb weren't as black as coal.

Diana hung up the phone. "Sorry about that. I just got new demographics one of our key salespeople needed."

They caught up for a few minutes, chatting about the station and industry news. When the conversation petered out, Hope glanced at the clock on the wall.

"I'm glad you called me in, Diana. I wanted to thank you again for giving me this opportunity. I'm really enjoying it, and I'm learning a lot."

"Well, you're very good at what you do, Hope. You have a way of connecting with people. Our numbers are remaining quite steady, which Darren was concerned about."

Darren was the station's GM, the head honcho. "Well, if he's pleased, I'm pleased."

"I called you in this afternoon because I have some wonderful news for you."

"Oh?"

"You may have heard that Dirk Crawford is retiring in a few months."

"Of course." Dirk had been on oldies for so long he was practically a legend in the region. He was the drive-time jock and a well-loved personality.

"Darren and I have spent a lot of time kicking around names for a replacement. We'd like to promote from within, but neither of us felt good about our options—until you came along."

Wait. What? Her heart was suddenly beating like the kick drum to an eighties dance tune.

"As I said before, you have a lot of talent. And, Hope, I really love the call-in show you did up north. You're very good with people. Tender, yet straightforward, and so wise."

"Thank you."

"I spoke to Darren a couple weeks ago about hiring you to fill Dirk's slot, and I'm excited about the possibility of bringing *Living with Hope* to our station on a nightly basis. As you know we're catering to middle-aged listeners, mostly women. Married, divorced, people with later-in-life problems. I think our listeners would benefit from a show like yours. You had a psychology minor—I have that right, don't I?"

"Yes."

"Darren agrees with me, Hope. So we'd like to ask if you're interested in Dirk's slot."

A full-body shiver passed over her. "Oh, wow. I-I don't know what to say."

"You don't have to say anything right now. I understand this would require a relocation, but we're several months away from October, so we have a little time. Take a few weeks and think it over." She checked her watch. "I'm sorry to have to wrap this up just when things are getting interesting, but I have a conference call in one minute."

"Oh. No problem." Hope stood, her eyes meeting Diana's and locking there.

Diana chuckled. "I think you're in a bit of shock. Just give it some thought, and we'll chat more later." She picked up her handset, clearly an indication that Hope needed to leave.

"All right, then. Thank you, Diana. I appreciate your belief in me."

"I'm confident you'll make the right decision."

Twenty minutes later Hope was floating on cloud nine as she entered the jewelry store. A full-time job at a large station. Somebody pinch her. Was she really ready for this? Ready to relocate and move away from her roots? Her friends?

The air-conditioning in the shop felt great in the sweltering June afternoon. The store smelled like flowers and money and boasted plush black carpet with sleek mahogany cases.

Hope waltzed up to the counter where a pretty

woman stood with her coiffed blonde hairdo and red lipstick. She smiled at Hope as she placed an expensive-looking watch back in the case. "May I help you, dear?"

"Yes, I'm here to pick up a ring that was being resized. Zoe Collins." She handed over the claim ticket.

"Let me get that for you, hon. Be right back." The woman slipped through the door at the back of the store.

Hope wandered to the next case and began perusing the sparkly diamond rings. Sometimes she envied Zoe and Cruz, so in love, with a darling four-year-old daughter in tow. Their lives were already underway, when Hope just felt . . . stuck.

You are not stuck.

She had her work, and an exciting opportunity at WKPC. If her love life lagged a little behind that of her friends, well, it would keep. She was only twenty-four, still young even by Southern standards. There was plenty of time for a husband and a few little cherubs.

But not plenty of time to get to Brady's. She checked her watch and said a quick prayer against the traffic. She'd made it all the way around the store before the saleswoman returned.

"Ah, here we are." The woman opened a box and slipped the ring from its sleeve.

Boy howdy, it was a gorgeous piece, winking

under the lights like the North Star. It was a princess cut with a band that was just a little old-fashioned. Cruz had chosen well.

Hope took the ring and slipped it on, forcing it over her knobby knuckle. She admired the ring, waggling her fingers a little so the lights caught it just right, imagining for a moment that it was really hers. From a man who was head over heels for her.

The woman was already packing away the box and slipping it into a pretty handled bag. She handed it to Hope. "I'm so sorry about the hassle. I put a bottle of jewelry cleaner in there for your inconvenience."

"Thank you." Shouldering her purse, she made her way for the door, pulling the ring off as she went. Only the ring didn't budge.

She managed the door and headed for the tiny parking lot behind the brick building, tugging at the ring as she walked. She could see now that her fingers were swollen, her palms red and blotchy. She was holding water. She'd gone to the diner last night and had their yummy ham special. Stupid ham.

She glared at the diamond. Stupid ring. She twisted and tugged. Tugged and twisted. It wouldn't budge past the knuckle. What if they had to cut it off? *Oh, Lord, please.* Zoe was going to kill her.

She gave up on the ring, buckled her seat belt,

and sent Brady a quick text. Then she headed north.

The ring was likely the right size. It had gone over her knuckle easily enough. She'd soap it up at Brady's. It would slip right off.

CHAPTER THREE

Brady straightened over the engine of the Porsche Boxster, stretching his back. He looked over his shoulder where Sam was cooing from the baby backpack.

"How you doing back there, Sammy?"

"Ba-ba-ba-ba!"

"I hear you, buddy. Almost done."

Brady dragged his hand across his face. It was hot as a furnace in this old barn. He had a brand-new metal building—air-conditioning and all—on the other side of his house, but he'd loaned it to Zoe when her barn burned down a couple months ago. It was the temporary home of his sister's new market, the Peach Barn, until her old barn was rebuilt. That day couldn't come soon enough for him.

He checked the oil, then topped it off and dropped the hood of the trunk. "Hope's coming over soon, you know that?"

"Ba-ba-ba-ba!" Boo Bear landed on the cracked concrete floor, and Brady fetched it, dusted it off, and handed it back.

When he shut off the engine, he heard the sound of an approaching vehicle. Too early to be Hope. The engine idled a little high, and it was no sports car either. He wiped his hands on a rag and left the shade of the barn.

A Buick sedan approached. At the sight of Calvin Jones's car, Brady's heart took off like a Maserati from the starting line.

He released a deep breath. *Dear God, please. Let it be good news.*

He'd been expecting the paternity test results any day, but somehow he'd thought the lawyer would call. Maybe the results were not what he hoped. Maybe Calvin had felt the need to deliver the bad news in person.

Brady's legs felt wobbly, and Sam's weight on his back suddenly felt like a ton of bricks. He watched as Calvin got out of the car, and he fought the sudden urge to flee.

The look on Calvin's dark-skinned face didn't make him feel any better. The lines on his forehead, the tightness at the corners of his brown eyes, the strained smile. Brady had a feeling the manila file in the man's hand could change his whole world. Could rip his son right from his arms. Drawing a breath seemed an impossible task.

Calvin extended a hand. "Afternoon, Brady."

"Calvin." His gaze flickered down to the file. "You've got the test results."

"I'm afraid it's not what we'd hoped, son."

Oh, God. Please no. This can't be happening.

Brady's breath left his body in a rush. Sammy

wasn't his. Wasn't his son. A burn started at the backs of his eyes. A thickness built in his throat, aching, strangling.

"I can't tell you how sorry I am," Calvin said. "I just got the results, and I knew you'd want to know right away."

Brady turned away, needing a minute. An hour. A month. A lifetime. He tipped his head back and closed his eyes. How could this be happening? Tears pushed at his eyelids. He felt so . . . lost. He'd lost the one person who belonged with him.

His real mom had ditched him. Though his aunt and uncle had adopted him as a baby, he'd always been keenly aware that he had a drug-addicted mother out there somewhere and a father who didn't know—and probably didn't even care— that he existed. His sister was really only his cousin, and his dad was only his uncle.

He'd never felt more alone. And that didn't even touch on the biggest problem. He might have no legal claim on Sam now. And he couldn't bear to think about his boy being raised under the Parkers' impossibly high standards.

It took him a long moment to blink back the tears gathering in his eyes, get himself under control. He cleared the lump from his throat before he faced Calvin again.

"I sure am sorry, Brady," Calvin said. "I wish I had better news for you."

A sweat had broken out on Brady's forehead.

He grabbed one of Sam's bare feet and held on tight. "But I can still fight for him, right?"

Calvin's gaze shifted away. "Well . . . sure. You can always try. But as you know, the hearing for temporary custody is next week. And the Parkers will no doubt be filing a petition to dismiss our counterclaim."

"What does that mean?"

"It means they'll be arguing that since you're not the biological father you shouldn't be considered for custody at all."

"But I'm the only father Sam knows!"

"We can file a response to their motion stating that the case should be argued as a best-interest case—doing what's in the child's best interest, regardless of the paternity test. The judge will hear the motions next week and make a determination about whether this ends here or goes on to a final hearing. If he finds in our favor next week, he'll also be deciding who gets temporary custody of Sam until the final hearing."

"And if he doesn't find in our favor?"

Calvin shifted. "Then he'll grant the Parkers permanent custody of Sam next week."

Brady's breath left his body. He could lose Sam next week? Lose him forever?

"Don't despair just yet. There's still a chance the judge will want to try the case on a best-interest standard."

How could this be happening? Brady curled his hands around Sam's feet as if he could hold him close forever.

"I have to be honest, though, Brady. Even if the judge decides to hear arguments about Sam's best interest, you've still got a mountain to climb. You're a young, single man with no blood connection to the child. You're up against biological grandparents, both of whom would be there full-time for Sam."

"But they're sixty years old! They'll be almost eighty when Sam graduates high school. And they weren't even good parents to Audrey and Heather."

Calvin cocked his head, his gaze sharpening. "Was there abuse of any kind?"

Oh, how he wished he could say yes. "Maybe not abuse per se. It's like I told you—they were distant and unaffectionate. Their standards were impossibly high. Their relationship with Audrey was strained because of it."

"Well, I'm sorry to hear that. But I don't think it's going to sway the courts much. We can look into it, of course, if things go our way next week, but without evidence of abuse, our chances aren't great. I'm sorry, Brady."

"But his mom just died, for crying out loud. And now you're telling me they could rip him away from the only home he knows?"

"I know it's not fair."

Brady scrubbed his hand over his face. "I can't believe this is happening."

Behind him, Sam began to fuss. Brady mindlessly unhooked the backpack and pulled the baby free of it, letting the empty carrier drop to the ground. The little guy's head was sweaty, and his sleeper was wet from being pressed up against Brady's back in the hot barn.

"Brady . . . I know this is a terrible shock. But maybe the Parkers would provide some stability. You've admitted you don't have regular childcare for Sam." His eyes swung to the carrier and back to Brady. "You can't expect to carry him around indefinitely. And I can't imagine any judge would approve of you working over a hot engine with a baby."

"Whose side are you on?" He'd never endanger Sam. He had to work, didn't he? And there'd been nobody to watch him today until Hope arrived. Anger burned and swelled inside. It didn't help that Calvin might have a point.

The attorney held up his hands. "I'm just trying to show you how the judge might view your situation. If I understand correctly, you've been passing childcare responsibilities around a bit. The court wants to see more stability than that."

"Audrey just died a month ago, and I was used to having Sam only on weekends. I'm still trying to figure out how to juggle work and child-

38

care. It's taken a while to get my feet under me."

"Well, I suggest you get them under you quickly. I said it before, but it's even more critical now. You should have a full-time care-giver before that hearing next week."

"I'll work on it." It wasn't as if he hadn't tried, but he was going to have to try harder.

Stupid Audrey. This was all her fault. She'd lied to him. Made a fool of him. Suckered him in, and like an idiot he'd swallowed her lies, hook, line, and sinker. How could he even be angry at her now, when she was gone? But he wanted to tell her exactly what he thought of her selfishness. He wanted her to know she was wrecking his life. Crushing his heart. That their baby boy might end up being raised by the parents she'd spurned.

And yet . . . if Audrey hadn't lied to him, he wouldn't have Sam at all.

His eyes fastened on Calvin's, desperation swelling inside. "Is there anything else I can do to have a better chance at becoming his . . . guardian?"

Guardian. It was a big step down from Daddy. Sammy grew fussier, and Brady glanced around for Boo Bear, finding him on the ground again a few feet away. He picked up the bear and brushed it off.

When he straightened, the crunch of gravel drew his attention. Hope's Civic was coming round the bend.

"The regular caregiver is priority one," Calvin said over Sam's fussing. "If the judge decides our way next week, we can go ahead with the petition, but you're looking at a lot of legal expenses—"

"This is my son we're talking about. Maybe not by blood, but he's mine just the same."

Boo Bear hadn't solved Sammy's crisis. His little body stiffened, and he began wailing in earnest.

"I know this is difficult. I wish I had better news."

Brady barely noticed Hope pulling up beside Calvin's sedan as he bounced Sam in his arms.

The car door slammed, and he was vaguely aware of Hope approaching as thoughts spun in his head. Crazy thoughts that had him packing bags and going on the run.

"Brady, what's wrong?" she asked.

His gaze swung toward her, but his head was still spinning. His stomach churned uneasily. The compassion in her eyes pulled at him.

"I-I got the test results back," he choked out. "He's not mine."

"Oh no. Oh, hon, I'm so sorry." She reached for Sam without taking her eyes from Brady's. The baby went willingly, snuggling into her neck, rubbing his sleepy eyes.

"I'm Brady's attorney, Calvin Jones."

"Hope Daniels."

Calvin's eyes sharpened on Brady. "I didn't realize the two of you were—"

Sam's wail drowned out the last of Calvin's sentence.

She looked at Brady. "Why don't I just take Sammy inside."

"I think he's hungry."

"I've got it covered. Take your time." With one last pitying glance she headed toward the house.

"You didn't tell me you were engaged," Calvin said once Hope was inside. "Brady . . . that might put a different spin on things."

Why in the world did Calvin think they were engaged? Brady gave his head a shake. "I'm not—Wait. What do you mean, a different spin on things?"

"Well . . . a judge tends to look more favorably on custody when there's a mom *and* a dad. The Parkers already have that going for them. This balances the scales a bit. It might help things go our way in next week's hearing. And it might also help in the final hearing. Especially if one of you could stay home with Sam full-time."

Brady's flagging hopes went buoyant. "So . . . I'd actually have a chance of permanent custody if—I mean because—I'm engaged? That's what you're saying?"

"That's exactly what I'm saying." Calvin clapped him on the shoulder. "This is good news,

Brady. It makes for a better argument to try this case on a best-interest standard."

Brady swallowed hard. "That is great news." And it was. If only he really did have a fiancée.

"I'll get that response filed and be in touch about next week's hearing."

"Okay. Sounds good. Thank you, Calvin."

"Hang in there, Brady. This isn't over yet."

They shook hands, and moments later as Brady watched the sedan roll down the drive, he wondered what in the world he was doing.

CHAPTER FOUR

"Here come your num-nums. Open up, baby doll. *Vrrrrroooom!*" Hope slipped the bite of baby food into Sam's mouth. He giggled at her sound effects, the pureed peas dripping from his lower lip.

Hope dabbed with the bib. "Is that funny? You think that's funny, huh?"

She stuck the spoon back into the jar and dished up another bite. But her smile fell from her face as she thought of Brady. She couldn't get the look on his face out of her mind. His knitted brows and bloodshot eyes, the strain around his mouth that told her he was about to lose it.

She hadn't seen that look on his face since Audrey had left him. And she'd seen enough of it then that she'd give a year's wages not to see it again.

"Muh-muh-muh-muh!"

She gave Sam another bite, wondering when Brady was going to come in. She'd heard the attorney leave a good ten minutes ago. He probably needed a few minutes to himself. This had to be breaking his heart.

As if she'd conjured him up, the kitchen door opened and Brady stepped inside. He didn't look much better. He gave her a tight smile and set the baby carrier and Boo Bear on the kitchen counter.

He gave Sammy a long look, a muscle flickering in his jaw, his eyes going a little glassy before he turned and opened the refrigerator door.

Hope sat back in her chair. "Are you all right? What am I saying, of course you're not all right. I'm so sorry, Brady. I just can't believe this is hap-pening."

"That makes two of us."

"Is there anything you can do? What did your attorney say?"

"Muh-muh-muh-muh!"

Hope fed Sam another bite, scooping up the bit that dribbled down his chin. The baby slapped his palms on the high chair tray and laughed at the noise it made.

Brady was still standing in front of the fridge, one hand on the open door, the other braced above the freezer.

"Brady?"

He straightened, shut the door, and turned, a puzzled look on his face. "Why'd he think we were engaged?"

"What?"

"My attorney. For some reason he thought we were engaged."

Oh. The ring. Hope held out her hand. "He must've seen this."

His eyes flickered to hers, frowning. "Where'd that come from?"

Hope gave a wry laugh. "It's Zoe's. I picked it

up for her, and it got stuck and then . . . Well, never mind." Bigger fish to fry. "So what did your attorney say? What's the next step?"

"He said the Parkers would be filing a motion to dismiss my counterclaim. Saying that since I'm not the biological father I shouldn't even be considered for custody."

Hope gasped. "That's not right!"

"If the judge agrees, they'll get custody of Sam next week, and it'll all be over."

"Oh, Brady . . . He doesn't really think that'll happen, does he?"

"At first he told me it just might."

"At first? He changed his mind?"

His eyes latched onto hers for a long minute. "When he thought we were engaged . . . he said a married couple would actually stand a fighting chance. That it evened things out a little."

Hope winced. "Oh. And when you told him you weren't engaged?" It was a real shame. Brady would be a better parent for Sam than the Parkers, married or not.

Sammy pounded the tray. "Muh-muh-muh!"

"Okay, okay, Mr. Impatient." Hope scooped the last bite into Sam's mouth. She glanced at Brady, who still hadn't answered. He had a funny look on his face. One she couldn't quite read.

"Brady? What did he say?"

His eyes looked everywhere but at her. "I-I didn't tell him."

45

"You didn't tell him?" Her voice rose at the end of the sentence. But then she bit her lip and cleaned up Sam's face and wiped the tray with a wet wipe.

Brady was suddenly in the chair next to her, his knees almost touching her thigh, an enigmatic look on his face. "Hope . . . I have a crazy idea."

She gave him a sideways look. "Oookay . . ."

He held her gaze for a long moment. Long enough for her to notice the flecks of silver in his blue eyes.

"What if we *were* engaged?" he said.

Hoo-boy. She reared back. "We, as in . . . you and me? But we've never—we don't even . . ." Hope shook her head. No words. She had no words. An awkward laugh escaped.

"Not for real. Just, you know, until . . ."

"Oh." Temporarily. Fake.

"The courts could very well side with the Parkers, Hope, right out of the gate. They might not even get a chance to hear why it's in Sam's best interest to stay with me."

She couldn't believe it. It seemed crazy. Any objective person could take one look at Sam and Brady and tell what a good father he was.

"A fake engagement won't even be necessary unless the judge finds in my favor next week. But if he agrees to hear the arguments for what's in Sam's best interest at the final hearing, Calvin said a two-parent household could be just

46

what we need to tip the scales in our favor."

We. Our. Oh, that sounded awfully nice.

But she imagined all their friends and family. How would they play this off with them? She and Brady had been friends forever. Just friends.

At first, in high school, he was just Zoe's older brother. Then after graduation Zoe had taken off to tour with her band, Brevity, and Hope had been so busy with college and working, she'd only seen Brady from time to time. But once she'd gotten her degree and taken the weekend job managing the Rusty Nail, she'd started running into him more often. They became friends, and even began flirting a bit here and there. Hope had started thinking that maybe . . .

But then Audrey had entered the picture.

Brady sank back in his chair and scrubbed his hands over his face. "I don't know what I'm thinking." He palmed his eyes. "I'm losing it. I'm flipping losing it."

Hope rubbed his arm, wishing she could take away his pain. Poor guy. He so didn't deserve this.

"No, you're not. Come on, hon, you're just upset. Who can blame you after the news you just got? It's really not such a crazy idea . . . I mean, if it would help you get custody, I'd do it in a heartbeat, you know?"

His hands fell away, his eyes locking onto hers for a long moment. "You would?"

"Of course I would." It was just a matter of weeks or . . . maybe months? If it would get him Sam, she'd be doing them both a service. She gave him a lame smile. "What's a little fake engagement between friends?"

His eyes fixed on hers until she warmed under his perusal. Brady might be only a friend, but he was all kinds of handsome with that black hair and those piercing blue eyes. It was pretty intense having all that attention laser-focused on her.

"Really?" he said. "You'd do that for me?"

"For you and Sam? Of course I would." She squeezed his hand. It was a small price to pay.

Sammy held out his arms, and she stood to lift him from the chair. "Now that that's settled, you'd better help me get this ring off or your sister's going to kill me."

CHAPTER FIVE

The honorable Judge Alders looked to be in his sixties. His bushy eyebrows perched over a pair of wire-rimmed spectacles, and he seemed to wear a perpetual frown. The courtroom lights shone off his balding crown as he hunched over his bench, peering at documents through his bifocals.

Brady squirmed in his chair behind the defendant's table and refrained from looking over at the Parkers. Both sides had just spent five minutes defending their positions—a total of ten minutes would decide whether Brady should even be considered as a potential guardian.

In a matter of minutes he could be ordered to surrender Sam and give up his rights to see him ever again or even know how he was doing or where he was living. It seemed impossible that it had come to this.

Calvin had done everything he could to sway things in Brady's favor. He'd informed the judge that Brady was engaged and that his fiancée was Sam's full-time caregiver. Since Hope's temporary job in Atlanta was now over she'd agreed to this. Brady had insisted on paying her a decent wage, and she'd still work weekends at the Rusty Nail. He was sure that babysitting wasn't her dream job, but she was a good enough friend not to say so.

The judge shuffled the papers and pushed his glasses up his nose as he looked out to address the nearly empty courtroom.

This was it. Brady clenched his hands in his lap. His lungs seemed to forget how to operate.

"Breathe," Calvin whispered.

Brady sucked in a lungful of air and blew it out, not taking his eyes off the man who would decide Sam's fate.

Judge Alders folded his robed arms on the bench. "This is an unusual case. To my knowledge a custody case has never been brought in Georgia between biological grandparents and a nonbiological father."

Brady's heart skipped a beat. Was that good or bad? He forced himself to remain still through the long pause.

"Mr. and Mrs. Parker, I'm deeply sorry for the loss of your daughter. As biological grandparents you certainly have the right to make a custody complaint." He looked back down at the documents. "According to the records, Mr. Collins was regular with visitation rights prior to the mother's death. And since then he's had permanent custody. Although the court-ordered paternity test was negative, he clearly cares a great deal for the child."

The judge cleared his throat. "The plaintiffs argue that since the defendant is not the biological father he reserves no custody rights whatsoever. However, I'm inclined to hear arguments on what's in the child's best interest. So in response to the first motion, I find in favor of the defendant."

That was him. He had a chance! Brady's heart rate hit a new level even as his breath left his body. *Oh, thank You, Jesus! Thank You!*

He heard a whimper from the plaintiff's table but couldn't bring himself to feel anything but relief and pure joy.

Calvin gave him a smile and a brief nod.

Before Brady could even process his good fortune, the judge moved into the temporary hearing. Brady's head swam as each of the attorneys made his case.

It seemed crazy that such monumental decisions were made in a matter of minutes, but that's what was happening. He clung to hope as the proceeding wrapped up.

And then it was all up to the judge again.

Brady fidgeted in his seat as Judge Alders once again cleared his throat. "This second motion is regarding temporary custody of the child, which will remain in effect until the final hearing. After reviewing the witness statements and hearing the arguments . . . I've decided in favor of the defendant."

That was him. Brady closed his eyes for a long moment, his head tipping back as a wave of relief washed over him. His eyes prickled with tears.

Thank You, God. Thank You.

Moments later he was vaguely aware of Patricia Parker's indignant voice as she scolded her attorney on their way down the aisle.

Calvin shook Brady's hand. His face had broken out into a wide smile. "Congratulations, Brady."

"Thank you so much. I couldn't have done it without you."

"Let's move out to the hall and chat a few minutes."

The hallway of the Murray County courthouse was clear by the time they got there. The building was fancier than one might expect, with cherry wainscoting on the walls and molded tray ceilings.

Brady was full of nervous energy from the adrenaline rush. There was a wooden bench along the wall, but he couldn't even think of sitting right now. They'd won. Sam was his, at least for the coming months, and the judge was going to consider him for permanent custody.

Calvin set his briefcase on the bench and angled a full smile his way. "A good day in court."

"The best. I'm still shaking. What's next?"

"Discovery. We'll prepare for the final hearing, which is a matter of months away—usually six to nine. But if both sides agree, we can do it sooner."

"The sooner the better, from where I'm

standing." He just wanted to get this over and get on with his life.

"We'll see about getting that done then."

"It's a good sign that the judge gave me temporary custody, right? I mean, for the long haul?"

"Well, of course. He understands Sam is being well taken care of. But it doesn't necessarily mean he'll find for you in the final hearing. He'll hear all the evidence. When's the wedding date?"

Brady blinked. "What?"

"You and Hope? When's the big day?"

"Uh . . ."

"Sometime soon, I hope. Before the final hearing. It could make all the difference. Didn't you see the change in Judge Alder's demeanor when he found out you were engaged? I believe it changed every-thing. I don't think we would've even gotten this tried on a best interest standard otherwise."

Brady's spirits plummeted. "We . . . we haven't set a date yet. We'll need time to plan and all."

"I suggest you make it soon. I'm sure your fiancée will be more than happy to be flexible when she realizes what's at stake."

"Um, of course. I'll . . . I'll talk to her. But really, wouldn't an engagement be just as convincing to the court?"

"A set wedding date might help a bit. But engagements are broken all the time, Brady. You want your best chance. Take my word for it: show up at the final hearing with a wedding band on that hand and a wife on your arm."

Gravity pushed at his shoulders. "Right."

Calvin clapped him on the back and grabbed his briefcase. "I'll give you a call next week, and we'll set up an appointment."

"Sure, sure. Sounds good."

Calvin's footsteps echoed down the cavernous hall, and Brady could only stand there like a statue watching him go. He swallowed hard. A wedding band. A wife. What in heaven's name was he going to do now?

CHAPTER SIX

Brady frowned at the Excel spreadsheet on his laptop. Of all the days to be doing this, his least favorite part of owning a business.

He glanced at Sam, who'd rolled his way across the living room—a new trick—and was now on his belly. He babbled at the squeaky toy clenched in his fist.

Needing a break from numbers, Brady got up and swooped the baby into his arms. An unwelcome aroma assaulted him. "Whoa, little dude. You reek."

He carried Sam over to the sofa and began changing his diaper. "You couldn't have waited for Hope, huh? Had to stick Daddy with a messy one."

Daddy. The word was like an arrow to his heart. He still could hardly believe he and Sam didn't share the same DNA. He couldn't love the kid any more, though, that was for sure. Sammy smiled up at him, those blue eyes sparkling, that gummy smile breaking his heart.

After the hearing this morning, Brady's hopes had been so high. But they'd quickly fallen as reality crashed in. Calvin had made it pretty clear what needed to happen. But Brady wasn't engaged. He didn't even have a girlfriend. How had he gotten himself into this fix?

Focus on the positive. He had temporary custody of Sam, and the judge was going to give him a fair hearing. That was something, wasn't it?

But Calvin was right. He was a single man with no blood ties to the baby. And though Sam had bonded to him already, the kid was only six months old. Babies adjusted quickly. Look how quickly he was recovering from Audrey's death. And she'd been his full-time mommy.

A dread built inside him like a brewing storm, dark and ominous. Somewhere in the background a clock was ticking down the hours he had left with Sam. He swallowed hard against the lump in his throat, his eyes stinging with tears.

God, help me. I don't understand why this is happening. I can't lose him. I just can't. And the thought of the Parkers raising him . . . You can't let that happen. Please, God. I love this kid so much.

He finished up the diaper, blinking back the tears. He'd shed more of them recently than he had since he was a child. Even the divorce hadn't left him feeling so raw. He'd called Zoe and Hope after the hearing as promised, and they'd been elated by his news. But he hadn't told them the bad part. If they sensed his lack of enthusiasm they didn't mention it.

He set Sam on his lap, and his heart melted

when the baby leaned forward and snuggled into his chest. Brady should be working right now. He had a clutch to replace and an engine to tune, but he suddenly wanted to soak up every possible moment with Sammy. Time with his son might well be running out.

⭒

Hope walked toward Brady's house, eager to hear all the details of the hearing. It sounded as though everything had gone his way in court today, but she'd sensed a gravity on the phone that she hadn't had time to explore. Maybe she'd only imagined it. He'd probably just been overwhelmed.

She hadn't even had a chance to ask him if they'd need to go through with the fake engagement. Maybe that's what was going on. Maybe he was worried about pulling that off.

Well, they'd have plenty of time to talk now. She was officially a full-time Sammy-sitter. Was officially finished filling in at WKPC. There were several months between now and October, and she worried Diana might change her mind. What if she lost the opportunity?

Stop that. God knew what He was doing. He'd taken care of her so far. He wasn't going to let loose of her now. She balked at the thought, remembering a time that belief had been shaken. But she didn't want to think on that now. Or ever, really.

Hope pushed back a loose strand of hair. She

57

was glad she'd worn it up today. The June temperature was pushing a hundred, and the humidity nearly stole her breath.

She pulled Brady's kitchen door open. "Knock knock!"

"Come in." Brady was on the sofa, Sam lying against his chest. "Hey there." Brady's gaze only flickered off hers, but she didn't miss the bloodshot eyes and look of defeat.

Her spirits sank. She'd been right. Something was wrong. "Hey, Collins."

At the sound of her voice, Sam turned and smiled around his pacifier, looking impossibly adorable. The baby held out his arms as Hope approached.

She took him, pressing a kiss to his cheek. "How's my favorite little punkin?"

"He has a new trick. He can roll across the entire room. You've been forewarned."

She poked Sam's soft belly. "Is that true, little man? Are you a big boy now? Are you a big boy, huh?"

As he giggled, Hope caught an odor. She wrinkled her nose. "Ew, I think someone messed his pants. Shoo—ee! Sammy's stinky!"

Brady pushed to his feet, waving a balled-up diaper before heading toward the kitchen. "Already taken care of. You're welcome."

Hope chuckled. "Way to go, Sammy! Save the good ones for Daddy!"

As soon as she said the word, she bit her lip. It

had only been a week since he'd gotten the test results. The wound was still pretty raw.

When Brady returned she set Sam down on the rug and sat beside Brady on the sofa. "Okay . . . Why do I get the feeling your hearing didn't go quite as well as you made it sound earlier?"

He gave a strained smile. "It did go well. The judge is going to hear our argument at the final hearing, and I got temporary custody."

She studied his face. Such a handsome face. And such a kind heart. She wanted to smooth the worry creases from his forehead and massage away the strain from his shoulders. He'd been through so much with Audrey and now this.

"But . . . ," she prompted.

"But . . . part of the reason for the judge's decision today was my engagement—" He shot her a look. "My nonexistent engagement to my nonexistent fiancée."

She gave her head a shake. "So . . . we'll just follow through with the plan. I already told you I'd do it. I mean, I admit we'll catch some flak from our friends. And we'll have to tell Zoe and Cruz what's really going on, but—"

Brady was shaking his head, staring at Sam, who'd already rolled halfway across the room.

"What?"

He gave a sigh that seemed to come from his toes. "Calvin doesn't think an engagement will be enough, Hope."

"What do you mean? You just said it was part of the reason things went in your favor today."

"Yes. Because presumably that engagement would end in a wedding that would provide two parents for Sam. Calvin said I should 'move up' the wedding date to before the final hearing—which, by the way, could be just a few months away."

Her spirits sank. "Oh. What did he say when you—"

Brady cut a look her way.

"Ah. You didn't tell him."

His lips tightened. A shadow flickered as he clenched his jaw. He punched a pillow. "Why didn't I start dating after the divorce instead of sulking around my garage? I could've at least had a girlfriend by now."

"Because Audrey wrecked your heart, and you weren't ready yet."

"I don't know if I'll ever be ready after this. She really did a job on me, Hope." His head fell back against the sofa cushion. "What am I going to do? I can't stand the thought of losing him. I can't stand the thought of the Parkers raising him. They'll smother the sweetness right out of him—" His voice choked off.

She took his hand in both of hers. It was so big, rough with calluses and permanently stained around the nails from his work.

"We . . . we could get married for real . . ."

He gave her a look. "Hope . . . come on. That goes way beyond the bounds of friendship."

He was right. A fake engagement was one thing. Marriage quite another.

And yet . . . she loved Brady. And she loved his little guy. For a moment she imagined being a mommy. Putting Sammy down to sleep every night and singing lullabies and teaching him his ABCs. Her heart rolled over in her chest.

And Brady . . . He was such a great guy and a wonderful father. How could she stand by and let the Parkers take Sam away from him when there was something she could do about it?

"Brady, there's nothing I wouldn't do for you." She meant it, she realized. He'd become such a dear friend the past couple years.

"That's really sweet, Hope. But I could never ask that of you."

She'd wanted marriage and family for a long time now. Even though she was a career woman, some part of her deep down longed for that home of her own, complete with husband and kids. She'd thought she had that once. But it had been ripped away from her.

But how could a marriage to Brady work when she was planning to take a job in Atlanta in October? She'd have to move, and he couldn't move his business. But maybe there was a way to work around that. And what could possibly be more important than Sam?

"We should at least think about it," she said. "There's too much on the line not to."

"I believe in the sanctity of marriage, Hope." He winced. "Despite the fact that I've got one divorce under my belt. I don't want another broken marriage, and I sure don't want to be your enemy. Not ever."

She squeezed his hand. "That will never happen."

"Things can get pretty crazy in a marriage—trust me."

"That's because you were married to Audrey. You and I—we're both fair, reasonable adults. We get along great."

"I'm not going to let you sacrifice your life on my behalf. You deserve a real marriage."

"It wouldn't be a sacrifice. I'd be getting plenty in return. You know I want to be married and be a mom—"

Brady seemed to take in her words. Then he gave his head a shake. "This is crazy. Marriage is hard enough when it starts with love."

"We do love each other."

He gave her a droll look. "You know what I mean."

"Maybe it'll be easier this way. Did you ever think about that?"

Without so much emotional risk. Without the possibility of losing someone you depended on more than your next breath. The more she thought about it, the more comfortable she felt about the whole thing.

She'd experienced deep loss, and so had Brady. She sure had no desire to go through that again. And though she'd been dating, trying to find that someone special, a part of her recognized that she pulled away whenever things started getting serious.

"Let's just pray about it," Hope said. "There's no need to rush here. It's a big decision."

He gave her a pointed look. "It's too much."

She nudged his shoulder with her own. "Let's just sleep on it, all right? What could it hurt?"

"You're going to wake up in the morning and realize you were having a moment of temporary insanity."

"Maybe so. But there's a lot at stake here. So we should at least give it the consideration it deserves."

His eyes drifted to Sam, who was on his back, pulling his feet to his mouth. He babbled, his sweet little voice ringing through the room.

Brady gave a sigh that seemed to come from deep inside. "All right. Let's pray about it."

He swiveled his head, locking eyes with her for a long moment. His blue eyes were the color of worn denim and just as soft as they peered at her. There was warmth and affection in his gaze. A tender caring that made her want to stretch toward him like a sunflower reaching toward the sun's heat.

She suddenly realized how close they were. Only a breath away. An odd flutter stirred in her belly as the moment drew out between them.

"You're a good friend, Daniels," he said softly.

His words warmed her from the inside out. "Don't you forget it. And no matter what we decide, I'm here for you every step of the way—and so are Zoe and Cruz. Just hang in there, all right? God's got a plan in all this. We just have to trust Him."

CHAPTER SEVEN

When Brady awakened the next morning, the sun was flooding through his curtains. He checked the time on his phone. Almost eight o'clock.

He groaned. He never slept past seven. Especially since Sammy normally woke at six on the dot. Worry niggling in his gut, Brady crawled from bed and went to the nursery across the hall.

The room was dim, lit only by a nightlight, but he could see Sammy on his tummy, his diapered butt pooching into the air. The baby's back rose and fell rhythmically.

His boy was fine, sleeping soundly. He left the room, the weight of yesterday settling over him like a lead cape as he descended the staircase. The judge's words, his attorney's advice, his conversation with Hope. He ran a hand through his short hair.

Downright crazy. What had they been thinking?

By now Hope was awake and getting ready. She was due over here at nine. No doubt she was feeling the same way about yesterday's talk. She was probably dreading coming over. Feeling like she was going to be letting him down or something.

He'd put her mind at ease. It was the least he could do. This was his problem, not hers. He hadn't even put much prayer into it last night. To be honest, he'd drifted off right in the middle of it.

He set up the coffee machine, toggled the Brew button, then sent Hope a text.

Temporary insanity officially over?

That should break the ice. Help put her mind at ease. He shook his head as pieces of their conversation from the day before played in his mind. He'd never thought of himself as impetuous. Besides the one night when he'd gotten Audrey pregnant—or thought he had—he was the embodiment of logic and reason. But he supposed distress had a way of bringing out the foolish in a person.

That was the week his grandma had let it slip that his birth mom was in town. And Brady, being a glutton for punishment, started thinking she had come for his birthday. The next night he got wind she'd already left; she hadn't even bothered to look him up. It really messed with him. It felt as if he'd been abandoned all over again. He'd impulsively hit a bar in Ellijay and done something he'd promised himself he'd never do—he'd gotten skunked. Audrey's timing couldn't have been more perfect.

He'd made a foolish mistake. And on one account he was so sorry. On the other, he couldn't bring himself to regret bringing Sam into his life. His eyes locked onto a photo of the baby he'd stuck to the refrigerator with a magnet. His goofy little smile and sparkling eyes got him right in the gut. Yeah, he was definitely a desperate man.

He got out a mug and poured some cream into the bottom as the coffee finished brewing. A moment later, as he reached for the carafe, a text dinged in. He checked the screen.

Nope. It's still hanging around.

He frowned at the screen for half a minute without blinking. He hadn't expected this. Before he could respond another text came in.

It might just be a permanent condition.

He pressed his lips together, still shaking his head.

Hope.

He clicked on Send with more force than necessary, frowning at the phone, his heart beating erratically.

We'll talk when I get there, okay?

Fine.

He set down his phone and decided to enjoy a hot cup of coffee before Sam woke up.

By the time he heard Hope pull up outside he'd changed and fed Sam. Brady normally loved mornings, when his little guy was bright-eyed and babbling. But today he was distracted, thinking about the conversation to come.

He carried Sam with him as he went to open the kitchen door. Hope was just walking up the steps of the stoop.

She wore a sleeveless black top and shorts that showed off her long, tanned legs. Her hair was up in a sloppy ponytail that made her look younger than her twenty-four years and cute as a button. She wore no makeup that he could tell, which made her wide, green eyes stand out. She could have any guy she wanted, it seemed to him. Why the heck would she settle for a marriage of convenience? And *his* convenience, at that.

Their gazes locked for a long moment.

"What?" she asked. "Why are you looking at me like that?"

" 'Cause you were supposed to regain your sanity overnight.

She leaned in close to kiss Sammy on his cheek, and her light perfume wrapped around Brady as she swept past.

"Now, now, that wasn't our agreement," she said as she dropped her purse on the counter. "We were supposed to give the matter some prayer. Do you have time to talk now, or do you want to wait until after work?"

The Audi R8's clutch could wait. He was tired of feeling so unsettled. "I have time now."

She'd already moved over to the sink and started rinsing this morning's bottle. "Okay, so let's talk. What exactly are your objections to this arrangement?"

Arrangement. He gave his head a shake. "I don't even know where to start."

"Start anywhere you please."

Sam squirmed to get down, so Brady put him on the living room rug with one of his toys.

"Listen, Hope, I'm not worried about me. You know the mess with Audrey put me off dating—and that was before I even knew she tricked me into thinking I got her pregnant." He scrubbed his face, mumbling to himself, "Idiot."

"You are not an idiot." She closed the dishwater and turned, crossing her arms.

After his bad judgment with Audrey he didn't trust himself to make a good decision where love was concerned. But he'd known Hope forever. And he trusted her. Really trusted her.

"I don't exactly have my whole future planned out," he continued, "but I was thinking love and marriage might be somewhere in my distant future. Possibly. But you . . . You deserve the real thing, Hope. True love, happily ever after, all that."

She held his gaze for a long minute, her eyes going soft and maybe a little sad.

She was thinking about Aaron, he realized suddenly. And though he hadn't known her very well back then, he knew Aaron's death had been life-defining for Hope. She never talked about it. Never talked about him. That right there said a whole lot.

"I had love once, Brady. Maybe I was only a teenager, but it was the real thing."

69

"I know you did. It was a terrible thing you went through."

Her eyes locked on Sam, but he didn't think she was seeing the baby. Her gaze was distant, in some faraway place that filled her with grief.

"It was really hard, losing him, you know?"

"I get that." No one understood what a risk love was until they'd been wrecked by its loss. "But you're young, Hope. Only twenty-four. Plenty of time to mend."

"Yeah, but—I don't think I ever want to go through that again."

"We've both been burned, in different ways. We're both understandably skittish to take the leap a second time."

"Maybe even downright opposed to, if I'm honest. I think I push men away. I'm starting to see that."

He studied her, remembering things she'd said in the past. Things his sister had said. "I thought you wanted love and marriage. Kids."

"I do, but . . . there's a reason I haven't found it yet—mainly all that pushing. But honestly, how many times can you expect to find true love, huh? And ever since we talked about this last night . . . the whole idea of building a life with someone I love and respect as a friend has settled around me in a good way. A really good way."

Brady walked across the room, putting some distance between them. Between her logic and his resistance. He ran a hand over his face. He hadn't expected this. Hadn't expected her to make so much sense. When she talked about a marriage between them it didn't sound crazy at all, it sounded . . . practical. Even appealing.

He stopped at the picture window and stared out at the distant mountains rising from the morning fog. He couldn't believe this was starting to sound logical to him. That he was starting to feel this arrangement with Hope was a legitimate idea.

But he didn't want any misunderstandings between them. "Just so we're being perfectly clear, you're actually relieved by the chance to have the things you want . . . marriage and family, without all the rest."

Her chin notched up. "Yeah, I guess I am. Maybe that makes me a big ol' chicken, but it's the way I feel. And I already love Sam, Brady. I hope you know that."

"I do. You'd be a great mom to him. That was never in question."

His gaze returned to the landscape, unseeing, praying. This was a big decision. No question, he'd do whatever was necessary to keep Sam. But he was trying not to be selfish here. Trying to think of Hope—what kind of a friend would he be otherwise? Could he trust himself to be objective about this when he had so much on the line?

But she seemed to want this. She had her own

reasons, and they seemed to blend seamlessly with his. But still . . .

"Hope, I feel it's only fair to warn you . . ."

"What?" she asked when he didn't continue.

"I don't think I'm very good at . . . at being a husband."

She waved him off. "Phfft. I'm sure that's not true."

"Audrey could've given you a long list of all the ways I failed at the job."

"And I wouldn't have believed a word of it. Brady, I don't know anything about your marriage, but I know you as a person, and there's no way you were a bad husband."

"Thanks for that." He wanted to believe her. Maybe Hope would bring out the best in him. Audrey sure hadn't. But that was probably a cop-out.

He felt Sammy at his feet. The baby was on his back, slapping at Brady's foot and looking up at him with a toothless smile. "Da, da, da, da!"

Smiling, Brady scooped him into his arms, and Sam grabbed his lips, pinching.

Hope approached, standing beside him. "So . . . does that mean we're on the same page here? It sure sounds like we want the same things." She lifted her slender shoulders. "Who's to say we can't have our own kind of happily ever after, you know?"

He looked at her with fresh eyes as she poked

Sam in the belly, eliciting a drooly smile. Imagined that she was his wife, the mother of his child. That they were a family. That he had a partner in this world. Someone he could champion. Someone he could count on. He'd never had that with Audrey.

But marriage comprised more than a tidy arrangement between two people. Marriage came with intimacy—at least it should. It came with sharing confidences, sharing a commitment, sharing . . . a bed.

This was an area they'd yet to touch on—but it was a big one in his book. Was she expecting some kind of sexless marriage? His gaze roved over her face, seeing not the friend he'd known for years but the beautiful young woman who was proposing a future with him.

She had beautiful eyes, large and green, with a warmth in them that made a person feel like she was really listening. When she smiled, that wide, trademark smile, she lit up a whole room.

And below the neck there was not a single deterrent.

He envisioned living side by side with Hope, day after day, week after week, year after year. Envisioned the intimacy of sharing life without the benefit of enjoying that intimacy to its fullest. Envisioned years of sexual frustration.

He was no saint. True, his libido had been nonexistent lately, but he couldn't sign up for

73

that indefinitely. Not when he was married to such a beautiful, feminine woman. A woman he legitimately loved and trusted and respected. Maybe he was a pig, but he couldn't see that working too well for either of them.

"Brady?" She questioned him with those big green eyes.

He blinked, realizing he was staring at her, probably like some perv. He tore his eyes away. Palmed the back of his neck. His skin was hot, and sweat had broken out on its surface.

Sam reached for Hope, leaning toward her, and she took him from Brady's arms, freeing him to put some distance between them.

❖❘❖

Hope watched Brady cross the room. He moved with a masculine grace she could only admire. There was confidence in the line of his shoulders, in the length of his stride. He was a man who could take care of himself. A man who could take care of his family.

But something was bothering him. "What is it? What's wrong?"

He faced her, stuffing his hands into his jeans pocket, giving her a look she couldn't quite make out. "Since we're actually giving serious consideration to this . . . I think it's important we be clear with each other about what this is—and what it isn't."

"Managing expectations." She nodded. "Very important."

He shifted. Moved to the coffee table where he'd set his coffee. Took a sip. Set it back down. He scratched his head.

"You seem like you have something specific on your mind."

"Yeah." He scrubbed his hand over his jaw. "I was just wondering . . . What about . . . you know?"

She arched a brow. "You know?"

He gave her a flinty look. "Yeah, you *know*."

Hope's lips twitched. She wasn't squeamish about the topic. It had come up regularly on *Living with Hope*.

But seeing the flush rising from Brady's collar, she couldn't resist the urge to tease him just a little. "You mean sex? Are you talking about sex, Collins?"

His cheeks flushed. "Stop saying that word."

He was kind of cute when he was shy. "If you can't even talk about it with me, how do you think we're gonna . . ."

He leveled her with a look.

She laughed, the flinty look completely incongruous with his blushing. "Okay, okay, fine. I guess I hadn't gotten that far. What are your thoughts on the subject?"

Brady gave a gruff laugh. "You have to ask? You're a gorgeous woman and—"

"Gorgeous, huh?"

"—I'm a man."

"I had noticed."

"That's encouraging."

"But while you might be a man, I, my friend, am a woman. We tend to move a little slower in that area, as I'm sure you've noticed. I think I'd need a little time to . . . get used to the idea. Settle into the relationship. We've been friends a long time. To my way of thinking, that requires a shift in thinking."

He gave her a thoughtful look, nodding once. "Fair enough."

"Maybe we can think of the beginning of our marriage as a courtship of sorts—physically speaking."

"We'll play it by ear then?"

"We're reasonable adults who care for and respect each other." She let her gaze sweep over his frame, noting his broad shoulders. The sculpted curves of his biceps, his long, muscular legs. "And you're not so bad yourself, Collins. I'm sure we can work something out."

He turned again and paced to the threshold of the kitchen, staring off to seemingly nowhere.

Sammy tugged on her ear, and she playfully snapped at his fingers until he smiled. Then she buried her nose in his soft neck and laid down a string of rapid-fire kisses until his melodious giggle filled the room.

Brady turned, a frown tugging his brows as his eyes locked on Sam.

She lifted her head, the smile falling from her lips. Sam buried his face in her neck, snuggling, his chubby hands fisting her shirt.

"Is that all that's on your mind?" she asked.

His chest expanded on a breath, and his shoulders fell as he expelled it. "What if—I really hate to say this out loud—but what if I don't get Sammy? What if we get married and, despite that, the Parkers are still awarded custody?"

She rubbed Sam's back. "I thought your attorney was pretty confident things would go your way if you were married."

"He was cautiously optimistic. I'm just trying to cover all my bases here."

Sam squirmed to get down, so she set him on the floor, then straightened, meeting Brady's gaze. "I'm looking at this as a real commitment, Brady. Marriage is serious business to me. I know it is to you too. Unless . . . you'd want out at that point . . ."

"No. We're in agreement there. I don't want another divorce."

"I just can't imagine that any judge would take Sam away from you. He couldn't do better for a father."

The corner of his lips turned up. "Thanks for saying that."

"Well, it's true. Anyone who looks closely enough could tell you that."

His shoulders sank a bit, the tightened corners of his eyes relaxing.

She thought of her job opportunity and wondered if she should bring it up now. If they actually did this, she'd either have to give up the job or commute, coming home on weekends only. She wouldn't be able to be Sammy's caregiver. But she knew Brady. He'd never let her give up the job. However, she was willing to make that sacrifice if necessary.

"Hope?" Brady asked. "What are you thinking?"

"I'm thinking this will be a commitment just like any marriage. Whatever challenges come, we'll work it out between the two of us."

His blue eyes pierced hers for a long, drawn-out moment. "It kind of sounds like we're doing this."

She smiled as excitement began to bubble inside, making her feel a kind of joy she hadn't felt in a long time. "Sounds that way to me too."

"We've still got a lot to talk about." He checked his watch. "Not the least of which is an engagement, a wedding, and how we're going to manage all this."

"Well, that can wait a few hours, can't it? I know you have work to do. Maybe it'll give us both a chance to think over some details."

"Good point." He scooped up Sammy and gave him a kiss on the cheek. "Be good for Hope."

In a few weeks or months it would be *Mommy*. She would be Sammy's mommy. That feeling of joy bloomed bigger, wider, as Brady transferred the baby into her arms. And it lasted all day long.

CHAPTER EIGHT

Hope squirmed in the passenger seat of Brady's car. They'd talked things over the night before and made a plan. They would "come out" as a couple tomorrow night at the Rusty Nail. They would treat their engagement announcement as a normal one. They didn't want to give the courts any reason to feel the marriage was invalid. Besides, it was no one's business that they weren't "in love," per se.

Except Zoe and Cruz. Their best friends. Brady's sister. They had to tell them everything—there was no way they'd buy this sudden engagement of theirs. And now Hope and Brady were on their way to break the news to them.

Hope had phoned her parents in Ecuador that morning, hoping to reach them before they started their day. They'd been a little surprised but seemed thrilled for her and Brady. Her mom had always had a soft spot for the guy.

"I always knew there was something special between you two," she said. Hope just went along with it.

"We could scrape together a little something to help with the wedding costs," her dad said.

"That's all right. We're planning to keep it simple. Besides, I'd much rather you save up to fly back for the wedding if you can."

"We wouldn't miss it, honey," her mom said.

Brady slowed down for the turn that would take them into town. They were meeting Zoe and Cruz at the Mellow Mug, which shouldn't be too busy this late in the evening.

"You're nervous," Brady said.

"I can't decide how this is going to go over with Zoe."

"In the end, it doesn't really matter. This is our decision."

"You're right, of course. Still."

If she could only make the butterflies in her stomach settle down. By the time Brady parked along the brick wall in the parking lot they seemed to be having a wild, wing-fluttering rally. She spotted Cruz's truck a few spaces down.

Brady shut off the ignition and turned to her. "Ready?"

"As I'll ever be."

A few moments later the robust aroma of java assaulted her as they entered the building. The Mellow Mug was an old renovated building located in the heart of downtown Copper Creek. It was a long and narrow space, dimly lit, with old creaky wood floors and a collection of eclectic furniture.

She spotted Zoe and Cruz in the back corner and gave a wave before stopping at the counter to place their orders.

Zoe had been Hope's best friend since ninth

grade. She had gorgeous auburn hair, electric green eyes, and fair skin. She was a beautiful foil to Cruz, with his olive Puerto Rican complexion and black hair. The newly engaged pair had been high school sweethearts of sorts, but had only this year reunited.

"Did you two come together?" Zoe asked as Brady took the corner of the opposite sofa.

"Um, yeah." Hope sat in the middle. Close enough to Brady but not too close.

"Where's Sam?" Cruz asked.

Brady scratched his jaw. "Ah, I got a baby-sitter."

"Same here," Zoe said. Their four-year-old daughter Gracie had been a recent surprise to Cruz, but he'd taken to fatherhood like a pro.

"To adult time." Cruz raised his mug of brew and they toasted.

"How're the new barn plans coming along?" Brady asked Zoe.

"Right on schedule. Completion date is only about a month away. Then you can have your building back. I don't know how to thank you for letting me borrow it."

"No big deal. I've operated out of my old barn for this long. Couple more months wasn't going to hurt anything."

While Zoe had inherited Granny's peach orchard, Brady had inherited a substantial amount of money. He'd invested it in the new building for his business, but by the time it was finished Zoe had needed it more than he had.

An awkward silence followed as Hope wondered how they were going to bring up the engagement. They hadn't really talked about it.

"So . . . ," Zoe said, her gaze toggling between Brady and Hope. "I got the feeling there's some agenda to this meeting."

Hope shared a look with Brady as they tried to silently decide who and how to start.

"Okay, definitely an agenda," Zoe said. "Is everything okay? You're scaring me. Did you find out something about the hearing?"

"I guess I'll start," Brady said. "And this is about the hearing, indirectly."

"Well, actually, pretty directly," Hope said.

"I guess that's true." He cleared his throat. "So you know how I told you both that the hearing this week went well?"

"Yeah . . . ," Zoe said.

"That was kind of only half the story," he said.

"Okay . . ."

Brady shared another look with Hope, and she encouraged him with a smile that felt a little unsteady.

"The judge was under the impression that I was engaged. And it turns out that had a lot of bearing on his decision to consider me for custody at all. My attorney feels that I have a great chance of getting custody of Sam—but only if I'm married."

Zoe's auburn curls shimmied as she gave her head a shake. "Wait. Why did the judge think you were engaged?"

"Because I told my attorney I was."

"Well . . . ," Hope said. "Not exactly. Actually, I showed up one day while he was talking to his attorney, and he saw your engagement ring." She nodded toward Zoe.

"*My* ring?" Zoe asked.

"Yeah . . . Remember when it got stuck on my finger that day I picked it up in Atlanta?" She turned to Cruz. "I'd eaten ham the day before, and my fingers were all swollen, and you know how it is with ham and the way it . . . Anyway . . ." She cleared her throat. She was getting offtrack here.

"So your attorney assumed you were engaged, and you just let him believe it?" Cruz said.

"And the judge made you think that was a critical factor in winning custody of Sam?" Zoe said.

"Exactly," Brady said.

"Yes." Hope exchanged looks with Brady before meeting Zoe's gaze. "Which is why . . . Brady and I have decided to get married."

Confusion clouded Zoe's eyes. Her lips parted. She tore her gaze away to look at Brady. Only to flitter back to Hope. The ticking of the wall clock seemed unusually loud. The music from the speakers stopped, ushering in a long, uncomfortable pause.

Hope gave an awkward laugh. "Say something."

Cruz ran his palms down his thighs. "Um . . . I thought you were going for some kind of fake engagement here, to be honest."

"Marriage?" Zoe looked between them, disbelief etched in the lines between her eyebrows. "The two of you are getting married?"

"That's right." Brady reached for Hope's hand, engulfing it.

Hope hadn't realized how cold her hands were until his warmth was wrapped around hers. "An engagement isn't enough. His attorney feels he needs to actually be married by the final hearing to have his best chance at keeping Sam."

"By the final hearing?" Zoe's eyes shot to Brady's. She leaned forward, planting her elbows on her knees. "Brady, you cannot use her like this. It's not right."

"Whoa, whoa," Hope said. "This was my idea. He's not using me at all. I want this." A knowing washed over her. She hadn't stated it so clearly out loud. But it was the truth.

"I don't think you two have a clue what you're getting into here," Zoe said.

"I know you probably don't want to think about this," Cruz said. "But what if, heaven forbid, you were to lose custody, Brady?"

"What if you drive each other nuts? Or fall in love with someone else? What then, huh?"

86

"We know what we're doing," Brady said.

"We're going into this with our eyes wide open."

"We've talked about it at length."

Zoe gave them a look of incredibility. "Over two whole days?"

"We're committed to this," Hope said firmly. "Committed for the long haul. Even if Brady were to lose custody, which is not likely. We believe this is the right thing for both of us, and we hope you can support us."

"You don't even love each other. For heaven's sake, that's the very foundation of marriage."

"We do love each other," Hope said.

Zoe's lips pursed. "You know what I mean."

Brady set his drink on the coffee table. He waited for a woman to pass on the way back to the bathroom, then lowered his voice. "We know this is unconventional, Zoe. But arranged marriages happen every day in other parts of the world between people who've hardly even met. They seem to work out all right."

Hope put her other hand on top of their joined hands. "And we have a lot more going for us than that."

"Arranged marriages?" Zoe fell back into her seat, eyes wide in disbelief. "Are you hearing yourselves?"

Cruz took Zoe's hand, probably intending to settle her down, but it didn't seem to work.

She nailed Hope with a look. "Why are you doing this? You have your whole life in front of you. I mean, I get the urgency, the desperation on Brady's part—we all feel that. And I know you love Sam and have a really soft heart. But, Hope . . . come on, this is above and beyond. Way beyond. What about everything *you* want?"

"That hasn't changed. I want a marriage and children. I'm getting both of those things."

Zoe's gaze sharpened on Hope. "So he's using you to get Sam, and you're using Brady to get a family?"

"Come on, Zoe," Brady said. "No one's using anyone. We have common goals, and we're helping each other attain them. Stop making this sound so crass."

At long length Zoe released a slow breath. "You're right. I'm sorry. I love you both so much. I feel defensive for both of you."

"You don't need to defend either one of us," Brady said. "We're adults. We're making a mutual decision."

Zoe crossed her arms, looking between the two of them, shaking her head. "Is this a joke? Because I feel like I'm being punked."

Nice. So her whole future was a joke. Just because it wasn't like Zoe's—soul mates reunited, happily ever after, yada, yada, yada—didn't mean Hope wasn't deserving of her own story.

"You know, Zoe, I'm your best friend. And this

is your brother. Do you think you might try to be happy for us?"

"I just want you to think this through." Zoe's eyes shone with concern. "I see such potential for . . . disaster."

"Every marriage has that potential," Brady said. "We have nothing but respect for one another. We do love each other, and—possibly more important—we genuinely like each other."

"We've thought about it, talked about, and prayed about it. It's what we want. We're doing this. We wanted you guys to be the first to know, and we wanted to be up front with you about everything."

"But as far as anyone else goes," Brady said, "this is just a regular engagement. An ordinary wedding."

"Albeit a little rushed," Hope added, giving the others a long moment to let everything they'd just said settle. "Can you get on board with this? Because we'd like the two of you to stand up with us."

Zoe and Cruz traded looks. The woman passed them again on her way back to her seat. The country tune flowing from the speaker picked up as the chorus began.

Brady's hand had tightened around Hope's, their damp palms pressing together.

Zoe's shoulders rose on an inhale and sank as the breath left her body. "Of course we'll support your decision if this is really what both of you want."

"It is," Brady said.

Cruz traded a look with Zoe, then gave a nod. "Then count us in."

"Well, that could've gone better," Hope said once they were alone in Brady's car. She drew a deep breath and let it out.

"Could've gone worse."

"They did come around." By the time they'd parted they were already talking wedding plans. "But, yikes. It was a little dicey there for a few minutes."

"They were just surprised. Zoe even offered to help with the planning."

"Yeah, but given the time constraints, an informal affair would be best, don't you think? Maybe after church on a Sunday or something. I have a white dress that'll fit the bill."

His gaze darted her way. "What? No. This is your wedding day. I want it to be special for you."

She met his gaze, softening. He was a sweetheart. "Real weddings are expensive, Brady."

"I can swing a small wedding, Hope. I'd be happy to."

"We could use the money for other things. Your business. Sammy's college fund. You're probably drowning in attorney's fees already."

"Just think about it, all right? You should at least have a new dress. Some flowers and stuff. Daisy'd have a fit if you didn't let her do up some flowers."

"I'll think about it. Where are we going?" she asked when Brady turned onto a road that led them up into the hills.

"We're taking a little detour."

"This road doesn't really go anywhere. And what about your sitter?"

"The sitter is kind of the point."

"What?"

"Stop asking so many questions."

Hope shrugged and leaned back in her seat. It was his dime. On the other hand, their dimes would soon be in the same pile. Finances. That was something they hadn't talked about.

But they could save that conversation for later. It had already been a long day for both of them. She looked out the windows into the growing darkness. The pine trees and hills were silhouetted against the sky. Overhead the stars twinkled on a midnight-blue canvas, and a full moon hung over the valley. Just another beautiful Georgia summer night.

The road wound and dipped and rose steadily. By the time Brady began braking, the tension from their meeting had fallen from her shoulders.

Brady pulled off onto a turnout and stopped when he reached the guardrail, the front of the car facing the valley. The town of Copper Creek spread below them, the twinkling lights like a mirror image of the night sky. They were at a spot commonly known as Inspiration Point.

She looked at him sideways. "Is this where you brought all your girlfriends to make out?"

"Not even once." Brady put down the windows and turned off the car. The sudden hush of the engine ushered in a symphony of night sounds. The air smelled of pine and woodsmoke, and a light breeze blew, teasing her hair.

She turned toward him. "So are you going tell me what—"

He was facing her, one elbow on the console, wearing an intense look she hadn't seen before. A whisper of moonlight filtered in, caressing the planes of his face, making him more handsome than ever.

"I couldn't think of another place to do this," he said.

He looked down, and she followed his eyes to see him opening a box. It took a moment to realize the spark of light was a diamond twinkling in the space between them.

She gasped. "Brady." She'd hardly even thought about rings.

"I know we're not a traditional couple . . ." He pulled the ring from its nest. "But you're a truly special woman, Hope. I'm so honored that you agreed to spend the rest of your life with me. I promise to spend the rest of my life working to be worthy of that decision. And I hope you know I'll always treat you with the respect you deserve."

Her heart softened at his words. Shoot, it may have actually melted just a tiny bit. She blinked against the sudden sting behind her eyes. He didn't have to do this. She sure hadn't expected it. But it was just like him. So thoughtful.

"Darn, Collins. You got game."

He looked down, and she suspected the darkness hid a flush.

"You deserve a real proposal, Hope. You probably deserve a lot more than I'll ever be able to give you. You know that, right?"

There was a thread of worry in his voice, and she wanted to alleviate his fear. "Is this the beginning of that courtship I mentioned earlier?"

He lifted his shoulders. "Gotta start sometime, I guess."

She gave him a sideways look and lightened her tone. "You're hoping for a real wedding night, aren't you, buddy?"

He rubbed the back of his neck. "Geez, Hope. I'm not going to rush you. You know me better than that."

She chuckled at his discomfort. "I know that. You're just such an easy target, I can't resist teasing." She held out her left hand, waggling her fingers. "Now bring that baby over here, and let's see if it fits."

CHAPTER NINE

Brady was packing up the diaper bag when the knock sounded at his door. Hope was upstairs changing Sam into a fresh outfit, so he tossed a clean burp cloth into the bag and opened the door.

His former sister-in-law wore a wary smile. "Hey there, Brady."

"Hi, Heather. Come on in. I have the diaper bag all packed, and I just fed him."

The Parkers had Sam for the weekend, and Heather had offered to be the go-between. Things were likely to be a little awkward between them after Thursday's hearing. Heather might like Brady, but the Parkers were still her parents. She was bound to feel loyal to them.

The stairs squeaked as Hope descended them. She'd dressed Sam in a pale-blue romper and brushed his baby-fine hair.

"Here he is," Hope said, her eyes landing on Heather.

"Heather, this is my fiancée, Hope Daniels. Hope, this is Heather."

"Nice to meet you," Hope said, extending her hand as she reached the bottom of the steps.

Heather cocked her head. "Hope Daniels . . . not the radio DJ?"

95

"The very one."

"Oh wow. I was so upset when the station changed ownership. I listened to your call-in program almost every night."

"Aw, thank you. That means a lot."

"Congratulations to both of you on your engagement. I hadn't realized you were even dating, Brady."

"Thanks, well . . . Hope and I have known each other forever, and things just kind of . . ."

"Progressed quickly. When you know, you know, right?" Hope turned Sam around so he could see his aunt. "Look who it is, Sammy boy. It's your Auntie Heather."

Sammy kicked his legs excitedly, and when he reached out, Heather scooped him up and kissed him on the cheek. "Hey there, buddy. How's our boy?"

"He's been fed and changed, so he should be good for a while."

"He's gotten pretty adept at rolling around, though," Brady said, "so you really have to watch him."

"Is that true, little guy?" Heather pinched Sam's dimpled chin, eliciting a smile. Her mouth wobbled, and her eyes grew shiny. "He's changed since I saw him last. His face has filled out a bit."

"You'll see him every other weekend now," Brady said. "How are your parents doing since the hearing?"

She gave Brady a strained smile. "They took the news pretty hard."

Brady took that to mean they were angry. That was their default emotion any time things didn't go their way. Their lawyer had already been in touch with his. They were going to put up a real fight, and heaven knew they had the money to do it.

A heaviness settled inside him, but he forced himself to shut it down. He grabbed the diaper bag and accompanied Heather to the door. "I'll walk you out and move the car seat over."

"No need. I have Dylan's, and I'm used to managing with three kids in tow, remember?"

"Right." Brady hooked the diaper bag over Heather's shoulder. "Okay. He should have everything he needs in here."

"If he doesn't, I'm sure I do."

"If you or your parents need anything, don't hesitate to call. He likes his blue bear when he gets sleepy. And he still takes a morning nap."

"Got it. Thanks, Brady."

He opened the door for her. "His pacifier is in the side pocket. He'll get himself to sleep, but he'll need that. And he gets hot easily, so dress him lightly at night."

Heather touched his arm. "He'll be fine. I promise."

He exhaled the breath he didn't realize he'd been holding. "Sorry."

She patted his arm. "Try to relax and have a

good weekend. I'll bring him back tomorrow around one."

"All right. See you then."

The door shut behind Heather, and he watched her through the window loading Sam into the car. Watched her minivan roll down his drive, a cloud of dust blooming in her wake.

"He'll be fine." Hope's touch was reassuring. "You said you trust her."

"I do. It's just hard to let him go." He tried not to think about how it might feel to let him go for good.

But that wasn't going to happen. Speaking of which . . .

He turned toward Hope and offered a smile. "I'd better get a shower. We've got a big night ahead of us."

"Yes, we do." She grabbed her purse from the counter. "I'll see you there in a couple hours."

Saturday night at the Rusty Nail was the perfect time and place for their engagement announcement. All of their friends came to hang out and listen to whatever band was on the schedule. Though Hope was usually on staff as weekend manager, she'd called off tonight.

Brady entered the building at nine o'clock, the smell of grilled burgers making his stomach rumble as he passed the crowded bar and headed into the dining area. The rustic feel of the place, with its beamed ceiling, wavy metal walls, and wood plank floor made a man feel right at home.

The din of chatter competed with the country tune blaring through the speakers. As much as he'd hated sending Sam to the Parkers for the night, he was glad he'd be able to focus on Hope and their announcement.

He found his group in the back corner, farthest from the stage. The round wooden tables had been pulled close to form an awkward chain. It appeared Hope had yet to arrive.

Zoe and Cruz were there, however, with little Gracie. Noah and Josephine, recently remarried, sat beside them. They were a gorgeous couple. Josephine owned the local barbershop, and Noah ran a home-improvement company with his brother. Noah was currently holding their sleeping baby against his shoulder and trying to one-hand a messy burger.

Next to them was Noah's best friend, Pastor Jack, and Daisy Pendleton, who owned the local flower shop. Those two would soon be the only singles of the group, Brady realized.

He greeted his friends and took one of the empty seats beside Cruz. He'd just caught the group up on the good news from the hearing when he spotted Hope skirting the tables on her way toward them.

She looked pretty in trendy jeans and a sparkly top that left her slender shoulders bare. Her left hand was tucked into her front pocket, no doubt to conceal her engagement ring. Her dark hair hung in loose curls over her shoulders, and when her smile fixed on him, he felt a little punch in his gut.

She was his. Or soon would be.

"Hey, y'all," Hope said over the music as she slid into the seat next to Brady. "What's up?"

"Hey, Hope." Josephine pushed her short blonde hair behind her ear. "Aren't you working tonight?"

"Nope. I got the night off."

"Brady was just telling us how well the hearing went." Noah set down his burger and patted baby Nicolas's back.

"I know," Hope said. "Great news, isn't it?"

"The best," Daisy said, then looked at Brady. "Sammy must be sleeping better. You look well-rested."

"He's sleeping through the night most of the time."

"Must be nice," Noah said. Though the tender way he looked down at Nicolas belied his complaint.

"At least there're two of us to take turns," Josephine said. "Brady's on his own."

Brady slid Hope a look from the corner of his eyes, and she gave him a private smile as the group segued into a conversation about the effects of insomnia on mental health.

"How are your folks doing?" Daisy asked Hope during a lull in the conversation. "Still in Ecuador?"

"Yeah, they're helping with a new church plant now."

"How long have they been missionaries?" Josephine asked. She hadn't grown up in Copper Creek like the others.

"They did some short-term trips while I was in college, and went full-time right after I graduated."

"Aw, you must miss them something fierce," Josephine said.

"I do, but we keep in touch. It helps to know they're doing exactly what they've always wanted to do. It truly is their calling."

When a server came around, Brady and Hope ordered. He tried to follow the conversation at the other end of the table. He was conscious of Zoe and Cruz's silence and knew they were probably nervous for him and Hope.

Service was slow, so a while later Hope left the table to get a refill at the bar. Brady watched her go. She had a nice, confident stride, and her legs looked even longer in the heeled sandals she wore tonight. She was trim but filled out those jeans just fine.

He appreciated that she dressed modestly. While other women their age tended to show off their cleavage and bare legs, Hope's clothing merely hinted at her figure—which he was beginning to notice was actually pretty darn sexy.

Cruz nudged him with his elbow.

When Brady looked his way, Cruz lifted a brow, smirking.

So he was checking out his fiancée. Hardly a crime. He scowled at his friend, but a minute later he found his eyes swinging back toward the bar where Hope waited for service.

Rawley Watkins was talking to her. Rawley was the lead singer of Last Chance, the local country band playing later tonight. He made some kind of frantic gesture, making Hope throw her head back in laughter.

Brady frowned as he watched the two of them. Rawley was tall and lanky, and being a musician, he drew a lot of interest from the ladies. Brady supposed his longish blond hair and dimpled smile didn't hurt matters either. He was known for dating around but generally was considered a nice guy.

But Brady wasn't feeling especially generous as he watched Rawley squeeze his fiancée's shoulder. Brady leaned forward, planting his elbows on the table.

Suddenly that engagement announcement couldn't come soon enough. The possessive thought surprised him. He hadn't expected to feel territorial about Hope. He was still a little peeved as she approached the table a couple minutes later. As her gaze collided with his, her smile dimmed.

"What's wrong?" she asked as she slid into her seat.

"Nothing."

She leaned in until her familiar scent teased his nostrils. "Are you worried about the announcement? It's going to be fine. The hard part's over."

"Not really."

"Then what?"

He took a sip of his Coke, his eyes darting around the table before he responded. "It'll probably be easier to convince them this is real if you aren't flirting with other guys, that's all."

She gave him a blank look, a slight shake of her head. "Flirting with . . . Rawley? Are you talking about Rawley?"

"There's going to be enough suspicion as it is." He was starting to feel a little foolish for even bringing it up. "It's not like we've been dating. This is going to seem sudden."

"I wasn't flirting with Rawley. We were just talking."

Hadn't looked that way to him, not with Rawley's casual touches and dimpled smiles. Maybe Hope liked him. They'd never gone out as far as he knew, but clearly Rawley was interested. Maybe Brady was getting in the way of something.

His gaze found hers, looking deep. Needing to be sure. "Are you sure you want to do this, Hope?"

She blinked, looking at him with disbelief. "What has gotten into you? Of course I'm sure. We've talked about this at length. I'm wearing your ring."

Hurt flickered in her eyes, making his chest tighten. What was he doing? Hope was as loyal as they came, and she didn't play games. She wasn't Audrey. Not even close. Maybe he had more baggage than he realized. He became aware of an ache in his jaw and realized he was clenching his teeth.

Under the table, Hope found his other hand and squeezed. "Are you okay?"

He'd just acted like a jealous idiot, and her only concern was for him. He ran a hand over his face. "Sorry. I guess I am nervous about this."

She gave his hand a squeeze as she smiled at him. "It's going to be okay. I promise. I'm committed to this."

He saw the resolution in her eyes and felt the tension drain from his shoulders. "So am I. I'll stop acting like an idiot now."

"Well, when do you want to make the announcement?"

"Maybe we should do it before the band starts. It'll be too loud to talk."

"Hey, you two," Daisy called to Brady and

Hope, pushing her long blonde hair over her shoulder. "It's looking far too serious at that end of the table."

Hope and Brady exchanged a look. He read the go-ahead in her eyes. Brady turned toward his friends. "Actually, it's turned very serious." He waited a beat, making sure he had everyone's attention.

"Hope and I have an announcement to make." He turned toward her, giving her a fond look. The certainty in her eyes urged him on. "As you know, we've been friends a long time. And lately, well, we've been seeing each other and things have grown . . . serious. We want everyone to know—we've gotten engaged."

The looks on his friends' faces might have been hilarious had he not been so nervous. Noah stopped eating midchew, his cheeks punched out like a chipmunk. Josephine's red lips parted, her eyes widening. Daisy's brows pinched together, and Jack's drink paused midway between the table and his mouth.

"Congratulations, you two!" Zoe said.

"This is great," Cruz said. "I'm really happy for you guys."

Brady was grateful for their enthusiastic responses. The others joined in, albeit sounding a mite confused.

"I . . ." Daisy looked between them, but a semblance of a smile was forming. "I guess I'm a little slow on the uptake here. I didn't even realize you two were dating."

"Me neither," Josephine said. She gave a sassy smile. "But I'll confess I just said recently you'd make a great couple. Didn't I, Noah?"

Noah nodded. "She did. Congratulations, you two. I'll admit to being clueless."

"They were always flirting," Josephine said.

"And they've been seeing so much of each other lately," Zoe said.

"I've been watching Sam a lot. And all that time together . . . I guess one thing just led to another."

"I love it when I'm right," Josephine said. "Let's see the ring!"

Hope pulled her hand from under the table, and the other women oohed and aahed at the ring. Brady was glad he'd taken the time to choose carefully. The diamond was a simple solitaire, and the white gold band, with its gentle twists and turns, suited Hope well.

She leaned in to make eye contact with Daisy. "We'll have to get together soon and talk flowers."

Daisy did a little golf clap. "Yay! Now you're talking my language. What were you thinking?"

"Well, I know it's not traditional, but I've always been partial to honeysuckle."

"Aw," Daisy said. "You know what that symbolizes?"

"Hopefully not death and doom," Zoe mumbled. Hope slid her a withering look.

"It means 'devoted affection.' Isn't that just the sweetest thing? So perfect for the two of you."

"Sounds great," Hope said. "Let's do it."

"How did he propose?" Josephine asked, leaning forward on her elbows. "Tell us everything."

"Yeah, no holding out," Daisy said. "Some of us have to live vicariously."

After exchanging a smile with Brady, Hope told the story, making it somehow sound better than it actually was.

"Very romantic," Daisy said with a sigh when Hope had finished.

"Well done, bro," Zoe said. "She wouldn't have wanted a big production."

"Give me some credit. I do know the woman."

"Yes, you do." Hope gave his shoulder a playful—flirtatious?—nudge.

His eyes locked onto hers, and he got caught in the seductive pull of them. In the inviting little tilt of her mouth. Her top lip had a gentle bow, and the bottom one was plump and supple looking. He wondered what they would taste like.

"Well, congratulations again," Jack said, pulling Brady from his straying thoughts. "Marriages that start with friendship have a real advantage, if you ask me."

"We're glad you think so," Hope said. "We were hoping you'd marry us."

Jack gave a deep nod. "I'd be honored."

"We're not wanting a long engagement, so we'll need to get it on the church calendar soon." Brady was glad he'd talked Hope into a real ceremony, though they'd agreed to keep it simple.

"Call the office Monday. We can get the pre-marital counseling on the calendar at the same time if you want."

"Premarital counseling?" Brady's mouth went a little dry at the thought. He exchanged a look with Hope, careful to keep his eyes off her lips.

"It's pretty basic. Just six sessions. Easy-peasy. Though if you guys would be more comfortable counseling with someone else . . ."

"No," Brady said. "That's fine. I guess we just—"

"Hadn't really thought about that yet," Hope said.

"Already completing his sentences," Cruz said. "That's so cute."

Brady elbowed his friend just as the server showed up with their food. He was glad for the distraction. The announcement was over. Now they just had to get through the meal. And apparently six sessions of marriage counseling.

CHAPTER TEN

They set the date for August twenty-fifth, which gave them only a two-month engagement. They would be married a month and a half when the trial came around. Because of the rushed time line, they decided to get right to the premarital counseling.

Hope shifted in the chair opposite Pastor Jack's desk. The office was small, though it boasted high ceilings, ornate paneling, and a wooden door that looked as if it had time-traveled straight from the medieval ages. An oriental rug hugged the plank floor, and the smell of lemons and church hymnals hung in the air.

Pastor Jack had stepped out for a moment, which gave Hope some time to collect herself. She was more nervous than she'd been since they'd hatched this whole plan.

More nervous even than when they'd met Brady's dad for breakfast before church Sunday and told him the news. His response had been reserved, though polite. He and Brady had never been close. Over the years Brady had tried so hard to please his father—getting good grades, finishing college, making a success of his business. But the man never seemed particularly impressed. Hope wanted to shake him. Mr. Collins wasn't close to

Zoe either, though heaven knew his daughter had never been bent on appeasing him.

Brady set a hand on her leg, and she realized she'd been tapping her heel at a rapid pace.

"Sorry. I don't know why I'm so nervous," she whispered, glancing around the office, feeling as though they were being watched, which was ridiculous.

"It'll be fine. We know each other pretty well, and you're good at all this relationship stuff— you practically wrote the book."

"It's just that Jack has that intense stare, you know? The one that makes you feel like he can see straight into your soul."

Brady chuckled. "He can't see any deeper than anyone else. Relax."

A rustle sounded behind them as Jack entered the room. He was in his midthirties and had never married, though it wasn't for lack of opportunity. He was built like an Armani model, and with his thick, black hair and blue eyes, he was easy enough on the eyes. Add to that a disposition of humility and compassion, and Hope figured it must be a God thing he hadn't found the right woman yet.

Jack shut the door and eased behind his massive desk. "I guess you meant it when you said you didn't want a long engagement."

"We didn't see any reason to wait once we were sure," Brady said.

"Of course. Well, I keep things pretty casual during these sessions. The purpose is to make sure you've looked at all the important issues that'll affect the health of your marriage. It's always a good idea to get everything out there on the table." He gave Hope a look. "I know I'm preaching to the choir here."

He started with easy topics, asking what kinds of things they enjoyed doing and how they were compatible. Hope began to relax as she saw they really did know each other quite well. It was easy to spell out the qualities she liked about Brady, and he didn't have any problems listing hers.

"She's kind, she's a good listener, she's wise and fun, and she's pretty darn sexy too."

Her eyes had darted to his at that point. She'd never forget the way his eyes flashed with awareness when they turned to her. It would be a long time before she forgot that list too. She'd underestimated him. He was good at this counseling stuff.

He'd reached over and taken her hand at some point, and their fingers were laced together on his thigh, their damp palms pressed together. She glanced at the wall clock, surprised at how their session had flown past.

Pastor Jack was nodding as Brady finished a thought. Then he turned toward Hope. "We have time for one more. Hope, why don't you tell me about the last conflict the two of you had and how you resolved it."

"Umm . . ." She looked at Brady, thinking back. They'd kind of argued about whether or not to get engaged, but she couldn't say that. Even as friends, they hadn't bickered. She'd always found Brady reasonable and even-tempered.

"We actually get along really well," Brady said. Hope nodded.

"Well, sure," Jack said. "But every couple disagrees now and then. You've surely had differences of opinion . . ."

"Of course." Hope looked to Brady, desperation probably shining in her eyes.

"Right," Brady said. "Well . . . Saturday would probably be the most recent conflict. I, uh, got a little jealous, I guess you might say."

Something fluttered in Hope's belly as her gaze sharpened on him. He hadn't exactly couched it in those terms on Saturday. She wondered if it was true or if he was just embellishing the story.

"Okay," Jack said. "Tell me about that."

Brady's neck was mottled pink. "Uh, it was the other night at the Rusty Nail. I thought someone was flirting with Hope when she was up at the bar getting a drink."

Jack looked at Hope. "How did Brady respond to that?"

She traded looks with her fiancé. "He, uh, seemed a little out of sorts when I got back to the table, and I was concerned. I asked him what was wrong."

"Did he tell you what was bothering him?"

"Yes," she said. "And I assured him I wasn't flirting. That I was completely committed to him and our relationship."

"Good." Jack's gaze shifted to Brady. "And how did you respond to that, Brady?"

He gave a sheepish smile. "I apologized for acting like an idiot."

Jack chuckled. "Well done. Was that the end of it?"

"Yes," they both said at the same time.

"Good." Pastor Jack nodded.

He reiterated the importance of conflict resolution and went into detail about what they'd done right. They talked about how disagreements could escalate if handled improperly.

When time ran out Jack wrapped up the session, and they set a date for later in the week.

⭙

"Man . . ." Brady pulled his shirt from his damp chest as they made their way across the parking lot to their cars. "I'm sweating bullets here."

"You were the one who said we had nothing to worry about. I thought it was pretty easy."

He shot her a droll look. "You're not the one who had to admit to being jealous."

She chuckled, the melodious sound making

something inside him light up. He had to pull his eyes from her stunning smile.

"So it was true," she said. "You really were jealous."

"Stop gloating."

"I can't help it. It's so much fun watching you squirm. And so fascinating that you were jealous." She eyed him for a long moment, ending with a saucy look. "Admit it, Collins. You like me."

His lips twitched. "Shut up."

"You do." She nudged his shoulder. "You totally like me. You think I'm sexy."

His smile broke into a laugh even as heat bloomed in his cheeks. "You're impossible."

"Impossibly sexy."

"I am never going to live this down."

"Not in a million years," she said. "I'm going to tell our children how smitten you were with me from the very start."

He nailed her with a look. "Our children, huh? Sounds like our courtship is progressing pretty quickly there, Hope."

She gave a little cough. Her chin dipped down as she rummaged through her purse for her keys, her hair like a curtain in front of her face. "Yeah, you keep thinking that, mister."

Interesting. He hit the fob to unlock his car, and his heart lurched when she tossed a smile over her shoulder.

"See you tomorrow," she said.

"See you."

He hadn't even turned the ignition key when her Civic rolled past him a moment later. He was too busy sitting there wondering when in the world things had shifted inside him. Wondering if things were shifting inside of her too. The thought brought a moment's hesitation. Was this shift a good thing or should he start dialing it back?

Naw, he thought, shaking his head, a smile curling his lips. It was just him and Hope doing their flirting thing. Perfectly harmless.

CHAPTER ELEVEN

Hope let herself into her apartment and turned up the air-conditioning. Three weeks had passed since their first counseling session, and she and Brady had fallen into a nice rhythm. She came over in the morning to watch Sam and stayed until Brady quit for the day. They'd squeezed in two counseling sessions a week, and tomorrow was their last.

She'd spoken with Diana Mayhew about the radio job a few days ago. Hope knew she needed to tell Brady about it, but she'd been putting it off. She knew she'd probably have to give up the opportunity, and he was going to feel just awful about it.

She didn't feel so great about it herself, to be honest. She couldn't help but feel she was letting someone else's fate dictate her own, and she'd already done that once before. Look how that had turned out. But Sam needed a full-time caregiver, and that's what she'd signed on for.

Her cell phone buzzed as she dropped her purse on the counter. She fished her phone from her pocket, smiling when she saw Brady's name on the screen.

"Hey there," she said by way of greeting. "Forget to tell me something?"

"Nope."

She smiled at the deep sound of his voice as she cranked up the air. "I just left your house five minutes ago."

"I know. I'm calling to ask you out on a date."

"A date, huh? So you can spend even more time with me? We see each other nearly every day. You should be sick of me by now."

"I can't court you without taking you out on dates. Sorry it's taken me so long to figure that out."

She laughed at the sheepish note in his voice. "Apology and invitation accepted."

"Great. I'll make a reservation for Saturday if that works for you."

"Oooh, goodie. I get to dress up. And yes, Saturday's fine. What about Sam?"

"The Parkers will have him overnight."

"Great. That'll help keep your mind off of it too. I know you fret when he's gone."

"I'll be fine."

"Plus, we can celebrate our graduation from premarital counseling."

"Hear! Hear!" There'd been more than one awkward moment in that office. "More importantly, Saturday is exactly one month from our wedding date. That's certainly worth celebrating."

"You are such a romantic," Hope teased. "See, I never would've guessed that about you."

"You ain't seen nothing yet, Daniels."

Brady could only stare when Hope opened her apartment door on Saturday night. Her eyes looked exotic, though she wore minimal makeup. Her red lips were her prominent feature tonight. She wore her dark hair partly up, in a style that was a little messy and a lot sexy. He'd been thinking that word a lot lately.

His eyes swept downward, taking in her little black dress and a pair of long legs that ended in slinky high heels. He was sure he'd seen her dressed up before, and for the life of him, he couldn't understand how he'd overlooked her.

"Wow."

Her smile widened as she stepped over the threshold and pulled the door closed behind her. "Wow yourself. You clean up pretty good, Collins."

He didn't imagine he could compare in his black pants and button-down. He escorted her to his Infinity and opened her door, not even trying to drag his eyes from her long legs as she tucked them inside.

They chatted about their days as they made the short drive to the Blue Moon Grill, Copper Creek's only fancy restaurant. It was situated on the outskirts of town, adjacent to the town's namesake creek.

The host led them through the dimly-lit

restau-rant to a booth beside the bank of windows at the back. The mountains were mere silhouettes against the darkening sky.

After the server brought their drinks, Brady raised his glass. "To our prewedding anniversary."

She clinked his glass. "Cheers." Her lips twitched as she took a sip.

"What?" He didn't want to take his eyes from her face. The candlelight shed a soft glow over her skin, making her look radiant. The soft, wispy curls around her face set off her eyes.

"I was just thinking how bizarre it is that we're celebrating an anniversary on our first date."

He shrugged. "So we're doing things a little out of order."

"You even proposed before our first date. That must be some kind of record."

"Not many women can claim that."

"We'll share a child before we share our first kiss."

He gave a playful scowl. "Since we won't officially share Sam until we're married, I can only assume you're shooting me down before I even walk you to your door."

She gave him a sassy smile. "I don't kiss on the first date, mister."

"Now you tell me."

She laughed, and he couldn't pull his gaze away from the sparkle in her eyes.

"You know, you're pretty charming when you want to be," she said.

"Charming enough to get a first-date kiss?"

She lifted a shoulder. "Policies are policies."

The server came and took their orders. Brady sank back in the booth, content to enjoy the soft music and relaxing atmosphere.

"So . . . ," Hope said. "People have been asking me where we're going for our honeymoon."

"Yeah, me too. I guess we should go someplace for a night or two, or it might seem a little odd."

She hitched a brow. "Won't being on a honeymoon with me seem a little odd?"

"We'll just think of it as an extended date. Heather and her husband will have Sam that weekend, so that'll make it easy. Where would you like to go?"

"I don't know. We probably shouldn't go too far away."

"Maybe Gatlinburg?"

She gave it some thought. "That would be perfect. There's great hiking there if you're up for that."

"I love to hike. All right then. I'll reserve a place—two nights?"

"Sounds like a plan."

The food came soon, and they enjoyed their tender steaks. Hope kept thinking of Diana and that job. Such a big opportunity. Should she bring it up? Or just tell Diana she couldn't accept it?

A few minutes later Brady pushed away his plate. "What's on your mind?"

"What do you mean?"

"You're distracted. You have that little frowny thing between your eyebrows and you've gotten quiet."

She gave him a look.

"What's going on? Are you having reservations? Regrets?"

"No . . . of course not. I just . . ."

He leaned forward on his elbows, those blue eyes laser-focused on her. "Tell me."

She had to get this out. Where would their relationship be if they couldn't talk about the important stuff? "It's nothing, it's just . . . There's this job opportunity at WKPC."

"The station in Atlanta? What kind of job?"

"Back when I was filling in, Diana called me into her office. She told me their drive-time jock is retiring in October, and they thought I'd be a good fit for the position. She also said they wanted me to bring *Living with Hope* to their programming."

"Hope . . . that's an amazing opportunity. Why didn't you tell me? That was weeks ago."

"I don't know. It just kind of got lost in all our . . . planning. And besides, I'm going to turn it down."

"What? No, you can't do that. This is the kind of job you've dreamed about."

"Brady, the job's in Atlanta. Your business is here, and I can't be both places at once."

He stared at her for a long minute. "You can't turn this down," he said finally.

Hope set her napkin on her plate. "See, this is why I didn't tell you. I knew you'd insist on my taking the job, and where does that leave us? And Sam? Don't lose sight of what's most important here—our marriage and the reasons for it."

"We can work around all that. You can commute. Come home on weekends. We'll work something out. I'm not letting you give up your dream job to help me."

Hope's heart softened as she looked into Brady's adamant face. Could that really work? "What about Sam? Who's going to take care of him?"

"I can find childcare for Sam. I never intended you to give up your life for us, Hope. Other couples live apart sometimes—military, sales-people." He took her hand and squeezed it. "We'll figure it out. All right? I want this for you."

Her lips turned up as relief flooded through her. She hadn't realized how much she wanted that job until this moment. "All right. Thanks, Brady."

The conversation lightened as the evening drew to a close. Hope felt immensely relieved about the job situation. Relieved to have the topic finally out on the table. Talking about it had even seemed to draw them closer.

So she didn't know why she was suddenly nervous as they walked up her apartment stairs. This was hardly a normal first date. She'd already told him about her first-date policy, so there shouldn't be any "will he or won't he" tension going on.

Nevertheless, her hands were trembling as she unlocked her door. She turned around wearing a ready smile to find him standing closer than she'd expected.

He got even closer as he set his palm on the doorframe over her head. The rich, spicy scent of his cologne was nice. Masculine. She breathed it in and took a moment to appreciate his smoothly shaved face and the sharp turn of his jaw.

"I do believe you're leaning," she said.

"Leaning?"

"Haven't you ever seen *While You Were Sleeping*?"

"I guess I missed that one. Does it have something to do with that first-date policy of yours?"

"No, it has to do with leaning."

"Is that against your first-date policy too?"

"According to Bill Pullman's character in the movie, leaning has certain . . . implications."

He gave her a sideways look. "Now you have me curious."

"We'll have to watch it soon then."

"You're not going to tell me?"

"Nope."

"Sounds like a second date to me. How about next Saturday. We'll have Sam, but I can make you supper, and we can watch it after I put him down."

"I do like a man who cooks."

"Not to mention a man who subjects himself to what I can only assume is a romantic comedy."

"You assume correctly, Mr. Collins."

He gave a playful scowl. "You may have to wake me up for the leaning part."

"I'll let you pick the next one—and I say that knowing full well you're a sci-fi fan, so that should tell you how very flexible I am."

He held her gaze, an inscrutable look on his face. She watched as he took her in, his eyes dropping to her lips, his lashes dark shadows against his cheeks.

"What's that look for?" Her voice wasn't quite steady. "You're not thinking of disregarding my policy tonight, are you?"

"Hmm . . . No. I think I'll save it until you just can't wait another minute."

"There's that male ego. I was beginning to wonder if you had one."

"I might even make you beg for it."

She laughed. "That's some imagination you have there, Collins."

She was still smiling a moment later as he leaned even closer. Until his scent wrapped around her. Until his warm breath caressed her face.

Then his lips were on her forehead. Soft and warm and sweet.

She told herself the tightening in her chest was surprise, not disappointment.

He slowly drew away, a tender smile on his lips. "I had a great time tonight, Hope."

"Me too. Thank you for a lovely first date." The best she'd had in years, she realized. He was just so much fun. And so easy to talk to. He wasn't exactly hard on the eyes either.

He pushed away and gave her one last smile before he headed down the stairs. She opened her door and entered her apartment, still feeling the imprint of his lips on her forehead.

CHAPTER TWELVE

Hope entered the small lounge off the ladies' restroom, smoothing the skirt of her white gown. It rustled quietly with each step, keeping tempo with the heavy thuds of her heart. She couldn't believe it was already her wedding day. The last month had flown past. Minutes from now she'd be Mrs. Brady Collins.

Deep breaths.

As she entered the room Zoe straightened from the mirror, her tube of lipstick poised midair. "Hope . . . You look gorgeous."

"Just look at you!" Josephine said. "That dress is perfection."

"Oh my lands." Daisy fanned her face. "I'm gonna cry, y'all."

"Don't do that," Josephine said. "You'll mess up all my hard work."

"Come over here in front of the mirror." Zoe ushered Hope in front of the full-length mirror, and her three friends gathered around. They wore short, black dresses of varying styles paired with silver jewelry.

Hope's eyes swung to her own reflection, hardly able to believe what she saw. "I love the way you did my hair, Josephine." The half-up, half-down style included complicated braiding and a waterfall of curls. It sure helped having a hair stylist for a friend.

Not to mention a flower shop owner. "And the flowers are gorgeous, Daisy. I took a quick peek before I started getting ready. I love the way the honeysuckle drapes from the arrangements. And I could smell the sweet fragrance the minute I walked in."

"It's going to be a beautiful wedding."

Hope's parents had arrived a week ago and helped with the last-minute details. It was so good to see them and catch up. They'd known Brady back in high school, but he'd done a lot of growing up since then. Her dad picked his brain about cars while her mom fussed over Sam. They all got on just fine. She wished they could stay longer, but Ecuador was their home. They were out greeting guests now, and soon her dad would escort her down the aisle.

Deep, deep breaths.

"That dress fits you like a glove," Josephine said. "You're simply stunning."

Daisy palmed Hope's bare shoulder. "Brady's going to faint dead away when he sees you coming down that aisle."

Hope bit her lip. She hadn't spoken to her fiancé all day, much less seen him. She'd never realized what a stupid tradition that was. She wanted to look into his eyes and reassure herself that they were on the same page. That he hadn't changed his mind. That he wasn't going to be a no-show at his own wedding. Were they crazy? Were they doing the right thing?

Hope's eyes fastened on her friends' in the mirror. "Is he here yet?"

"Of course he's here." Zoe fiddled with Hope's skirt. "This material is like a cloud. So pretty."

"So you've actually seen him?"

Josephine chuckled. "Listen to you."

"He's in the back room getting into his suit with the other guys," Zoe said. "Relax, everything's fine."

"Is he nervous?"

"He's excited."

"Is that code for nervous?"

Josephine laughed. "It's code for he's the luckiest man in the world, and he knows it."

"Oh!" Daisy said. "That reminds me. I just went in to put on their boutonnieres, and he gave me a message for you. He said to tell you he still has a 'raging case of permanent insanity.' I think I got that right . . ."

Hope froze for a long beat, then threw her head back and laughed. The weight of worry slid right off her shoulders. That guy. She could hug his neck right now.

Zoe was looking at her, wearing a speculative smile. "That's more like it."

Hope couldn't seem to stop smiling. She couldn't believe how just a few words had lifted her spirits. Assured her that this was right. That's how it was with Brady. She'd truly enjoyed their closer relationship these last two months.

She touched up her lipstick. "I can't believe it's already my wedding day. It seems like he just put the ring on my finger."

Zoe smirked. "He did, honey. You had a two-month engagement. If you'd told me a few months ago that you'd be getting married before me, I would never have believed it."

Hope's eyes found Zoe's, worry of a different kind pressing in. "It doesn't bother you, does it? I hope you don't feel like we stole the spotlight."

Zoe squeezed her hand. "Not at all. I just want what's best for you and Brady. My own wedding day will arrive soon enough—in six weeks, to be exact."

"And it's going to be perfect."

Daisy checked her phone. "Speaking of arriving, y'all. It's about that time."

"All right, ladies," Zoe said. "Let's do this."

Brady stuck a finger under his stiff collar and tugged. He straightened his bow tie, then fiddled with his hair. Stupid cowlick. Couldn't do a thing with it today. He shrugged into the black suit coat, giving himself a once-over in the mirror.

He wondered if it was normal to be this nervous. Wondered if Hope was feeling the same way. Then he started second-guessing the message he'd sent through Daisy. What if Hope had taken it the wrong way? What if they were making a big, huge mistake?

He closed his eyes, whispering a prayer until he felt peace settle over him like a spring fog over the valley. *All right. It's going to be okay.* He drew in a deep breath as the need to hyperventilate left him. Smells mingled together in his nose: cologne, flowers, musty hymnals.

A hand clapped down on his shoulder, startling him.

"Dude. Relax," Cruz said, meeting his gaze in the mirror. "It'll all be over soon."

"Wow. Thanks for that."

Cruz chuckled, giving his shoulder a squeeze. "Everything's fine. Pastor Jack said it's time to get out there."

Two minutes later Brady, Cruz, Noah, and Pastor Jack stood in front of the small crowd. Mrs. Hammond began a sweet melody on her violin, and the attendants started down the aisle. Brady tried to look around them, hoping for a glimpse of Hope. He needed to see her face. Lock onto her eyes, see that confident smile blooming on her face.

Zoe and Cruz's daughter, Gracie, came down the aisle next in a white sundress. She was cute as could be, her red curls framing her face, her skirt bobbing with each careful step. Her eyes found her daddy's as she neared the front, looking a little lost and uncertain. Cruz pointed toward Zoe on the other side of the aisle, and the crowd chuckled as Gracie scuttled toward her.

As Gracie settled into place beside Zoe, the violin music segued smoothly into the rousing notes of the "Wedding March." The crowd stood, turning toward the back of the sanctuary.

Brady's heart lurched in his chest as his eyes fixed on the doorway. Hope stepped into the space on the arm of her father.

Brady's lungs took a breath and held it hostage. She was gorgeous. Like an angel in her white dress with the light flooding in all around her. Her eyes locked on his, a smile stretching her lips. That smile. It could calm every fear. Brighten every corner. Negotiate peace treaties.

Mine, his heart whispered.

She wore no veil, allowing him free access to the twinkle in her eyes as she neared. She was thinking about his message right now, he just knew it. She'd understood. Why had he ever worried? They'd always been on the same wavelength.

His lips twitched, and she winked at him as Pastor Jack asked who gave her away. Mr. Daniels performed his duties, then took a seat in the pew beside his wife.

In the next few minutes Brady barely heard a word Jack said. He was too busy thinking about

Hope, standing so close beside him. About the amazing gift she was giving him. About how beautiful she was—he was dying to take another peek.

Instead, he brushed the back of her hand with his, and she laced her fingers with his, squeezing tight.

A few minutes later her voice was steady as she repeated her vows. And after he recited his, he slid the band onto her finger. It stuck a little on her knuckle, and heat surged up his neck before the ring finally glided over, slipping into place. He released a breath.

The crowd gave a nervous chuckle as Brady met her smiling eyes. He somehow knew she was thinking about the stuck engagement ring and the ham-swollen fingers that had gotten them both into this.

⇒❖⇐

Hope's eyes were locked onto Brady's as Pastor Jack gave a few last thoughts. Brady's thumb swept over the sensitive skin on the back of her hand, somehow calming her. She took in his solemn face, his steadfast gaze, and knew a moment of pure certainty.

Here was a man who would not let her down. A man who would put her before his own desires. A man she could trust and respect. They didn't come any finer than Brady.

Her eyes swept over his familiar face, from the smooth line of his jaw to the straight slash of his brows, and upward to the adorable cow-lick. It was stiff with product. He'd tried to tame it for their big day. Her heart softened at the thought.

"Therefore," Pastor Jack was saying, "by the authority vested in me, and in the name of the Father, Son, and Holy Spirit, I now pronounce you husband and wife. What God hath joined together, let no one put asunder." He turned to Brady with a crooked smile. "You may kiss your bride."

Brady turned toward Hope, his eyes serious and searching hers. He leaned down, his breath a mere prelude, before his lips swept over hers, slow and soft. Her pulse skipped a beat, reminding her how long it had been since she'd been kissed.

It would've been enough, that gentle whisper of a touch, to satisfy the requirement. But he drew her closer and swept his lips over hers once again as if the first taste hadn't been quite enough. And this time she realized the little pulse-like flutter hadn't merely been her lack of recent experience.

Collins could flat-out kiss.

His lips were the perfect blend of pliant and firm. Reverence and passion. Brady kissed like kissing was the whole point, not a brief stop on a journey to some better destination.

When he drew away, her eyes fluttered open to

meet his heavy-lidded stare. Oooh, those eyes.

"Not bad, Collins," she said on an unsteady breath.

"Not so bad yourself, Daniels."

She arched a saucy brow. "It's Collins now, mister."

Something flickered in his eyes. But before he could reply Pastor Jack turned them to face the crowd. His voice boomed across the sanctuary. "I now present to you . . . Mr. and Mrs. Brady Collins."

Hope gave Brady a sideways look as the crowd cheered. "Told ya so."

Hope's toes were pinched, and her jaw ached from smiling by the time Brady drew her onto the dance floor for what she assumed was the last slow dance of the night.

Her boss at the Rusty Nail had hosted the reception as his wedding gift. The food he'd provided at cost, making the whole thing ridiculously affordable. Her parents and attendants had strung the place with white twinkle lights and tulle, transforming the space into a rustic wedding celebration.

They'd made it through the first dance, the toasts, and the cake. They'd made the rounds, gulped down their food, and joined the wedding party on the dance floor for numerous line dances. It was loads of fun, this wedding stuff. And exhausting.

She'd only thought about her high school sweetheart twice today. Once when she'd awakened this morning and again when Aaron's parents had come through the receiving line. Both times she'd pushed the thoughts into the recesses of her mind. It was all such a long time ago. There was no point reliving the past. She had to move forward now. With Brady. And you know what? She could think of worse things.

She slipped into his arms, sliding her hands up his shoulders, pausing only to straighten his bow tie. She drew in a deep breath, catching a hint of spicy cologne that was all Brady.

They still had a long drive to Gatlinburg tonight. He hadn't told her a thing about where they were staying, but after the rushed planning and the tiring day, she was ready for a little getaway.

"Have I told you how beautiful you look tonight?" Brady's arms came around her as the nostalgic strains of "The Way You Look Tonight" began. His hand made little circles on the small of her back. "Really, Hope. I feel pretty darn lucky—for a lot of different reasons."

Her aching jaw managed another smile. "Me too, Brady. And you look awfully handsome yourself. Half the women in Copper Creek are probably going into grief therapy tomorrow."

He laughed. "You're outrageous. And I love that about you."

He twirled her around, spinning her gracefully.

136

Flashes flared in the twinkle lights as she came back into his embrace. He tightened his arms, bringing her against him as they moved together as one.

She'd known he was a good dancer, but he was taking it to a whole new level tonight. "Smooth, Collins. I had no idea you had so many moves."

"You ain't seen nothing yet."

She arched a brow at him, but he only chuckled as he led her through another graceful spin. The dance floor grew crowded, so they finished out the dance with Hope's cheek pressed to his shoulder.

As the last notes rang out, the memory of his sweet kiss lingered in her mind. A smile curled her lips as she wondered what the rest of the night would bring. What the rest of the weekend would bring. And just for tonight, she didn't bother looking any further ahead than that.

CHAPTER THIRTEEN

Brady unlocked the cabin door and pushed it open, letting Hope enter first. Behind him, beyond the cozy porch, crickets and katydids chirped from a darkened pine grove.

"Oh!" Hope stopped just inside the door. "I love it!"

He set down the bags as she spun around, taking in the high-beamed ceiling, the floor-to-ceiling stone fireplace, and the log railing leading to the second-floor loft. The cabin smelled pleasantly of pine cleaner and woodsmoke, and a crackling fire pushed back the evening chill.

He never would have booked such a rustic place for Audrey, who'd liked things sleek and shiny. But this somewhat luxurious little charmer seemed right up Hope's ally. He was delighted his instincts had been right on target.

"Who lit the fire?" She stopped on her way to the hearth, gasping at the bouquet of fresh flowers, which included a cascade of white honeysuckle. "And brought the flowers?" She shot him a you-shouldn't-have grin.

He lifted a shoulder. "Just did a little pre-arranging."

She paused to take a whiff of the nearest bloom. "Mmm. Thanks, Brady. You're such a sweetheart.

You're making me feel guilty for taking you off the dating market."

He gave a gruff laugh. "What dating market? I've been out of circulation a long time."

"Well," she said, "I'm a lucky girl, and I know it." She put her hand over her mouth to cover a wide yawn. It was well after midnight, and it had been a long day for both of them.

"A tired one too, by the looks of it. Why don't we go ahead and hit the hay? There's a trail nearby that boasts a beautiful sunrise view."

Her smile fell. "Sunrise? As in the hour when the sun comes up?"

"That would be the one."

"You're going to kill me this weekend, aren't you?"

He gave her a look. "You said you loved to hike."

"In theory. I like to walk . . . I like pretty views."

"Well, you're going to get plenty of both."

"Um, are there going to be spiders?"

"What? In the woods? In the mountains? Of course not."

He ignored her adorable whimper as he walked over and made sure the firebox was well covered. The flames were already low and would extinguish themselves soon. He hefted their bags and started up the stairs.

Hope followed behind him, soon forgetting

the hiking as she began oohing and aahing over the knobby railings and the hand-stitched quilt hanging against the wall.

He stopped at the first door at the top of the stairs and ushered her in. "Madame, your room." She stepped inside, taking in the generously sized master suite, tastefully decorated in neutral tones. "Oh, it's beautiful."

He set her suitcase just inside the door as his gaze swept over the huge rug that hugged the wood floor and the king-size bed that dominated the room. It was so high that, even with those long legs of hers, she'd almost need a stepladder to crawl into it.

She wandered over to the adjoining bathroom, which he knew featured a large garden tub and a walk-in shower. "Wow." She disappeared inside the room. "I'm used to water stains and a clingy shower curtain, you know. This is quite the step up."

When she returned, she stopped on the bathroom's threshold. "So . . ." She leaned against the wooden jam with an enigmatic look. "We never really talked about, uh, sleeping arrangements . . ."

He cleared his throat and nodded his head toward the hall. "I'll be right across the hall. I have my own bathroom too."

Her eyebrows hiked up below her sideswept bangs. Her hair was still in that messy, sexy updo, exposing her graceful neck. He wondered what she'd do if he pressed a kiss to the tempting spot between her neck and shoulder.

"Are you sure? I mean . . . It's a big bed. I might not even know you're there."

"When I share a bed with you, wife, I most definitely want you to know I'm there."

Surprise flickered in her eyes before she gave him a most sexy smile. "Well said."

"I'm courting you, remember? Maybe it's been a while, but I wasn't in the habit of sharing a bed with my dates."

She cocked her head. "Well, you weren't exactly married at the time either."

He smirked. "Sorry, Mrs. Collins. I'm afraid you're just going to have to wait."

Her laughter floated like a melody as he turned to leave the room.

"Waiting for me to beg? Like I had to beg for that kiss today?" she taunted.

"That was an order from an ordained minister," he said over his shoulder. "It was strictly obligatory."

"It sure didn't feel obligatory."

He paused in the hallway, his lips curling at the sass in her voice. "Careful, sweetheart. I might start thinking you enjoyed it."

In the beat of silence he could count the ticks of the mantel clock, hear a quiet series of snaps from the fire below. Where was the saucy laugh? The snappy comeback?

"You got nothing, Collins?" he asked. Something warm engulfed him as he used her married name. *His* name.

"Good night, husband," she called in a sing-songy voice.

He could picture the indignant thrust of her chin that probably accompanied that tone. "Good night, wife." His smile widened as he set his feet in motion. "Don't forget to set your alarm for six o'clock."

She groaned, and he heard the unmistakable *whoosh* of a body falling onto a mattress.

He chuckled. And he was still smiling minutes later when he drifted off to sleep.

CHAPTER FOURTEEN

When they finally reached the peak of Mount Torture, Hope was a wreck. She'd hit snooze when her alarm went off and had to choose between a shower and coffee. She'd chosen poorly. So poorly.

She blamed lack of caffeine for the fact that her legs wobbled and her eyeballs hurt, and also that she was about to die.

She stopped a few feet behind Brady, placing her hands on her knees. "I'm equally in need of caffeine and water. And oxygen. The air's thinner up here, huh? It's like I'm breathing, but there's no oxygen." She sucked in four quick breaths. "I think I'm hyperventilating."

Even in the predawn dimness she could see his droll look.

"We're barely at three thousand feet, Hope."

"So I'm out of shape, is that what you're saying?"

He put his palms up. "Hey, I may be a rookie husband, but I'm not stupid. Besides . . ." His gaze raked over her, from her messy ponytail to her hip-length T-shirt to the tight yoga pants, and northward again. "Your shape looks pretty good from over here."

Her lips tugged upward in a smug smile; she

145

suddenly felt much better. "You catch on quick, Collins."

He slid the backpack from his shoulders and set it on a boulder that was large enough to seat twelve. "Come sit down."

"You don't have to ask me twice."

As Brady unzipped the backpack, Hope surveyed the view while she caught her breath. A valley opened before them, immense, she assumed from the magnitude of the climb she'd just endured.

Across the valley the dark mountains shielded the sun. But a golden orange glow swept low across the sky, heralding the eminent sunrise. The colors faded upward into light blue, then into the inky darkness that the sun would soon push back. In a few minutes it would be a stunning panorama.

She drew in a lungful of fresh mountain air, catching the scent of pine and loamy earth. Somewhere nearby a bird chirped good morning, and a cool breeze rustled the canopy of leaves.

"Here you go." Brady handed her a Thermos mug, filled with precious coffee.

Praise Jesus. "I love you," she said heartily, then took a careful sip.

"My plan is working already." He settled on the rock next to her, balancing his own cup.

"And just what plan is that?"

"Always leave them wanting more, baby."

She laughed. That he could make her laugh, uncaffeinated, at o'dark hundred said a lot.

A glowing sliver of orange peeked through a break between two mountains. "Look. Here it comes."

As if by agreement they watched in silence as the orange ball rose slowly over the horizon. Even the sounds of nature seemed to hush in awe of the moment as the sun became a half circle and then a globe, resting like a glowing ball between the two mountains.

"Wow," she said, looking at Brady when the sun grew too bright. "That was stunning."

He arched a brow. "Worth the hike then?"

"If I say yes, are we going to make this crack-of-dawn climb again tomorrow?"

"I might let you sleep in." He reached into the backpack, withdrew a white box, and pulled back the lid for her.

Half a dozen gourmet pastries were nestled inside. She sucked in a breath. "Where did those come from?"

"Prearranged. Pick one."

"Just one?" She selected a raspberry Danish, looking at him sideways as she chewed the sweet, gooey pastry.

"What?" he asked.

"Do you have any flaws? Any at all?"

"What? Of course I do."

"What are they?"

He took his time chewing a bite of the chocolate muffin he'd selected. "Well, for starters, I'm obsessed with sports cars, and I tend to care too much . . ."

"That's a flaw?"

"And I can be a little insecure sometimes. What about you?"

She wanted to explore that last one, but later. "Mine aren't exactly a secret. Sometimes I speak without thinking. I tend to exaggerate. I can be a wee bit bossy. And also my thighs."

He choked. "Your thighs?"

"Did I say that out loud?"

"There is nothing wrong with your thighs, Hope." His gaze dipped south and back up. "Not a thing. Geez. Women are so hard on themselves."

"We'll talk again after you've actually seen them."

"Thighs," he muttered, shaking his head, a crooked little smile on his face. "And for the record, I didn't know we were opening this up to physical flaws."

She snorted. "As if you have any." She'd seen him shirtless on more than one occasion. He had a six-pack, arms of steel, and tanned, flawless skin. Not that she'd noticed.

"I have a crooked nose—and I can't even make it cool by saying I got it in a fight. I have a deviated septum. Sexy, huh?"

She laughed. "Where? You do not."

He pointed. "Right here."

She ran her finger over the alleged crook. "You're crazy. It's straight as an arrow."

"And then there're my hands." He held them out, palms up.

She looked, though she didn't need to. She'd noticed his hands a long time ago. They were quite nice. Strong, capable, manly hands. "What's wrong with your hands?"

"They're all calloused and stained. No matter what I scrub them with I can never get them completely clean."

She ran her fingers over his work-roughened palms. "I don't know how to break it to you, buddy, but women find hands like these pretty hot."

"They do not."

"Trust me. They're very manly and rugged and definitely do not count as a flaw."

"Well, I haven't even mentioned my cowlick."

"That's not a flaw either. It's cute."

He gave her a rueful smile. "It's pointy, and it sticks up high enough to perch a bird."

She threw a wadded-up napkin at him, laughing. "You're ridiculous."

Maybe it was the fresh air or the caffeine or the delicious sustenance. Or maybe it was simply Brady. He was so much fun to be with. And so sweet. He'd gone to a lot of trouble for their pseudo honeymoon. She hadn't expected that.

What she had expected was a moment or two after the ceremony when she questioned her sanity. When she wondered if she'd just made the biggest mistake of her life. A mistake that couldn't be easily corrected. But so far, no signs of that. At least for her. She was enjoying herself too much.

She nudged his shoulder, waiting until his eyes locked onto hers. The sunlight made the blue flecks almost silver. "No regrets?"

He held her gaze for a long, pulse-stirring moment. "No regrets."

His eyes were smiling. He'd have laugh lines as he grew older. Probably go a little gray at the temples and be more handsome than ever, the jerk.

"You'd tell me if you did?" she asked.

"I would. But what about you? Has your sanity returned yet?"

She laughed, remembering his message the day before. "I guess not. And, by the way, thanks for that pre-ceremony message. I was fretting a bit."

His gaze sharpened on her. "Doubts?"

"Not about me. I was afraid you'd changed your mind. Getting downright neurotic about it, in fact."

"You didn't have to worry about that, Hope. I think life with you is going to be pretty darn fun."

"Well, it won't be boring, I can assure you of that."

His gaze roved over her face until heat flared up inside her. "I think you're right."

Something fluttered in her belly. She remembered his wedding kiss—who could forget? She could almost see the reverent way he'd looked at her as he leaned in. Feel the gentle brush of his lips. Once. Twice. Not enough. She'd like to try it again, without the audience.

As if reading her mind, his eyes dropped to her mouth.

Her heart thumped, and her lips parted in anticipation.

But instead of leaning forward he turned back to look at the valley.

Her breath *whooshed* out. She told herself the clenching of her stomach was just hunger. Right. Hunger. She needed sustenance. She took a tasteless bite of the Danish.

Brady finished off his muffin. "I didn't realize how hungry I was."

"We burned a lot of calories this morning." She took a sip of her coffee, rebounding from the moment. "And supper last night was a little rushed, huh?"

"It was a crazy night. Good, though. I think our friends enjoyed themselves. I know I did."

He'd been a prince about the whole wedding thing. She was glad she hadn't settled for a quick after-church ceremony. She would've regretted it, and her mom would've been disappointed.

"Thanks for going through with all that. I'm glad we had a real wedding."

He grinned at her. "Me too. Thanks for not being a bridezilla."

She smiled, thinking of all the late-night planning talks after his long days in the garage. He'd never once become impatient with her indecision or argumentative about details.

She thought of all he'd been through the last year with Audrey. How the woman had jerked his heart around. He hadn't deserved that.

"I don't mean to speak ill of the dead," she said softly. "But Audrey was crazy. I hope you know that. She had no idea what she had in you."

He shot her a look before taking another muffin. "Thanks for saying that."

"It's true."

As they finished breakfast they talked about their plans for the rest of the day. Hope was glad he had more than hiking on the agenda. They decided to do the scenic chairlift in Ober Gatlinburg, catch lunch in town, then go back to the cabin for a nap. Now that was a plan she could get on board with.

After taking some selfies, they started down the trail. The hike down was much easier, Hope was happy to find. They even managed to carry on a conversation.

"So this car obsession of yours . . . ," she said as he helped her over a log in the path. "Do you have a favorite? A dream car?"

"The McLaren F1."

She laughed. "That was quick. What makes it your dream car?"

"Well, first of all it's rare. Only sixty-four of them ever made. And it's fast, of course—has a top speed of 243 mph."

"That is fast. So is that what you're working toward someday? To own a McLaren F1?"

"I'd be happy just getting to work on one. Buying one would set me back about ten million."

Hope's eyes bulged. "Ten million dollars? Yeesh!"

"I'd settle for a McLaren 720S, though, if you're making my Christmas list."

"I'm afraid to ask what that one costs."

"It's only $254,000. But it can take you from 0 to 60 in a mere 2.8 seconds. See, I'm willing to compromise."

She laughed. "That's more than your house is worth."

"*Our* house. Told you . . . obsession." He checked his watch as he maneuvered around a boulder in the path. "I want to check my phone when we get back. Make sure Sam's all right."

"I'm sure he's fine. But I miss him."

"Me too." Something in his tone tugged her

eyes to him. He had the worry frown between his brows.

"Hey, none of that worry stuff. We're on our honeymoon. Just check in with Heather when we get back, and you'll see Sammy's doing just fine."

He spared her a smile as he held a branch for her. "You're right. Is your schedule clear this week to stay with him?"

"All except for Thursday. I have that interview at the oldies station. Maybe we can ask Ruby if she wouldn't mind—"

He stopped so suddenly she almost ran into him. "An interview? I thought that job was a done deal."

After their first-date conversation about the opportunity, he'd brought up the job regularly. He really wanted this for her. "It is. This is just a formality."

His eyes pierced hers, concern in the blue depths. "You sure?"

"Stop worrying. It's all in God's hands."

The frown between his brows didn't go away. Nor did the worry in his eyes. "The commuting thing isn't bothering the folks at the station? Hope, I'd feel like dirt if you lost this job because of what you did for me."

Didn't he realize how much he had to offer? What a terrific human being he was? And that was before she even added that adorable baby of his into the mix.

An ache welled in her throat, and she touched his arm. "I'm starting to see what you meant by insecurity. Brady, the job will be great. Commuting won't be an issue. But even if I lost it somehow, I wouldn't regret marrying you. The real gift is you and Sam and the promise of a great future as a family."

She meant that—and it worried her a bit. Was she falling back into an old pattern? She'd been willing to follow Aaron to Duke, and all of that had fallen through with his death. She'd ended up settling for a local college. Was she settling again? No, she wouldn't have to settle. The job was hers, and Brady was willing to make sacrifices to see that happen.

Brady's frown lines had smoothed out, the worry in his eyes beginning to morph into acceptance.

"I'm excited about our future, job or no job," she said. "I mean, I definitely *want* the job . . ."

He huffed a laugh. "You deserve the job. That job has your name written all over it."

"And I'll get the job. So let's just take one step at a time, all right?" She poked him in the side. "And stop fretting over everything."

He gave her a wry grin. "I'm starting to see your bossy side."

"Well, get used to it, mister. There's plenty more where that came from."

CHAPTER FIFTEEN

They decided to spend their last day in Gatlinburg hiking to Midnight Hole. So Brady took the dirt road to the trailhead, and they started the one-and-a-half-mile trek down Big Creek Trail.

As they walked, Brady looked up at the towering white pines shading the needle-strewn path. Branches creaked in the wind, and the air was heavy with the smell of decaying leaves. It was easier than yesterday's hike, with only a moderate incline.

When they came to a spot where the trail dropped steeply to one side, he took Hope's hand and pulled her away from the drop-off. Even after the danger was past, he kept hold of her. It felt natural to have her hand in his.

He couldn't help but compare their short time here to the seven-day honeymoon he'd taken with Audrey. Though she'd agreed to a courthouse wedding, she'd settled for nothing less than a luxurious honeymoon. They'd gone to Gulf Shores and stayed in an upscale condo he could scarcely afford at the time. She wanted to spend all day lying on the beach, and when he suggested anything else she pouted until he gave in.

He glanced at Hope, his mouth inching upward.

She was so easy to please. So easy to be with.

"What?" she asked when she caught him staring too long.

"Nothing. I like you, that's all."

Her smile widened. "Aw. I like you too, Collins."

A while later he heard the rush of water. It was only late morning, but the temperature was nearing ninety degrees. His T-shirt clung to his back, and his hairline was damp with sweat. He was glad for the shady trail, and the cool water was going to feel even better.

The path that led toward the swimming hole split off to the left, and he led her down the trail until it opened to the deserted water hole. Boulders, probably ten feet high, surrounded a small waterfall. The cascade fed a deep blue pool before meandering downstream into a rippling creek.

"Looks like we have the place to ourselves." He set the backpack down on a large rock, kicked off his sandals, and tugged off his T-shirt.

Hope was already headed toward the rocky shoreline. She pulled off her T-shirt, revealing a red swimsuit, slender shoulders, and that tiny waist of hers. She dropped her shirt on a nearby rock and paused to shimmy from her shorts.

His mouth went dry as he looked his fill at his wife.

His *wife.*

Her square shoulders tapered down to a narrow waist that flared out to the subtle curve of her hips. Her long, shapely legs, smooth and tan, seemed to go on a mile. The temperature seemed to go up about twenty degrees, and that cool water was calling his name.

Hope slipped off her sandals and started for the water, not stopping to look back. "Are you checking me out, Collins?"

"You're my wife—I can check you out all I want."

She turned now, her mouth turned upward in a sassy smile. "Turnabout's fair play, you know."

"Have at it, woman."

He hoped she was doing just that—and liking what she saw—as he climbed the boulders, making his way toward the highest one by the waterfall. He was suddenly very grateful for the hours he spent working out.

"Be careful!" she called as he reached the top. "You're not going to—"

He leaped off the edge and heard Hope's shriek just before he hit the water. He kicked to the surface, barely registering the cold water swirling around him.

"You're a nut!" she said as he surfaced. "And you scared me half to death!"

He wiped the water from his eyes, kicking to stay afloat. "A million people have jumped from that boulder and survived."

"And I wonder how many didn't." She was tip-toeing into the water, walking carefully across the rocky creek bed.

He treaded to where his feet reached bottom, his eyes falling over the front of her. Over the red swimsuit, the eye-pleasing curves, and lower still to those legs.

He raked back his wet hair. "So where is this physical flaw you spoke of?"

She gave him a rueful look, finally submerging her body into the deeper water. "Oh, it's there, buddy. It's there."

"Remember what you said about my hands? Well, that goes double for your thighs."

She gave him a patronizing smile. "You're very sweet."

"Well, say what you want. But I haven't seen a single thing I don't like." His face went ten degrees warmer at the admission, but he forced himself to hold her gaze as she neared. His heart was beating like a jackhammer as her eyes pierced his.

She lost her footing and gasped as she sank.

"Careful." He grabbed hold of her before she went completely under and pulled her up.

She latched onto his wrists, and water swirled around his legs as she kicked to stay afloat. "That's a drop-off. I can't reach here."

He walked her backward until her feet touched bottom. But his hands felt quite at home there on the curve of her waist. They tightened reflexively.

She was still holding on to him too, and her gaze was like a caress. "Thanks," she said softly.

She seemed closer than she had been just a few seconds ago. Had she moved, or had the water pushed them together?

The ends of her hair hung ropelike over her bare shoulders, and that feminine scent of hers swirled around him, making him crazy. His eyes trailed up her graceful neck, past that tempting spot in the cradle of her shoulder, past those supple lips and straight to her eyes.

Her lashes were dark and spiky, a luscious frame for her mossy-green eyes. The amber flecks sparkled, an invitation swirling in those green depths.

He followed a water droplet down the curve of her cheek to the corner of her lips. He was unable to deny himself a taste any longer. He leaned down and brushed her mouth with his.

She tasted faintly of coffee and fruit. He nudged her lips open for more and thrilled to her response, a gentle tangling, a sensuous dance that quickened his breath.

Her hands slid up his arms, around his neck, and his skin tingled with want. He forced his hands to stay put, though he wanted to pull her flush against him.

Take it easy, buddy. She was only a friend just two months ago.

But she's your wife now.

Patience. They had all the time in the world. He wasn't going to rush her, even if it killed him. And it just might.

⊰‖⊱

Hope threaded her fingers through Brady's wet hair, loving the warm, wet, slippery feel of him. His scent wrapped around her like a hug, making her want to press closer. She'd loved his wedding kiss. Had relived it a time or two or hundred. But this. He was even better without an audience. So. Much. Better.

Her heart was pounding so hard she was pretty sure a tsunami was in the works. Thank heavens for the water's stabilizing force around her wobbly legs. It had been a long time since she'd been kissed like this.

Had she ever been kissed like this?

She felt him withdrawing a few seconds before he actually pulled away. His blue eyes were hooded, dark, and smoldering. His breaths came in short puffs. Okay, maybe that was her.

"I didn't beg," she said in a breathy whisper. "Just saying."

"I believe your eyes did the begging, young lady." Had he always had that low, lazy drawl?

"True enough, I suppose. I'll give you the point, but it's hardly my fault."

His gaze drifted over her face, and she felt the

look like a touch. Speaking of touch. His thumbs, moving at her sides, were making her insides hum.

"Aren't you going to ask me why it wasn't my fault?" Her fingers moved lazily over his neck. "The wedding kiss was nice, Collins, but this . . ."

His lips curled. "Good to know."

"I see why you had all the girls swooning in high school. Clearly you've had a lot of practice."

"Hope . . . ?"

"Yeah?"

He leaned closer, his lips a breath away. "You talk too much."

And then he found a most effective way to silence her.

CHAPTER SIXTEEN

Brady eased up on the accelerator as he passed the *Welcome to Dalton* sign. In his peripheral vision he caught sight of the vase of flowers Hope had buckled into the back seat and smiled. *Well, they're too pretty to leave behind.* She was a trip. The very best kind.

He'd done a lot of smiling this weekend. They'd done a lot of talking, a lot of laughing, and yeah, a little more kissing since this morning. It had been kind of sad, packing up their things and closing up their cozy little cabin. He could've easily stayed another week, getting to know her quirks, her history, her heart. But it was time to return to real life, and that meant picking up his son.

Their son.

He spared her a glance, realizing anew that Hope was now his son's new mommy. Not that he wouldn't keep Audrey's memory alive for Sam. It was important to him that Sam know who she was, just as Brady had always known who his biological mother was. Reality wasn't always pretty, but it was the truth, and that mattered.

Hope squeezed his hand, and he felt her gaze on him. When he turned to look at her, she was smiling.

"Thanks for the amazing weekend. I had a

really good time. I know it wasn't a real honeymoon but . . ." Her voice trailed off almost apologetically.

He squeezed her hand. "I had a good time too. And for the record, it beat my first honeymoon by a long country mile."

Her brows hitched upward. "No kidding?"

"No kidding." He turned onto Heather's road, coasting to a crawl as her driveway neared. "But that's for another time. We're here now."

He pulled into Heather's driveway. She and her husband lived in a modest ranch in a nice neighborhood. The homes were well-maintained, shaded by a variety of mature trees, and the smell of freshly cut grass hung in the air.

"I'll be right back," he said as he cut the engine. The front door opened as he approached the stoop, and his heart bottomed out at the sight of Patricia Parker. She wasn't supposed to be here. That was the whole point of using Heather as a go-between. His mood sank like a lead brick.

Tension lined Patricia's attractive features and stiffened the slender set of her shoulders. Her ash-blonde hair was shoulder length, but today it was clipped at the back of her neck. She was tall like Audrey had been, and though Brady dwarfed her, the woman's regal bearing felt imposing nonetheless.

He nodded as she stepped down from the stoop. "Patricia. I trust you had a nice weekend."

The corner of her lips curled. "Not as nice as yours, apparently."

He gave her a benign smile. "Is Sam ready to go?"

"Is that her?" Patricia was glaring at his car.

"That's my new wife, yes. Maybe we should just take Sam and go." He edged around her, took the one step, and knocked on the door.

"I have a right to meet the woman who's taking care of my grandchild."

When he turned, he saw Hope had already gotten out of the car. She walked up the sidewalk, seemingly impervious to Patricia's scowl.

"Hi." She extended her hand toward the woman. "I'm Hope."

Brady sighed. "Hope, this is Patricia Parker, Sam's grandma."

The woman crossed her arms over her chest, pointedly ignoring Hope's extended hand.

Hope let her hand fall to her side.

"Mom!" Heather scolded as she stepped outside. Sam was perched on her hip, and the diaper bag hung from her shoulder. "I told you to stay in the house."

Sammy was fussing, and the baby reached for Brady, who took him into his arms. Sam squirmed, rubbing his eyes.

"He's cutting a tooth," Heather said to Brady. "I gave him Tylenol an hour ago."

"Do you actually expect me to believe this farce

of a marriage is real?" Patricia said. "I know just what you're up to, Brady Collins."

"I think we'd best go." Brady turned to leave.

"You won't get away with this!"

"Want me to take him?" Hope asked as she took the diaper bag from Heather.

"I've got him." He ushered Hope off the stoop.

Patricia stood in their way. "What do you even know about her? How dare you bring another woman into our grandson's life so soon after his mother passed!"

Brady reached deep for patience, reminding himself that Patricia was still grieving her daughter. "Hope's a good woman, and she'll be a good mother to Sam."

"And our Audrey wasn't, is that what you're trying to say?" Her voice wobbled with emotion.

"All I'm trying to do is pick up my son, Patricia."

"You never gave her the benefit of the doubt! You always thought the worst of her."

"She tricked him into marrying her," Hope said. "And she lied about Sam."

Brady squeezed Hope's arm. "Please move out of our way, Patricia."

Patricia nailed Hope with a glare. "You have no say in this! I know all about you—looking to make your way up in the world by marrying a desperate man."

"That's enough," Brady said.

"Mom, come on." Heather took the woman's elbow and pulled her aside. "This isn't productive. Let's keep it civil."

When the older woman was out of the way, he and Hope continued toward the car. Brady put a fussy Sam into the car seat, and Hope got into the back seat with him, ready to entertain him with toys.

Brady got into the driver's seat and started the car. He couldn't get away fast enough.

❖

Hope's hand trembled as she retrieved Sam's pacifier from the diaper bag. Brady pulled from the driveway and accelerated down the street.

The confrontation had left her shaken. She put the pacifier in Sam's mouth. It took a little persistence, but finally he took it, and his eyes began to flutter shut.

She caressed his baby-soft cheek. "Thatta boy. Is your tooth hurting you, honey? My poor little punkin."

Brady said nothing as he headed toward Copper Creek, but agitation rolled off him in waves.

She forced herself to give him a few minutes to calm down. It couldn't have been easy hearing all that. It hadn't been easy even for her, and Patricia was a stranger. Though clearly the woman knew something about her.

Looking to make your way up in the world . . .

It was hardly the first time she'd been looked down upon, but the words had hit fresh today. She'd tried hard to put her past behind her, and sometimes she managed to forget where she'd come from. Having Brady witness the insult was especially hurtful. She didn't want him to view her that way, and she surely didn't want his pity.

But far worse than the personal insult had been Patricia's implied threat. Clearly the woman was suspicious of their sudden vows.

Ten minutes was all the silence she could handle. "Brady . . . can we talk about what happened back there?"

He rubbed his jaw. "I don't know what she was doing there. Having Heather in the middle was supposed to prevent that kind of thing. I'm sorry you had to hear that."

"That's the least of my concerns. Brady, she's obviously suspicious of our relationship. What if—"

"She can speculate all she wants, but she can't prove a thing. Anyway, our marriage is perfectly real in the eyes of God and the law. We may have gone about it in an unconventional way, but that doesn't change anything. We're committed to each other and committed to Sam. That's all that matters."

She hoped he was right. She thought of the movies she'd seen where couples had married to secure citizenship. About the interrogations they'd gone through to prove their love was real and not just convenient. But she and Brady hadn't broken any laws.

Hope picked up the shoe Sam had kicked off and tucked it into the diaper bag. "The judge might not be too happy if he found out we only married because of Sam."

"We married for other reasons too. Besides, that's none of anyone's business."

She hoped the judge would see it that way, if it came to that. "I'm sorry I got a little huffy back there. I wasn't exactly helpful."

He spared her a smile. "Your heart was in the right place. I appreciate your support. But there's no reasoning with Patricia when it comes to Audrey. I learned that a long time ago."

"I suppose parents tend to be blind to their children's faults."

"And it sure doesn't get better when the child passes away, believe me. I'll have a talk with Heather about avoiding scenes like that in the future. But sometimes the Parkers have minds of their own."

"I don't envy Heather being in the middle of this."

"Neither do I." Brady accelerated as he came to a long, straight part of the road. "And I'm sorry about what Patricia said to you. She was out of line."

Hope gave a careless laugh, though just the

memory of her words made a vise tighten around her heart. "No worries. It was a long time ago."

But the prickle of pain felt fresh enough. It was stunning how quickly the words had awakened the insecure girl she'd been. The girl who'd reached outside her comfort zone once upon a time only to find her heart shattered in two.

CHAPTER SEVENTEEN

Nine years ago

Aaron Bailey was new to Copper Creek High School. Maybe that's why he'd taken a shine to Hope so quickly.

She spotted him across the lunchroom in early December of her sophomore year. Even though he was sitting, she could tell he had a tall, lanky build. His longish brown hair flopped over his forehead in an adorable manner, and when he smiled his whole face came alive.

"Hey," Hope said to Zoe between bites of pizza. "Who's the new guy at the jock table?"

Zoe tucked her auburn hair behind her ear. "Aaron Bailey. He's a sophomore transfer from Pickens. He made the varsity basketball team, which you'd know if you actually went to the games with me."

Hope didn't think about Aaron again until later that week. She was putting books in her locker, in a rush between classes, when she felt a hard shove. Her shoulder hit the locker with a *thunk,* and her books clattered to the floor.

Hope turned to see Monica and Allison scowling at her. Mostly Hope attempted to blend into the crowd in the high school halls, but these two always singled her out. Monica had been her best friend in elementary school, back when it didn't matter if you lived in the crummiest part of town.

"Nice shirt," Monica said. "Goodwill special?"

"What color is that, 11B?" Allison said. "Puke beige?"

That was her address in Orchard Estates: 11B. It stung to know that Monica had shared this with her new friend. She hadn't seemed to mind the shabby apartment when they'd played Barbies on her living room floor.

Her parents could've afforded better, but they were philanthropic to the extreme, always finding people less fortunate to give their money to. Sometimes Hope wished they weren't so generous.

Allison was so busy sneering at Hope as they passed that she walked straight into somebody.

That somebody was Aaron Bailey.

"Sorry." Allison's voice was all breathy, and her face turned a deep shade of pink as she looked up, up, up into Aaron's handsome face.

Aaron looked at Hope, at the pile of books at her feet, then locked onto her eyes. She got caught in his smoky-gray gaze, and her face heated as he sized up the situation.

He gave Monica and Allison a charming smile. "I think our friend could use some help with her books, yeah?"

Seemingly hypnotized by his smile, both girls stooped to help Hope with her books.

"Here you go," Monica said, shoving textbooks at Hope.

Allison handed over her biology book, hardly looking away from Aaron. He was retrieving Hope's English journal, on which she'd written her name in every font ever created, like some silly sixth grader.

Once their task was done, Monica and Allison rushed off to class, looking over their shoulders at Aaron as they went.

Hope shoved her books into her locker, her heart beating up into her throat. She wished she could slide inside the locker and close the door behind her.

"Here you go." Aaron's voice was deep and somehow soft too. He towered over her shoulder, and he was standing near enough that she caught his clean, soapy smell.

"Thanks." Her face went warmer as she took the juvenile-looking notebook and stuffed it into her locker, never mind that she had English next.

Why, oh, why did he have to come along just as she was being bullied? Why couldn't he have noticed her during gym class when she was spiking a ball over the net or during the last assembly when she'd been recognized for her academic achievements?

"Walk you to class?" he asked.

"Um, my next class is on the other side of the

school. I don't want to make you late." She shut her locker door.

"I actually have a dentist appointment so I'm about to leave anyway."

"Lucky." Her eyes climbed up to his face. He must have been at least six foot four or five. And he was as lanky as she imagined. But for all those long limbs, he moved so gracefully.

"Lead the way," he said.

She started for class, setting a quick pace, hoping she might still beat the bell and also wanting to be rid of a guy who surely viewed her as some pitiful project.

"So who were those girls?" He looked off in the direction they'd gone.

Ah. He just wanted to the scoop on the class hotties. Her stomach gave a hard twist even as she told herself she was being stupid.

"Monica has a boyfriend, but Allison's not dating anyone. She's the blonde. I'm sure she'd go out with you—her eyeballs were practically glued to you."

He gave her a mock scowl. "I'm not interested in going out with them. I was wondering why they were giving you a hard time."

Her face heated. "Oh. They were just messing around."

She wondered if her ears were red and looked down so the curtain of her hair hid them. She wished she could teleport to English class. Or simply melt into the ugly tile floor. She wasn't picky.

"I haven't seen you around," he said as if sensing she needed a change of subject.

"I'm mostly in AP classes. And I don't go to the games. I usually have to work at the diner on weekends."

"Maybe I'll have to come see you there then."

Her jaw dropped a little. That didn't make her sound like a project at all. But teenaged boys were confusing sometimes. Maybe he was just the friendly sort.

She realized she was staring and jerked her eyes away. When she reached her class, he waved good-bye with a friendly smile.

He did come to see her at the diner that very weekend. He came with one of the guys on the basketball team and flirted with her every time she came to his table. She was so flustered she almost spilled his coffee right in his lap. The next week he caught up with her in the hallway and asked her out.

Aaron was the nicest boy she'd ever known. He somehow fit in with everyone: the jocks, the popular cliques, the mathletes . . . Everybody liked him. Their first date led to another and another, and by spring the two were officially a couple.

Everything changed for her somehow, being Aaron's girlfriend. She was accepted into new circles. No one, not even Monica and Allison, teased her about where she lived or her second-hand clothes. But the best part of being Aaron's girlfriend was Aaron himself.

He could just look at her and make her knees go all wobbly. When he kissed her, the rest of the world disappeared. She realized why people talked about "falling in love." Indeed, it felt like a breath-stealing free fall from the top of the world. Exhilarating. Wonderful. Powerful.

The summer passed in a glorious haze, and before she knew it, they were starting their junior years. While she concentrated on her grades, Aaron was laser-focused on training. He came from a middle-class family, but they had four kids to put through college. He needed a scholarship and was hoping to be recruited by Duke.

That fall he became a starter on the varsity team and was, in fact, the star of the team—a real feat for a junior. The team only lost two games the whole season, and everyone was talking about Aaron's future.

In the spring they went to junior prom, and when school let out they began another summer together. But midway into June his beloved grandma fell ill. He worked during the day but devoted his evenings to her, making sure she had company and food and that her lawn was mowed. He was with her at the end when she slipped quietly into heaven.

Watching his tender heart break, Hope fell more deeply in love with him. She held him when he cried after the funeral, thumbing tears from his face and pushing his hair back from his forehead.

By the time their senior year started, Hope was glad he had a distraction from his loss. And then, in December, he got the news he'd been waiting for: he was offered a full scholarship to Duke.

Hope was so proud of him. But the university was six hours away, and he'd be too busy with school and training to return to Copper Creek to see his girlfriend on weekends. Aaron was loath to be apart too. He encouraged her to apply to Duke and try to get an academic scholarship. He believed in her, and before long they had a plan in place.

For the first time in her life Hope started to imagine a life bigger than Orchard Estates. Bigger than Copper Creek.

She was going to get an academic scholarship at Duke and major in communications. She wanted to have a real career and forget where she came from.

It was just the two of them, working toward a better, brighter future. When she was accepted and offered a nice scholarship, Aaron surprised her with dinner at the Blue Moon Grill. They were floating on air.

But they were so deeply in love, and four years seemed like too long to wait to get married. By mutual agreement they began dropping hints to their parents about getting married during their sophomore year in college. Mr. and Mrs. Bailey were resistant at first.

But it would be cheaper to share student housing, Aaron argued. His full-ride scholarship would cover tuition, room, and board. Aaron, with his training schedule and classes, wouldn't have time to work, but Hope could get a part-time job. They could make it work somehow. By February his parents were beginning to capitulate.

Their future together seemed like a beautiful Christmas present, complete with a big red bow, theirs for the unwrapping. Even the basketball season, which was nearing an end, had the state championship in sight. The Copper Creek Miners easily claimed the sectional title, and the last week of February brought the regional game, which would be played on home turf.

Spirits were high in the school's halls. Aaron was a rising star on a winning team, but it didn't go to his head like it did some of the other players. He was the same old Aaron, high-fiving even the lowly freshmen in the hallways. The school cheered the team on with a rousing pep assembly.

That night the crowd was fired up on both sides of the gymnasium. A quick start by the Miners put them ahead early. Aaron was in fine form, putting up fourteen points by halftime, leaving Copper Creek ahead by two.

The crowd was energized as the second half began. Hope stood next to Zoe in the student section. The smell of popcorn hung in the air, mingling with the tang of sweat and floor wax. The players' soles squeaked on the wood court, and the cheerleaders chanted in unison.

The crowd cheered as their guard sank a free throw, nothing but net, and a few minutes later the stands shook with stomping when the Generals stood at the line. The free-throw shooter missed the shot, and the Miners rebounded the ball.

"Let's go, Miners!" Hope shouted.

Beside her, Zoe munched nervously on her popcorn, but Hope could only wring her hands as Aaron dribbled the ball across the court, calling out a play. The Miners darted around the court, guarded closely by the Generals.

"Come on, Aaron!" Her call mingled with all the others.

Aaron passed the ball to a teammate and shuffled into a new position. Hope's eyes were on the ball: Lewis to Gavin to Jared. A movement in her peripheral vision caught her attention.

Her eyes darted to Aaron as he hit the ground. His head hit the wood floor, and his body stilled.

"Foul!" someone called.

"Aaron!" Hope's hand shot to her mouth as the referee's whistle pierced the air.

The player who guarded Aaron stepped back, hands raised.

Zoe grabbed her arm. "It's okay. He just needs a minute."

"What happened?" Hope said.

"I didn't see it."

"He's not moving!" Hope said, her voice just a whisper.

Her heart stuttered at her boyfriend's still form. At the sight of Coach Watkins running onto the court. She was vaguely aware of the players taking knees. Of the deadly hush of the crowd.

"He hit his head," Zoe said. "He probably has a concussion. He'll be fine."

Right. A concussion. He'd wake up in a few seconds, and the crowd would applaud as he was led to the locker room to get checked over really well.

Someone dashed across the court, and Hope realized it was Jared's dad. He was an EMT with the local fire department. He knelt beside Aaron, blocking their view. He seemed to be checking vitals, but a moment later he began chest compressions.

A shiver passed over Hope's entire body, and her legs buckled beneath her. "Oh no."

Zoe's hand tightened on her arm, but Hope broke loose. She stumbled down the stands, pushing fellow students aside. She flew across the court and was a few feet away when the assistant coach caught her.

"Whoa. Stay back, Hope. Give them room to work."

"What's happening?" She fought for release, needing to be near Aaron more than she needed her next breath. But Coach Drury had her around the shoulders, his grip like manacles.

Oh, God, please!

He wasn't breathing. His heart wasn't beating. Her hands flew to her face. Her legs trembled beneath her, and the arms that imprisoned her now worked to keep her upright.

"Aaron!" Her scream echoed through the quiet gym.

Please, God. Oh, please. I'll do anything. I'll trade places with him!

The minutes passed in agonizing slowness. Someone else was looking through Hope's eyes, seeing Aaron's lifeless body, his scarred knee lying so close. Seeing his mom on the other side of him, his dad holding her, horror etched in the planes of their faces.

Minutes, hours, days later a muted siren sounded. Then people were rushing, lifting him on a cart, taking him away.

"I have to . . ." She tried to follow, but her legs gave out.

Coach Drury caught her around the waist. "Do you have a friend who can take you to the hospital? Hope?"

"I'll take her." Zoe was there, and minutes later she was in her friend's car.

A coldness had swept over Hope. She felt

chilled from the bones out. Her breath was caught in her lungs as if the air had solidified in her chest like cement.

What if he died? What if he was already dead? No, it wasn't possible. Not Aaron. This was just a nightmare. She'd wake up soon. She closed her eyes against the burn, and suddenly her breath came back. It rushed in and out until she felt dizzy.

"Hang in there, honey," Zoe said. "We're almost there."

"Aaron . . ." It was only a squeak.

"I know. I'm praying hard. Just keep praying."

She did pray . . . if halted words, incomplete sentences, and disjointed thoughts counted as prayer.

In the waiting room she rushed to the front desk. "My boyfriend was brought in, Aaron Bailey, he collapsed during a basketball game, is he all right?"

Hope barely registered the sympathy in the lady's eyes. "Let me just—"

"Hope!" Mrs. Bailey rushed forward and pulled her into her arms. "Oh, Hope, this can't be happening."

"Is he okay? Have you heard anything?"

"No word yet." Mr. Bailey had come to stand by his wife.

"He just fell, though, and hit his head. He'll be fine, right?"

Tears slipped from Mrs. Bailey's gray eyes, so like Aaron's. "They . . . they were still doing CPR in the ambulance, Hope."

"But now that he's here, they'll be able to properly treat him." She had to hang on to that hope.

The Baileys led her into the waiting room, and Zoe sat beside her, taking her hand.

Please, God. He's my heart. My everything. I can't lose him.

She thought of Aaron, of his expressive smile, of his unrelenting kindness. God wouldn't take him. Not Aaron. He was a shining light in a dark world. He had a bright future ahead of him. *They* had a bright future ahead of them.

She thought of Aaron's mom, Susan, who'd lost her mother not long ago and who was the most devoted mom she knew. Her heart ached at the thought of them losing their baby and only son.

Time slowed to a crawl, every sense on high alert. Hope felt as if days had passed by the time a doctor came through the doors. The Baileys were taken to the back while Hope paced the small waiting room.

"He must be fine now, right?" she asked Zoe. "They're taking them back to see him."

Maybe they'd come get her soon. She needed to see his precious face. See his eyes wide open, his chest rising and falling. She was going to let him have it for scaring her so badly!

But when Mark Bailey came back through the doors his shoulders were slumped, and there was a horrible look of shock on his face.

Hope didn't even realize she'd approached him until he stopped in front of her. His eyes were bloodshot, and he looked ten years older than when he'd left.

Hope couldn't speak. Couldn't even breathe. Zoe was at her side, slipping an arm around her.

"He . . . he's gone, Hope," Mark said, his tone flat, disbelieving.

No.

No, he couldn't be gone. He was just dashing up the court. Giving Jared a high five, that contagious smile spreading across his face.

Hope shook her head. Her vision blurred. An ache bloomed in her chest, wide and consuming, and she pressed against it.

It couldn't be true. Not Aaron.

"Susan's with him now. I have some phone calls to make."

"I don't understand . . . ," Hope said. "He just fell. He has to be okay."

"They don't know what happened. But they did everything they could. He's gone, Hope." His words wobbled as he pulled her into his arms and clung to her.

Hope choked back the sobs that built in her chest, and they filled her throat with a lump the size of Texas.

He pulled away a long minute later. And it was the bleak look on his face that broke through her denial. Her eyes burned, and her legs wavered beneath her.

Zoe took her arm.

"I-I want to see him," Hope said.

"Of course." Mark knuckled away his tears. "I'll take you back."

She followed silently through the double doors and down the long, sterile hallway. She heard Susan's sobs before Mark even opened the door.

"Why don't I wait out here," Zoe said.

Hope went inside, her wobbly legs carrying her toward Aaron's bedside. He still wore his basketball uniform. His head lay flat on the bed, and the harsh fluorescent lights made his skin pale. His hair was still damp with sweat.

Mark set his hand on her back, and she realized she'd stopped halfway to the bed. She took three steps and stopped again, staring down at her beloved's face. His long, dark lashes fanned his cheeks, and his lips were parted as if for a breath. She reached out and took his hand, curling her fingers around his.

He looked as if he were merely sleeping. But his chest was eerily still. His hand was limp and cool against her palm, and the paleness was not an effect of the lighting.

He was gone. He was really gone.

She couldn't breathe.

Then Zoe was there, holding her, and the sobs she'd choked back before clawed their way out.

The next few days passed in a numb blur. Aaron's autopsy showed he'd died of sudden cardiac arrest brought on by an undiagnosed heart condition. The disorder apparently killed about 150 athletes every year.

But having an answer didn't help. He was still gone. Arrangements were made; the funeral was held. Hope said good-bye to Aaron and left him in a vault suspended over the hole where his body would rest.

Everyone was sorry. Everyone was available to lend a hand. Everyone was praying for her. She'd never known how empty the platitudes were until now.

She was dead inside. As dead as Aaron.

In the weeks that followed she took each moment as it came. She couldn't think past the present. Aaron was supposed to be here. He was supposed to be in this moment with her. But he wasn't. Where was God in all this? Why had He allowed this? She'd trusted Him with her future, and He'd gone and done this horrible thing.

Weeks faded into months, the days bringing panic attacks, the nights long and riddled with nightmares. When summer was drawing to a close, Hope canceled her registration to Duke. She couldn't bear the thought of going there without Aaron. Without her heart. She'd hitched her dreams to Aaron, and they'd evaporated like fog under the morning sun.

But she had to have something to keep her mind occupied. Something to remind her she was still here. Something to live for. With her parents' urging, she registered last minute at Dalton State, a local college. She'd pursue a degree and find a way to go on somehow. It was what Aaron would've wanted.

CHAPTER EIGHTEEN

Hope turned on the oven light and checked the rolls. Almost done. The timer began ticking away the last minute, and she gave the green beans a stir. It was their first married meal at home, and she hoped the Crock-Pot chicken would turn out all right. The savory smells filling the kitchen were promising.

Behind her, Sam patted his high chair with both palms, making his Cheerios dance on the tray. "Ga-ga-ga-ga-ga!"

"Are you eating your cereal?" Hope poked his belly, making him laugh.

She almost had to put the little bugger in his chair to cook or get anything else done these days. He was crawling like a pro. Brady had installed a baby gate at the bottom of the stairs a month ago.

"Abee-babu!" Sam worked his index finger and thumb to pick up a Cheerio and put it into his mouth.

"Yummy, yummy! Good for your tummy!"

Hope went to the Crock-Pot and lifted the lid. She breathed in the garlic and oregano. She poked the meat with a fork and found it tender, so she turned it to warm and replaced the lid.

When the buzzer went off, she turned off the stove and grabbed a potholder. As she pulled open the door the delicious smell of yeast escaped.

"Hi, honey, I'm home."

Hope started, the back of her hand coming in contact with the inside of the oven door.

She jerked her hand back. "Ouch!"

Brady shut the kitchen door. "You okay?"

"I'm fine. Love the greeting—very domestic of you." Hope removed the rolls and went to the sink. The back of her hand burned like the dickens. She held it under a stream of cold water.

Sam slapped his tray. "Ga-ga-ga!"

"Sorry I scared you." Brady had come to stand close beside her. The faint smells of motor oil and garage prevailed over his spicy cologne. "Let me see."

"It'll be fine. How was your day?"

"Speaking of domesticated greetings." He gave her a sideways smile as he took her hand from the stream of water. The spot had reddened. He held it back under the flow.

"My day was just fine until I gave my wife an injury," he said facetiously. "I have a cream for burns upstairs."

He wiped his hand on his pant leg, stopped to drop a kiss on Sam's head on his way upstairs.

Keeping her hand under the flow of water, Hope stirred the green beans with the other, then turned down the heat. Brady was back a minute later. She shut off the water and was drying her hand as he set the first-aid kit down on the counter.

He took her hand. "Let me see."

"No blister or anything. It's fine."

He uncapped the cream, squeezed out a dot, and began rubbing it in, his thumb running in gentle circles.

"I can do that myself, you know."

"I broke it. I should fix it. Want some ibuprofen?"

"It's not that bad."

He lifted her hand and pressed a tender kiss to the spot. His lips were soft, and the gesture was so sweet her heart gave a little roll.

"How'd that taste?" she asked.

"Not so good."

His eyes met hers, sparkling with laughter. She'd missed him today, she realized. Over the last two days she'd gotten accustomed to sharing her every thought with him. So this morning when Sam had pointed with his finger for the first time, she wanted to run and tell him. And when she'd printed out her final résumé, she'd wanted to show it to him.

But now, as the amusement faded from his eyes and his hands came to rest at her waist, she was glad she'd waited. Because she was starting to think maybe he'd missed her too.

"Bet this'll taste better." He leaned close and

slowly brushed her lips with his. "Yep," he whispered and went back for seconds.

She leaned into his touch, returning his kiss, and her heart suddenly seemed ready to pound its way out of her chest.

A slapping sound pulled her back to reality. Sammy, pounding on his tray.

Brady eased away, his eyes sleepy. His lips happy. It was a beautiful sight.

"You know," she said, "this being married stuff isn't so bad."

"Right?" He gave her a charming smile and moved to run a hand over Sam's head.

Hope stepped over to the stove and gave the green beans a stir. "Supper's ready. I hope it turned out all right."

"It smells great. Would you mind if I took a quick shower first? I'm ruining all the good smells."

"No, that's fine. It'll keep a few minutes."

"Perfect." He stopped by the stove to drop a kiss on her head. "After supper we can open wedding gifts."

"Yay! Presents."

❖❖❖

Hope brushed away the wrapping paper and held up a heavy black object. "Um . . . what is it?"

Brady smiled at the look on Hope's face. That

little frowny face she made was adorable. "It's an elephant," he said helpfully.

She gave him a look. "But what's it *for?*"

Brady reached into the box and pulled out its match. "Bookends."

"Oh." She set them on the coffee table opposite each other and considered them. The elephants were sitting, their feet extended forward, their trunks lifted high, poised to hold up a heavy row of books. "Well, that makes sense, I guess."

Brady gave a wry smile. The gift was from his dad. "It's the same thing he got Audrey and me for our wedding."

"What? Are you kidding me?"

"He probably gets the same wedding gift for everyone."

Audrey had taken the bookends in the divorce, though, so they could still use them. He wadded the paper up in a ball and tossed it on the floor where Sammy was having fun with the boxes.

"I'm sorry," Hope said. "That must not feel very good."

"That's just the way Dad is. I'll use them to prop up my sci-fi collection, though he'd never approve. Novels are a waste of time according to him. But at least he came to the wedding, you know?"

His birth mom hadn't even known about their nuptials. They hadn't known where to send an invitation since she moved around a lot and didn't keep in touch.

"When's the last time you saw April?" Hope jotted down the gift on her notepad.

"About five years ago. She showed up at my grandma's place and stayed just long enough to upset everyone, and then she was gone again. She came back about a year and a half ago, but she didn't bother to look me up. Actually, that's what had me so upset the night I lost my head and slept with Audrey." He shook his head. "Stupid."

"I remember that. It was your birthday."

"Right. Not my finest hour."

"You were hurt, understandably." She gave him a sympathetic look. "It's terrible what drugs do to people."

Brady opened an envelope. "Yes, it is. This one's from Ruby Brown." He began ripping off the paper. "Granny took care of Mom for a long time, but she finally had enough. You can't blame her."

"That must've been hard, but she did the right thing. Enabling a drug addict doesn't help anyone."

"I know. It's just weird having a mom out there somewhere who couldn't care less about you. She just gave me up like I was nothing."

Hope touched his hand. "I'm sorry, Brady. You deserved so much better."

Her green eyes tugged at him. Made him feel she understood. No wonder her friends poured their hearts out to her.

"At least I had Mom and Dad, you know? They were good parents. And I got a sister out of the deal." Maybe he'd never felt like he'd quite belonged in the family, but he was blessed, he knew. It just seemed like a raw deal that the woman who'd actually raised him was killed in a freak bicycle accident while his birth mom got to live, strung out on drugs and caring for nothing but her next high.

"That's why you couldn't give up Sam, isn't it?" Hope said softly. "You know what that feels like."

His chest constricted, a long-buried pain surging to the surface. "You're a smart woman, Hope."

"You'd never let Sam grow up thinking you didn't want him."

"That's the difference between me and my mom. I actually do want him."

Her smile was warm and affectionate as she patted his leg. "I know you do. You're a good man, Brady Collins. But we don't have to talk about this anymore if you don't want to. I don't want to get you down."

Brady gave his head a shake. "Right. We're opening wedding presents here. This is supposed to be a happy occasion."

Hope's eyes lit on the box he'd just unwrapped. "Especially when it's a gift like this . . . a Keurig! Yay! I've been wanting one of these."

"Speaking of addictions . . . ," he teased.

She nudged his shoulder.

"Ga-ga-ga-ga!" Sam patted the side of a box, smiling at the loud noise he was making.

"See, Sam likes it too." Hope smiled at the baby. "You have such good taste, don't you, punkin?"

"He'll like the box better."

"Well, that goes without saying." She jotted down the gift. "Miss Ruby, you do know what a girl needs."

Brady snatched another envelope from a package. "So are you nervous about your interview tomorrow?"

"No, not really." She bit her lip as she put the card with the others.

He gave her a look until she broke.

"Okay, yes, I am. I printed out my résumé today. Any chance you'd take a look at it for me?"

"Sure, I'd be glad to. And I'll also remind you of what you said just a couple days ago. 'It's just a formality.' Also, 'It's all in God's hands.' "

She nudged his shoulder again, her lips twitching. "Thanks. I think."

"You've got this, Hope. This job was custom-made for you."

"Yeah?"

"Yeah."

Her lips had tipped up in a little smile, and he loved that he'd put it there. "You're going to do great."

CHAPTER NINETEEN

"So, how's married life treating you?" Diana Mayhew asked. The operations manager had taken a seat behind her big desk, a friendly smile on her face.

"It's great. We had a wonderful time in Gatlinburg, and I'm getting settled in at Brady's house." They'd used some of Hope's furniture to fill in the gaps left from his divorce. The rest they'd donated to the Hope House, a local girls home.

"Glad to hear it. It sure was a whirlwind engagement."

"Well, we both wanted a small wedding. And we've known each other forever, so it's not like we didn't know what we were getting ourselves into."

"Friendship first is always a great way to go."

They made small talk for a few minutes, then spent time discussing the direction the station wanted to take with the available position. Diana wanted to know Hope's thoughts on her program and told her about advertising goals they'd like to keep in mind.

The interview was going well. Like Hope, Diana shared a desire to help listeners make wise decisions and set healthy goals for their lives. The thought of impacting so many lives gave

Hope an adrenaline rush. She could talk about this subject all day.

But Diana was easing back from her desk, and Hope wrapped up her final thoughts, not wanting to take too much of the director's time.

"Well, it sounds as if we're on the same page, Hope. As you know, I'm a big fan of your program, and I hope to offer you the job. But we'll also be interviewing another candidate, so I'll be letting you know soon which direction we're going to go."

Hope worked to keep the smile on her face. "Oh. I didn't realize you were looking at someone else."

"I hadn't planned on it, to be honest. But Darren got wind of another jock out of Chicago looking to relocate. He wants to put him in the running too." Diana stood, smoothing her blouse. "He's not as good a fit, if you ask me, and I'm pulling for you."

Hope stood, her legs suddenly shaking. "Thank you, I appreciate that."

Diana extended a hand. "I'll be in touch soon. Hopefully it won't be too long."

"I look forward to hearing from you."

As Hope exited the building a moment later, she couldn't help but wonder what the heck had just happened. She was supposed to be a shoo-in for the position. She'd been counting on it.

It was after five by the time she crossed the town line into Copper Creek. Her emotions during the drive had morphed from despair to mere dismay. At Old Mill Road she turned left, making a last-minute decision to swing by the Peach Barn and talk to her best friend.

Zoe's new red barn hunkered back off the road beneath a grove of oak trees. It had been completed a month ago, and they'd moved all the merchandise from Brady's building. Zoe was happy to have her new barn, and Brady was glad to finally take ownership of his new garage.

Hope found Zoe stocking the bakery case. The sweet smells of fresh cobbler and muffins rose above the scent of cut lumber.

"Yum. Something smells good."

Zoe popped up from where she'd stooped. Her auburn curls were pulled back from her face. "Hope! How'd your interview go—oh, I don't like that look on your face."

"They're considering someone else."

"What?" Zoe's indignant tone validated Hope's feelings.

"Yeah, that was pretty much my reaction. I'm in the running, but still. Some guy out of Chicago."

"Pull up a chair, hon. This calls for sugar."

"Not going to argue." Hope took a seat at one of the small café tables, and a minute later Zoe brought over a pie tin filled with peach crisp and two forks.

"We're not even going to be civilized about this?"

"You're right. We're missing the ice cream."

"Forget the ice cream. Give me the fork."

They dug into the crisp, which was still warm. Hope let the flavors blend and melt on her tongue. The confection was almost good enough to make her forget she'd just been sucker punched.

"Start talking," Zoe said.

Hope swallowed the bite and told the story, starting with how well the interview seemed to be going and ending with Diana's unexpected announcement.

"Well, that bites. But at least she seems to favor you. That's good."

"But she's not the head honcho. That would be Darren, and he's the one pushing for this Chicago jock."

"Chicago." Zoe waved her off. "He's a Yankee. What's he know?"

"He's from a large market, which actually makes him more experienced than I am."

"Well, you're one of us, and you're brilliant at what you do. They'd be crazy to turn you down." Zoe took a generous bite of the crisp. "What did Brady say?"

"He texted me after the interview, but I haven't responded yet. I didn't want to bother him at work."

Zoe's eyes pierced hers, but Hope looked down. She stirred her fork around the gooey peach filling.

"What?" Zoe said.

Hope shook her head. "I'm dreading telling him. He was upset to hear I actually had to interview for the position. I'm a little embarrassed for assuming the job was mine. I'll feel like a loser if I don't get it."

"You're not a loser, and he'd never think that. Never."

"I just feel so foolish. I even went out and bought these stupid shoes. I don't want to admit how much they cost." So she had a tendency to compensate for her childhood. Who could blame her?

"Is that a new purse too?"

Hope gave Zoe a dark look. "Never mind." She was going to have to tell Brady she'd put the purchases on their credit card. Of course, when she'd bought them she'd assumed they'd soon have an extra paycheck coming in.

Zoe squeezed her hand. "Listen, you're getting all worked up, and for all you know you're going to get the job. Besides which, we both know this is all in God's hands, and if you're meant to have the job you will."

"I know, I know." Hope made a pouty face. "Why doesn't that help?"

"Because we have our own wishes and wants, and they don't always line up with His. But trust a girl who's made plenty of mistakes in this area . . . He knows what He's doing. Remember when I got pregnant at nineteen? And when I ran off with

Brevity to become a star? But now I'm engaged to the father of my baby girl, and I'm running Granny's orchard. God took all my mistakes and worked them for good. You can trust Him with your future, Hope."

But she thought of Aaron and how God had taken him away from her so suddenly. Had completely obliterated their future together. She'd trusted Him then, and look what had happened.

She shook her head. That was a long time ago. Hope felt her heart lighten a little as she looked at her friend. Zoe was right. Maybe she just needed to do a little realigning.

She felt better by the time she'd left—and devoured a healthy serving of peach crisp. Brady had texted to let her know he'd taken Sam to Murphy's Park, so she replied that she'd meet him there.

The tot was happily ensconced in a baby swing when she walked up the knoll to the grassy square on the edge of town. Towering maple trees offered a shady reprieve from the August heat. A squirrel nattered and scurried along a branch, and children's laughter rang out from the various pieces of playground equipment.

Unobserved, she watched Brady and Sam as she approached. Brady was giving the boy gentle pushes from the front, making silly faces and giving spontaneous belly pokes all the while.

Her guys. A smile curved her lips.

Brady turned at the sound of her footsteps. His gaze sharpened on her as his smile hit pause.

"Hey," she said.

"Hey. How'd it go?"

"Pretty good." Hope tickled Sammy's foot as he swung forward. "Hey, little guy."

Sam's eyes lit up and he kicked his bare legs. "Ga-ga-ga-ga."

"Is Daddy pushing you in the swing? What a good daddy!"

"So . . . don't keep me in suspense. Tell me everything."

She caught him up on the details about the program. "So, overall, Diana and I seem to be on the same page, and she even came out and said she definitely wants me for the position."

His eyes pierced hers. "Why do I feel a *but* coming."

"Well, because there's a little unexpected snag. It seems there are two of us in the running."

His brows collided, two commas forming between them. "What? She said the interview was just a formality."

Hope nodded. "She did. But there's a jock from Chicago looking to relocate, and Darren likes him for the position. He wants to interview him too."

"And Darren is . . ."

She made a face. "The station's GM."

Brady's lips tightened. "Well, that ticks me off. They shouldn't have all but promised you the position if they weren't prepared to offer it. When will you know something?"

"She didn't say exactly. But soon, I'm sure. Dirk retires in seven weeks."

"I hate this. This job is perfect for you, and anyone with half a brain can see that."

"I'm not going to lie. It was totally unexpected, and I'm pretty disappointed." She was surprised how hard that was to admit out loud. How vulnerable it made her feel.

He slipped his arm around her and hugged her against his side. "Of course you are. You've been counting on this."

She looked up at him, relieved that he'd drawn her close. That he'd known just what to do and say to alleviate that vulnerability.

But one look in his eyes, and she could see the potential consequences of the situation settling on him. Weighing on him. She remembered his words from their honeymoon and wanted to put him at ease the way he'd just done for her.

"I need you to remember what I said before. Job or no job, I have no regrets about marrying you, Brady. I got a pretty sweet family out of the deal. I'm content with that."

He let out a breath. "That means a lot to me, Hope. But I still want this job for you."

"Thanks for saying that. I just feel kind of stupid for assuming it was mine already."

"Hey." He squeezed her waist, his eyes inviting pools of blue. "There's no reason to feel that way. It's not your fault."

"Thanks. But I'll be okay either way, all right?"

He gave her a long, searching look, then tugged her close enough to steal a soft kiss. She felt the touch in the shiver that raced down her arms. In the quickening of her breath. In the tingle of want in her belly.

A string of emphatic baby babbling interrupted their brief interlude. Sam had drifted to a stop, and he was flapping his arms. They laughed at his impatience and decided it was time to go home and get supper started.

As Hope scooped Sam from the baby seat, her own words rang in her head. She'd be okay if she didn't get the job. Wouldn't she?

She'd started her radio career at her college station her freshman year and had fallen in love with it. After graduation, getting on at the local station had seemed like a no-brainer. And shortly after her arrival, when she introduced her *Living with Hope* program, she discovered that the prospect of helping people was a real bonus.

But her career now seemed to be on the brink of disaster. With the local station shutting down and her life firmly rooted here now, what would she do if she lost this opportunity?

CHAPTER TWENTY

Three weeks later Brady felt they had settled into a comfortable routine. During the week Hope took care of Sam while he worked in his garage. On the weekends he took care of the baby while she worked at the Rusty Nail. Most Saturday nights he showed up, Sammy in tow, and sat with their friends. Hope would take a break sometime during the night, then slip back into her managerial role after supper.

He had met with his attorney, who was busy preparing his case. Brady had reported Mrs. Parker's belligerent behavior, and Calvin had said to keep him apprised.

Hope still hadn't heard from the radio station except for a brief email saying there would be a delay since the candidate from Chicago was flying in for the interview.

Brady was pleased with his business. He had as much work as he could handle, and he could get lost for hours under the hood of a car. Coming home to Hope and Sam each night put an extra bounce in his step. They'd somehow managed to blend their lives together with minimal effort.

There were little things. She was a bit of a neat freak, so he made an effort to pick up after himself. Late at night she tended to get wound up just as he was winding down, so maybe he didn't hang on to her every word.

On TV he watched only *The Grand Tour* and ESPN while she favored *Dr. Phil* and the Hallmark Channel. She read widely—anything she could get her hands on—while he was content with the latest sci-fi novel or just the newspaper.

But variety was the spice of life. They agreed on the important things. Their faith, a routine for Sammy, open lines of communication.

Their roles were being negotiated and established. Hope kept the house clean and running smoothly. She did the grocery shopping because she enjoyed it and he did not. She cooked on the weeknights, and he took over on the weekends. He managed most of the yard work, took out the trash, and did the bills.

Which was what he was doing tonight, following a long but productive day. He was in the dining room, the bills strewn across the table.

Hope sat on the living room floor with Sam, helping him with a shape-sorting cube while a legal drama played out on the TV.

"Oh, you know he did it," Hope said to the TV. "Get your head out of the sand, woman."

Sam babbled around the fingers in his mouth while he worked the cube.

"Try this one, honey," Hope said, moving the circular block to another hole. "Good job! He did it, Daddy!"

"He's a smart boy." Brady opened the credit card bill.

He paid it off each month religiously to avoid interest, but tonight his eyes bugged at the balance. Whoa. What in the world? He hoped it wasn't a fraudulent charge. That had happened to him less than a year ago, and it had been a pain to update all the auto payments and bills with the new card.

He scanned the list of purchases, and his eyes zoomed in on a charge he didn't recognize.

"Um, Hope? You know anything about this charge to Bluefly.com for three hundred dollars?"

She glanced up and froze. "Oh, yeah . . . that. I meant to mention it. Also, I probably should've mentioned that I may have a tiny little shoe fetish."

He looked down at the balance again and back at her. "Okay . . ."

"I'm sorry. I should've told you about the shoes. I was nervous about the interview—I may have gone a little overboard."

Just a little. His last shoes had cost him thirty-five dollars on sale at Payless. "Maybe you can put your fetish on hold until your job comes through?"

She made a face. "*If* my job comes through."

"It will. I have every confidence. But in the meantime . . ."

"I know. I really am sorry. I guess I'm not used

to sharing money." She winced. "And, um, you might see one more little charge on there from my friend Kate Spade."

He scanned the purchases, coming to a stop toward the bottom. He worked hard to keep the censure from his voice. "Two hundred and seventy-three dollars? She must be an awfully good friend."

"It's a purse. It's really pretty. It was an outlet sale."

"Hope."

"I'd take them back, but I've already broken them in." Her eyebrows popped upward. "You know what? What's fair is fair. I spent six hundred . . . so why don't you go spend the same on yourself. New tools . . . a few laps around the race track in a Ferrari or something . . . It'll be good for your soul."

"But bad for our bank account, because then we'd have spent over a thousand frivolous dollars."

She grimaced. "Yeah . . . there's that."

"Hope . . . I mean, we're hardly destitute here, but we're not exactly rolling in cash either. We just paid for a wedding, there are lawyer bills, and we also agreed that building a savings is a priority."

"I know, I know. In my defense, I told you it might be a good idea to keep the money separate."

She had. But somehow that just didn't seem like a real marriage to him.

"I'm not trying to be a killjoy here. I want you to have nice things now and then. But I think maybe we should sit down and work out a budget."

"Now, now . . ." She chuckled uncomfortably. "There's no call to go throwing around the *B* word."

He gave her a long look. Audrey had been a spender, but he'd never dreamed Hope would be too. She was so down-to-earth and reasonable. At least, he hoped she was reasonable.

"Fine," she said on a heavy sigh. "You're right. We'll work out a budget."

CHAPTER TWENTY-ONE

Brady received his drink from the server and took a sip, his eyes drifting around the Rusty Nail in search of his wife. The band hadn't taken the stage yet so the rowdy Saturday-night crowd talked over the country song blaring from the speakers. The dance floor was filled with couples, some swaying, some attempting the two-step.

The smell of grilled burgers and onion rings made Brady's stomach howl, but he was set on waiting for Hope to take her break so they could eat together.

"Look, he's pointing at Hope." Daisy had commandeered Sammy as soon as she'd arrived. She and Zoe had kept the baby occupied for the past twenty minutes.

"That's his new trick," Brady said.

"It's so cute," Daisy said.

Sam was smiling, still following Hope with his eyes, the slobbery finger now in his mouth.

Brady followed his eyes and watched Hope chatting with a customer at one of the front tables. Next she zipped over to the hostess stand to have a word with the girl manning it. A moment later she was heading into the kitchen.

"She's busy tonight," Zoe said.

"She'll take a break when she can. You all go ahead and order. She won't mind."

"I can wait," Jack said. "Had a late lunch."

"We did too," Cruz said.

"We already ate," Noah said.

Daisy was too wrapped up in Sam to respond. She gave him neck kisses until he giggled.

The slow strains of "My Best Friend" came on. Josephine excused herself to go to the ladies' room, giving Noah a peck on the lips before she departed. They'd left little Nicholas with his grandparents for the evening, and Cruz and Zoe had the night out alone too. Brady should probably schedule a date night soon. Sometimes he forgot he was still courting his wife.

Across the table Cruz took Zoe's hand and, with a tender smile, pulled her up. Other couples joined them on the dance floor and began swaying to the romantic song.

Bryce Carter approached Daisy, and a moment later she was handing Sammy back to Brady and rising to follow him.

Brady shifted Sam to his other arm and caught an intense look on Jack's face. He was watching, wistful eyes tight at the corners, as Daisy followed Bryce to the dance floor, hand in hand.

Brady caught Noah tossing Jack a sympathetic look before excusing himself to get a refill.

Jack's hands had curled into fists on the table, and a shadow moved over his jaw.

Brady nudged him. "Hey . . ."

All traces of pain disappeared as Jack turned his way. A benign smile—his pastor face—had replaced his frown.

What had just happened? Brady couldn't find the words, so he gave Jack a long, searching look until Jack blinked and looked away. Took a sip of his Coke.

"What's up with that, buddy?" Brady said.

"What's up with what?"

"You . . . That look. There something going on between you and Daisy?"

Jack gave an awkward laugh as he rearranged his silverware. "Get real. She's way too young for me."

Brady guessed there were nine or ten years between them. "Not that much."

"Well, apparently she likes them young." Jack's eyes flashed toward the dance floor where she and Bryce were swaying and talking.

Daisy was several years Bryce's senior. "It's just a dance, man."

"Doesn't matter anyway." He pushed his Coke back. "She's a member of my congregation."

"And yet you're staring after her like you're a starving man and she's the last loaf of bread."

Jack scrubbed his hand over the back of his neck. "What, you're married four weeks and now you're an expert on love?"

Brady's brows shot up. "Love, huh?"

Jack gave him a look he'd never seen from a pastor. "Knock it off."

Touchy. Brady raised his one free hand. "Don't kill the messenger. I'm just saying, you could ask her to dance if you wanted."

Hope slid into the seat beside him. "Whew! Busy night."

Brady was glad for the interruption but probably not as glad as Jack. "It's hopping, all right. Everything okay in the kitchen?"

"Running like a well-oiled machine."

"I do love a good simile."

"Thought you'd relate to that one." She reached out for Sam, and the baby leaned toward her. "How's my big boy, huh? Oh, you look so handsome tonight! Did Daddy dress you up?"

"Ga-ga-da-do!"

"I know! Are you hungry?"

Josephine returned as the song drew to a close, and the band readied onstage. Daisy and Bryce moseyed over to his circle of friends, and from the corner of his eyes Brady watched Jack trying not to watch.

How had he not noticed this? He wondered if anyone else knew. Then he remembered Noah's look.

Once everyone except Daisy had returned to the table, they ordered their food. Last Chance rolled into their first number. The group chatted as best they could with the loud music blaring, catching up and reminiscing.

Brady grabbed Hope's hand under the table and held it on his thigh. He loved the way she glanced at him when something made her laugh, as if she wanted to share the moment with him.

The server came, setting down his burger and fries and Hope's grilled cheese. After all the food arrived, they tucked in, but the chitchat continued, occasionally erupting into boisterous laughter.

Brady didn't even notice a visitor approaching the table until he felt a touch on his shoulder.

"Hi there, Brady."

He looked up, and the dregs of a smile slipped.

April's face was barren of makeup. She was still attractive, though she looked older than her forty-six years. Her dark-brown hair was threaded with gray and pulled back into a long braid that fell over her shoulder. A red V-neck T-shirt hugged her thin frame.

"Aren't you glad to see me, baby?" she said over the music.

Hope's hand had tightened on his. Conversation at the table had come to a screeching halt as everyone stared at April Russell—or whatever her last name was now.

Brady fought the urge to shrug off her hand. "What are you doing here?"

"Honey . . . I came to see you." She squeezed

his shoulder before working her way around the table and sliding into Daisy's empty chair. She leaned forward on her elbows. "Catch me up on what I've missed."

Like his entire life? The last time he'd seen her was between his sophomore and junior years of college. He'd been just a boy, still living at home during the summers, working at Gunner's Garage. She'd barely managed to look him up before she was off again. And last time she hadn't even managed that.

"Brady?" April said. "What's been going on with you, hon?"

Everyone was staring at her. At him. He was glad the band was too loud for most of the others to hear anything that might be said.

"Granny died, for starters." It was a callous thing to say. But it just came out somehow in a clipped tone that gave away too much.

Something flickered in April's brown eyes. She fiddled with the strap of her oversized purse, her eyes darting around the table. "I heard that a while back. I would've gone to the funeral if I'd known."

"Well, we didn't know where you were." Granny had given April a phone last time she was in town, but she must've sold it.

April chuckled. "Oh, well, you know how it is. I can hardly stay in one place for long. The world's so grand. So much to see. I've been all over since I seen you last—Louisiana, Texas,

Arkansas. But enough about me. What have you been up to, honey?"

He gave her a wry look. "Quite a bit, actually. I'm married. I have a son now."

April sucked in a breath as her gaze slid to Hope, then to the high chair next to her where Sammy was munching on something with slobbery fingers.

"Oh! I'm a grandma! Is this him? He's just darling!" She leaned across the table and rapped her blunt fingernails on the table like she was trying to get the attention of a cat or something. "Hi, sweet thing. I'm your grammy. Oh, Brady, he's such a fine boy."

Brady felt the urge to sweep Sam into his arms, but April was already introducing herself to Hope. Some of the others had deserted their suppers and left the table. Only Jack, two chairs down, remained. Maybe he thought they'd need mediation. Maybe they would.

April gazed at Sam. "He looks just like you when you were a baby—that chin, those blue eyes."

Brady pressed his lips together. There was so much wrong with that sentence he didn't even know where to begin. If he had been of a mind to correct her, that is—and he wasn't.

"How long are you staying?" He didn't care if he was being rude. She'd never shown much interest in him and his life. Why start now?

April tilted her head at him, her eyes going soft. "I know I haven't been around much for you. I did what was best for you, though. My sister was a good mother to you, wasn't she?"

He gave his head a shake. That's it? All's well that ends well?

The server stopped by to check on them and asked April if she wanted anything.

"Oh, no, I'm not staying long."

Thank God for small favors.

Hope pulled Brady's hand into her lap. "Where are you staying while you're in town, Mrs. Russell?"

"You can call me April, hon." Her gaze shifted back to Brady. "What's become of Mom's place?"

"Granny left the orchard to Zoe. She and her daughter live there now." His tone clearly said she wouldn't be welcome there.

"Oh my, everyone's just grown up so fast. I'm not sure where I'll be staying just yet. I guess I hadn't thought that far."

"I'm sure you can find an old friend who'll put you up," Brady said. He sure wasn't having a drug addict under the same roof with his son.

"Probably right."

He could tell she was disappointed, but the safety of his family came first. Besides, she had no right to expect anything from him. He felt a prick of guilt. He should have more compassion.

Like it or not, she was his mother, and drug addiction was a horrible disease.

April looked between Brady and Hope. "So how long y'all been married?"

"Only a month," Hope said. "We got married August twenty-fifth."

"Oh, I wish I'd known! I was just down Roswell way. I could've come back for it."

"If only you'd kept your phone," Brady said, his ire getting the better of him.

A thoughtful frown pinched April's forehead as her gaze drifted over to the baby and back to Hope.

"It was a beautiful wedding," Hope said. "We went to Gatlinburg for our honeymoon."

Hope started prattling on about their trip, and April listened attentively, making appropriate comments.

Brady was grateful for the distraction. He started on his burger, which was now lukewarm and not the least bit appetizing. Hope ate between comments and broke off tiny pieces of her sandwich for Sam.

"So what are you doing for work these days, Brady?" April asked when her conversation with Hope petered out. "You must be out of college, I'm guessing."

"For several years now."

"My, how time flies."

Especially when you were high as a kite.

"He owns his own business." Hope looked at

225

him with pride. "He works on supercars, and he's built up quite a name for himself around here."

Heat prickled the back of his neck. Part of him—the little boy who still needed his mom's approval—wanted April to know he was doing well for himself. Another part of him didn't think she deserved to know anything at all.

"Oh my word," April said. "Supercars . . . I don't even know what those are exactly, but it surely sounds exciting."

"They're the really expensive ones," Hope said. "Ferrari, Lamborghini, Porsche . . . You name it. He's the best at what he does."

Brady gave Hope a look. She was laying it on thick. "All right."

"That sounds amazing," April said. "College really paid off for you, huh?"

"Sure." Actually, college hadn't done much other than appease his dad and give him a little business sense. He'd learned cars by working on them. By being a little obsessed with them. But April wanted to justify giving her son away to her sister.

The band kicked up another song, and the noise level went up several decibels, making conversation more difficult.

April hitched her purse strap onto her shoulder. "Well, I just dropped by to say howdy and let you know I was in town. I'll leave you two to your supper and your friends. Maybe we can get together soon."

"Sure," he said.

A moment later, as April was striding toward the door, Brady realized she'd never said how long she was going to be in town.

CHAPTER TWENTY-TWO

Hope watched Brady as he took a bite of his burger, his eyes going to the band onstage. His mom had just slipped out of the Rusty Nail.

"Are you all right?" she said over the music.

"I'm fine."

He didn't seem fine. His face was an enigmatic mask, and his hand shook as he took a sip of his Coke.

Beside her, Sammy slapped the table with his palms. "Ba-ba-ga-da!"

Hope broke off tiny bites of her grilled cheese and put them on his plate. She tried to imagine how Brady might be feeling. She'd never been abandoned by a parent, but she'd studied the subject. And having that parent suddenly slip back into his life as if she'd never left had to stir up some major hurt. He couldn't have an appetite after what he'd just been through, but he kept eating. Maybe he didn't know what else to do.

"You want to go? I can take off the rest of the night." He didn't need to be alone tonight, and Alan Morgan was on the clock. He'd filled in for her a time or two.

If Brady heard her, he gave no indication. His eyes hadn't left the stage. The lead singer, Rawley, broke into the chorus of a rousing country tune. A cheer came from the room behind them where a pool game was underway.

She touched his arm. "Brady."

He turned her way, and she nearly melted at the vulnerable look in his eyes. But they shuttered almost instantly.

"Why don't we go home? It's almost Sam's bedtime anyway."

Brady normally hung around until closing, Sammy often falling asleep in his arms or on the way home, but she sensed he needed to decompress.

"You have to work."

"Alan can fill in. It's just a few hours."

"Okay, sure." He tossed some bills onto the table and pushed back.

"Hey, man . . ." Jack leaned closer. "You all right?"

"Yeah, I'm fine."

"Well . . . if you need to talk, my door's always open."

"Yeah," Brady said. "Thanks. We're going to take off now."

Five minutes later they got into Brady's car. He'd dropped Hope off at work earlier so they could ride home together. He drove them through town and headed down the road that took them to his place. He'd quietly put Sam into his car seat and hadn't said a word since.

"You want to talk about it?"

He gave a dry laugh. "I don't even know what to say."

"It must be confusing to have her turn up so suddenly and show an interest."

His hands gripped the steering wheel. "On the contrary, that's what I've come to expect from her."

"I'm sorry."

"It's not your fault."

It didn't take a psychology course to see his walls were up high where April was concerned. And who could blame him? Self-preservation demanded it. Hope wondered if talking about it might help.

"I don't know much about what happened back then. She was young when she got pregnant with you, wasn't she?"

"Eighteen. But she slept around so much she didn't even know who my father was. She was pretty wild. I'm sure my grandparents weren't too happy about the pregnancy, but they let her stay. They supported her."

"She didn't do drugs while she was pregnant, did she?"

"No, that started after I was born. She was in a car accident—I was actually in the car too. But she didn't have her seat belt on, and she broke a couple of ribs. They put her on narcotics, and she got hooked."

"Oh, that's terrible."

"Once she couldn't get refills of her pain meds, she found suppliers and eventually moved on to harder stuff. She started going out a lot, neglecting me, and my grandparents figured it out. They confronted her, but by then she was too far gone. She didn't want their help."

"How did the Collinses end up adopting you?"

"There was some big blowup over the drugs, and April left town with her friends. My grandparents had the orchard to run, and it was harvest season. Mom and Dad had recently married, and Mom took over my care. When April came back months later they convinced her to sign rights over to them. I found out several years ago that my parents actually paid her off. Nice, huh? My birth mom sold me to her sister."

An ache bloomed inside of Hope. Drug addicts weren't capable of caring about anything but their next high, but hearing that wouldn't ease Brady's hurt.

It was impossible to read his face in the darkened car. "I'm so sorry. I'm sure Zoe's mom was totally smitten with you and willing to do whatever was necessary to keep you."

"She was a good mom," he said wistfully "I was blessed to have her."

But she didn't think he was feeling very blessed at the moment. Mrs. Collins had died in a bicycle accident on a family spring break trip out in California. The mom who loved him was gone, and the one who didn't wouldn't go away.

When they pulled up to the house, Brady got out of the car and took Sam from his seat.

"Want me to put him down?" she said.

"I'll do it."

She watched Brady carry the sleepy baby up the stairs. It wouldn't take him long. Sam had already had his bath, and he had a full belly. He only needed a diaper change and a fresh sleeper.

Hope flipped on the TV, and a few minutes later Brady padded down the stairs. He looked tired in the yellow glow of lamplight, his shoulders slumped, his steps slow.

He stopped at the bottom of the stairs, looking beaten. His arms hung down at his sides, and he looked around as if wondering how he'd gotten there.

"You okay?" Everything in her wanted to erase the forlorn look from his face.

His gaze swung to her as if just noticing her presence. "Yeah. I, ah, think I'll just go to bed, though."

She pulled her feet onto the sofa. "But it's barely after nine."

He gave her a wan smile. "I'm not good company tonight, Hope."

"Well, I'm not expecting you to entertain me," she said softly. She patted the sofa. "Come on. Let's watch a movie or something."

He shifted, looking undecided.

"I DVRed *While You Were Sleeping* recently. You could learn about leaning."

When the corner of his lips turned up, it felt like a major win. "I confess I'm still curious."

She smiled at him. "Come on, then. I saved you a seat."

While he made his way to the sofa, Hope found the movie and started it. She turned out the lamp.

"Want some popcorn?" she asked as he settled beside her, slumping down in the fluffy leather sofa.

"No, thanks."

"Sammy settle down all right?"

"Yeah, he'll be out like a light."

"You're not going to fall asleep, are you?"

"Depends how lame the movie is."

She nudged him with her elbow. "It's not lame. It's one of my favorites."

He gave her a skeptical look. "Didn't you also like *You've Got Mail*?"

She gasped. "That's a classic!"

Brady's lips twitched, probably at the affronted look on her face. He relaxed into the sofa, his shoulder coming to rest against hers. "When does the leaning part come up?"

"It's a ways in. Just stick with it."

The movie started, and they both grew silent as they followed the plot. Lucy, a lonely token taker on Chicago's rail system, rescues Peter from the track and is mistaken for his fiancée at

234

the hospital. While Peter's in a coma the family takes her in, and she connects with his brother, Jack.

Hope peeked over at Brady a few times. His eyes remained opened and focused on the TV. His face looked relaxed in the flickering glow of the screen's light. When the "leaning" scene came, his gaze sharpened, the moment onscreen drawing out with sexual tension.

Brady's eyes flickered briefly over to hers, hanging for a long moment. But a moment later he turned back to the screen.

The rest of the movie passed quickly. Hope's eyes stung when Jack finally kissed Lucy. Didn't matter how many times she'd seen it, she still went all mushy inside. The credits began to roll, and that's when Hope realized Brady was watching her instead of the TV screen.

"What?" she said.

"That was enlightening."

"Does that mean you liked it?"

"It wasn't as lame as I expected." He shifted until he faced her, placing his elbow on the sofa behind her head. His face was in the shadows now, but she read his intent in his body language. In the subtle shift of his focus.

"So," he said softly, his breath a whisper on her skin. "This leaning thing . . ."

"You, uh, seem to have it down pretty well there, Collins."

" 'It implies wanting . . . and accepting,' " he quoted.

"That about sums it up," she whispered. "You're a quick study."

He moved closer, their lips almost touching but not quite. Her heart pounded against her ribs. The spicy scent of his cologne beckoned her.

"Do those things apply only to the lean*er* or also to the lean*ee*?"

"I, um, think we can assume it applies to both."

"Yeah?"

"Yeah."

He closed the distance between them, and her pulse fluttered as their lips came together. He was in no hurry, kissing her like they had all night.

Her hand slid up the hard curve of his bicep, past his shoulder, and threaded into his short, soft hair. Then she felt his hand under her, and she went weightless as he scooped her into his lap. She sank into his solid chest, relishing his reverent touch.

Oh mama. Her husband was good at this kissing stuff. He could narrow her world to just the two of them in ten seconds flat. Make her forget where she was. Who she was.

A moment later an unwelcome sound filtered into her brain, and the external world came crashing back in. Sam was fussing, his cries growing more insistent through the baby monitor behind her.

She and Brady parted, their breath coming heavily between them. He leaned his forehead against hers, groaning.

She concurred.

"I'll get him," they said at the same time.

Giving him a shaky smile, she palmed his face, loving the feel of his raspy jaw. He'd had a rough night. Had a lot on his mind and needed some time to process everything.

She kissed his forehead. "You go on to bed. He probably just needs a little cuddling."

She sank into his chest as his lungs emptied on a heavy sigh. "You sure?"

"Positive."

"Thanks. Take some Tylenol with you just in case."

She reluctantly eased off his lap, wishing she could recapture the last few minutes. "This teething stuff is for the birds."

"For everyone involved." He flipped off the TV, and the room went dark except for the glow from the stove. "Night, Hope."

"Night, Brady." When she turned partway up the stairs, he was still watching her.

CHAPTER TWENTY-THREE

The next week passed uneventfully. Hope was sure Brady was relieved that his mom hadn't come around. Zoe had seen her at the grocery store, but other than that, she seemed to be keeping a low profile. Hope was caught between wishing the woman would slip quietly out of town and wanting her to make a real connection with Brady. But if she was still on drugs, that was pointless.

Hope still hadn't heard from the oldies station and was starting to feel discouraged. Brady tried to reassure her, but surely they'd interviewed the guy from Chicago by now. She wished Diana had given her some kind of time line.

She'd called her parents earlier in the week and caught up. April's reappearance made Hope appreciate them in a fresh way. They weren't as close as she'd like, certainly not geographically, but they loved her and made sure she knew it.

She snapped the legs on Sam's outfit and scooped him up from the changing table. Heather was going to pick him up in an hour so he could spend the weekend with his grandparents.

With only a week left before Zoe and Cruz's wedding, there were a million details to be handled. The couple was having their bachelor and bachelorette parties tomorrow. The boys were taking a road trip to see the Braves play, and the girls were going to Spaaaah! in Chattanooga to be pampered within an inch of their lives. Afterward they were going out for a tame but undoubtedly fun night on the town. It would be good to have some girl time.

"What else do you need in your bag, huh, punkin?"

Sammy tugged at her ear. "Ba-ba-ba!"

"I've already got Boo Bear. How about your paci? Your clothes, your bibs . . . Do you want your blankie?"

"Ba-boo!"

"Yes, you do!" She swept up his favorite blanket and tucked it in the bag, giving Sammy neck kisses until he laughed.

He babbled happily. Tylenol. She needed to stick that in the bag too, and she needed the teething ring from the freezer.

She bopped down the stairs, purposely bouncing Sam the way he liked. After shutting the gate at the bottom of the stairs, she set him down on the living room floor and went into the kitchen.

The savory smells of garlic and oregano filled the room. She had a new recipe in the Crock-Pot. Later, Brady was taking her out for dessert at the Blue Moon Grill. He'd offered to take her out for a supper date, but she still felt guilty for spending all that money on the heels and purse. She was determined to stick to their new budget.

She was retrieving the teether from the freezer when a knock sounded at the door. Heather already? It was way too early.

She peeked through the screen door and saw April standing on the stoop. Her dark hair was pulled back into a braid again, and her eyes scanned the outside of the house before they lighted on Hope.

"April," Hope said. "I wasn't—was Brady expecting you?"

"No, honey, I was just in the neighborhood."

Hope glanced at the ancient green Toyota in the drive. It had obviously taken numerous knocks, and rust was waging a slow but fierce battle on the side panels.

April followed her eyes, waving a hand. "That old car of mine . . . It's making a funny noise, and I hoped Brady could take a peek, but he wasn't in his shop."

"He's running an errand at the mo—"

Sam cried out, and Hope turned to see he'd maneuvered himself under the end table and gotten stuck.

"Hold on a second." She let the screen door fall shut, feeling a little rude. But she didn't know if Brady would want April in his home.

She got down on her knees, pulled an unhappy Sam from under the table, and lifted him into her arms. "There we go, sugar. Did you get yourself stuck?"

His big blue eyes blinked up at her, his wet lashes clumped together, his chin rumpled. She wiped the tears from his cheek. "It's okay. You're all right now."

When she turned to put him safely in his swing, she saw that April had entered the house. The screen door snapped shut behind her.

"Oh, he's such a handsome little fellow. Can I hold him?"

"Um . . . I should probably call Brady and let him know you're here." She reached for her phone.

But April was already at her side, hands out. "Come to Grammy, baby doll."

Sam smiled at the friendly face, leaning forward.

Oh well. Hope supposed it wouldn't hurt anything, since she was right here. She started to punch in Brady's number, but just then she heard a car pull up.

He was home. Thank goodness!

She shifted on her feet, not wanting to leave April alone with Sam, but she also felt the need to warn Brady that his mother was here. He probably wouldn't recognize her car.

April was playing peek-a-boo, and Sam seemed to be content. He was pulling April's hands from her face and smiling his silly, toothless grin.

Hope headed to the door to intercept Brady.

But when she got there, her breath tumbled from her lungs. It wasn't her husband approaching the house, but Patricia and Ned Parker.

Oh no. What were they doing here? She stepped out onto the stoop and came down the two steps. "Mr. and Mrs. Parker. What are you doing here?"

Patricia halted several steps away, her husband at her back. "We're here to pick up our grandson, of course."

"But . . . Heather was supposed to pick him up." Hope checked her watch. "And not for another forty-five minutes."

"She got delayed," Patricia said. "And she already notified Brady. He knows we're coming to pick up the baby."

Was that even true? She heard Sam's giggles and felt torn.

"We're in a bit of a time crunch," Ned said stiffly. "If you wouldn't mind getting Sam, we'll just be on our way."

"Brady's not home yet, and he didn't say anything to me about—"

"For heaven's sake." Patricia straightened to her full height. "So we're a little early. He knew we were coming."

"I should just call him." Hope reached for her phone and dialed his number. "He should be here any minute, and I'm sure he'd like the chance to say good-bye to Sam."

"We'll only have him for two days!" Patricia said. "Brady gets him all the time."

"I'm sorry, I just feel I should let Brady know what's going on." But Brady wasn't answering his phone. Maybe he was out of range, or maybe the phone had gone dead. She left a voicemail for him to call her ASAP and ended the call.

What now? Patricia was glaring at her, arms crossed. Ned's brows were pinched together, looking formidable as he towered over them both. And Brady's druggie mom was inside the house, alone with Sammy.

A wave of tension rolled over Hope. "He should be here any minute. Maybe you should wait in your car until he arrives."

Patricia looked over her shoulder. "Ned, do something. This is ridiculous."

Ned stepped toward Hope. "You have no right to keep our grandchild from us."

"I'm not trying to do any such thing."

"We're going to be late to our engagement!"

"If you'll just wait a few minutes—"

"As if you have any rights to Sam at all! Your marriage is nothing but a charade anyway!"

"That's not true."

"You get to spend every day with our grandchild, and you have even less of a right to him than Brady does."

Heat flushed through her body. "Well, I'm afraid the judge feels differently."

"He's our grandchild," Ned said. "You can't keep him from us. The judge said—"

"Everything all right out here?" April appeared in front of the screen door bouncing Sam on her hip.

Oh no. This wasn't happening. Hope closed her eyes in a long blink.

"And just who is this?" Patricia said.

"Howdy, y'all." April stepped out onto the stoop. "I'm April Russell, Brady's mama. And you must be . . . ?"

Hope tried to warn April off with a look, but the woman was paying her no mind.

Hope was vaguely aware of the crunch of gravel. Brady . . . Thank God. "April, maybe you can go inside and get Sam some Cheerios. They're in the pantry. I'll be right in."

"Wait . . . ," Patricia was saying. "I thought Brady's mom passed away when he was in college."

Ned's eyes narrowed on April. "She did."

April tossed her braid over her shoulder. "That was his adoptive mother, my sister. I'm his real mama. I'm in town visiting for a while. Are you Hope's parents?"

Hope's hand went to her throat where a warm tingling sensation had begun. Hopefully the Parkers knew nothing about—

"Wait just a minute." Ned took a few steps closer, passing his wife. "You're that drug addict who gave him up for adoption."

April's chin notched up. "Well, how diplomatic of you. I'll have you know that's all in my past now."

When Ned reached the steps, Hope moved in front of him, blocking his path.

He stopped but scarcely paid her any mind. "Is that why your pupils are dilated right now? Why you can't seem to stop fidgeting?"

April's eyes hardened. "You don't know what you're talking about."

"I'm a retired police officer. I've seen more addicts than you can shake a stick at."

"How dare you judge me," April said. "You don't even know me."

Ned's eyes shifted to Hope. "How dare you put my grandson in the care of some druggie."

It took everything in Hope not to shrink away. "That is not what's happening here."

"Who do you think you are?" April said from the safety of the stoop.

"You're not helping, April," Hope said. "Go back inside, please."

"Oh, no she won't." Ned grabbed Hope's arm, jerking her to the side. "Not with my grandson."

"Let go of me!"

"Hey!" Brady was there, pushing Ned away. "Back off, Ned."

The men faced off, their shoulders leaning in, their brows pulled tight. Brady was half a head taller, but Ned was stout and in good shape for his age.

"What's going on here?" Brady said. "Why are you so early?"

"We simply came to pick up our grandson," Patricia said, "just as we told you we would, and we find your druggie mother in possession of our grandchild! Is this what you call good parenting, Brady? I'm sure the judge will be very interested to know about this!"

"She's never even been here before, Patricia," Brady said.

"Give me my grandchild." Ned started to push Hope aside again.

But Brady grabbed him by the collar. "So help me, Ned, if you put a hand on her again, I'll lay you flat on the ground."

Hope had never seen Brady so riled. She placed a hand on his arm. "Okay, everybody, just calm down. Mr. and Mrs. Parker, April stopped by unexpectedly. She was here for all of five minutes before you arrived, and I was with her every moment."

Patricia's eyes narrowed on her. "So you say."

Brady turned loose of Ned's shirt, his jaw clenched, his eyes piercing the older man's. "Take your wife and get in your car, Ned. I'll bring Sam out in a minute. It didn't have to happen like this."

After a long, tense moment Ned started backing away. Before he reached the car he turned. "You haven't heard the last of this, Brady."

Hope was afraid of that very thing.

Brady couldn't sit down. He paced the length of the living room, the adrenaline still flushing through his system. He'd delivered Sam, along with the bag, to Ned and Patricia. They hadn't exchanged a single word before the car took off down the lane.

April was harder to get rid of, but Hope had finally made her understand that now wasn't a good time for Brady to take a look at her car.

"I'm so sorry, Brady," Hope said.

So was he. How had that gone south so fast? He couldn't believe this was happening. The Parkers would use it against him in court. He just knew it.

He laced his hands behind his neck. "Just tell me what happened."

Hope started at the beginning, going into more detail about April's arrival.

A headache throbbed in his temple. "I really didn't want April in the house, Hope."

"I didn't let her in the house." She explained that Sam had gotten stuck, and April had slipped inside while she went to help.

"All right, but then you just handed Sam over to her?"

Hope's eyes flashed. "What was I supposed to do? I'm not the enemy here, Brady. Yes, I let her take Sam for a few seconds. But I was standing right there. I didn't know what to do. And then the Parkers showed up."

"And what, you thought it would be a nice family reunion?"

Something flashed in Hope's eyes. She pressed her lips together. Her shoulders had gone rigid, and she crossed her arms over her chest.

What was he doing? Brady scrubbed a hand over his face, taking a few deep breaths. "I'm sorry. I know this isn't your fault."

She stared at him from across the room, her posture stiff and defensive.

He was an idiot. He gave a long sigh and approached her slowly. When he reached her he stopped, but her gaze was locked onto his shirt-front.

"Hope . . ." He tilted her chin upward until her eyes met his. He wasn't used to seeing those green eyes distant and flinty. And more than a little hurt.

Guilt pricked hard. She hadn't asked for this. Any of it. She'd done nothing but try and help him. She'd even married him, for crying out loud.

"I'm really sorry," he said. "You didn't deserve that."

Her shoulders sank as a breath tumbled out of her.

"You've been great. This was a . . . situation you couldn't have avoided."

"We never talked about how you wanted to handle April."

"I know. That's my fault. And it's just my luck she'd be here when the Parkers show up." He bit back a word he hadn't said in a long time. "They're going to use this against me in court, and it's not going to look good."

"We'll talk to Calvin about it. Tell him exactly what happened. Ned didn't do himself any favors either, losing his temper like that. Putting his hands on me."

"It's our word against his. I wasn't sure if she was still on drugs. It was dark at the Rusty Nail, but Ned's right. Her pupils were dilated. She's clearly on something, and we can't let her anywhere near Sam again."

"Agreed."

"I'll have a talk with her."

"She's not going to like it."

"Too bad. I just hope the damage hasn't already been done."

The Parkers had the money to look into April's past. Maybe hire a private investigator and dig up more dirt to use against him. Like the way she'd neglected him when he was a baby, and the charges her parents had filed so that his mom and dad could get custody of him. Maybe they could even call witnesses who knew of April's destructive behavior.

No, he'd never allow April near his son again. But if Patricia and Ned had their way, it wouldn't matter. They'd spin this one event into so much more than it had been. And with the hearing only a week and a half away, it might be the very thing that tipped the case in their favor. He could lose his son because of an absentee, drug-addicted mom who'd probably come back into town on some whim.

Brady's breath felt stuffed into his lungs, and his heart felt near to exploding. "I can't lose him, Hope. I just can't lose him."

Her eyes softened on his as she reached for him. "Hey . . . That's not going to happen."

He drew her into his chest, the soft feel of her against him like an anchor.

She held him tight. "Have faith. This will all work out. You'll see."

He could only pray she was right.

CHAPTER TWENTY-FOUR

Hope held Zoe's short wedding train as the bridal party headed toward the back of the church sanctuary. The slim-fitting bridal gown made the most of Zoe's trim figure. Josephine had tamed her auburn curls and left them flowing down her back. A circlet of flowers crowned her head. She looked like a fairy-tale princess.

Ruby Brown, whose job it was to keep this shindig running smoothly, manned the sanctuary door. Four-year-old Gracie was at her side, twirling in her frilly white dress, awaiting her part in the ceremony.

Ruby's face lit up when she saw Zoe. "Oh, look at you, child! I declare, you're just the prettiest thing. Your granny's looking down from heaven with a big ol' smile on her face right now."

Zoe gave Ruby a hug. "Thanks, Ruby. I'm so glad you're here. Everything going smoothly so far?"

"Just like clockwork. Don't you worry about a thing."

Ruby ordered the bridesmaids to take their places in the lineup, and Hope rearranged Zoe's train as the strains of "Loved Like That" filtered through the door. The parents were probably seated by now, and it was only a matter of waiting for the song to end.

Zoe had chosen to walk solo down the aisle. Partly because her relationship with her dad was strained, but also because it represented her rediscovered independence. After falling for the wrong guy, Zoe had cut ties with Copper Creek and lost her way for a few years. But she was back now, and happier than Hope had ever seen her.

Finished with the train, Hope straightened and faced her best friend. They'd been through a lot together, and she was so honored to be by Zoe's side today.

Zoe's makeup was flawless, and her green eyes sparkled under the dim chandelier. Her creamy skin glowed against the white satin of her gown. She was a beautiful bride. Perfection.

Hope gave a wistful smile. "Have I told you how absolutely gorgeous you look?"

Zoe fiddled with the taupe ribbon dangling from her elegant bouquet. "Several times, but I sure appreciate the sentiment."

"Cruz is going to faint dead away at the sight of you." The two had waited a long time to be together. But Gracie had her daddy now, and the three would finally be a family.

"Do you have the ring?" Zoe asked.

"Of course I have the ring."

Zoe's eyes narrowed on hers. "You didn't put it on your finger, did you?"

Hope gave her a look. "I have my own ring now, thank you very much."

"I don't know why I'm so nervous. Look, my hands are shaking." The ribbons hanging from her bouquet trembled.

Hope took Zoe's free hand in her own and gave her friend her best, confidence-inspiring smile. "All of those jitters are going to go away the second you lay eyes on that man in there. He loves you more than life itself. I have never known two people more meant for each other or more deserving of a happily ever after."

A tremulous smile curved Zoe's lips as her eyes went glassy. "Oh, Hope. Thank you. You always know exactly the right thing to say."

Hope made a face. "Well, I just stole from my matron of honor speech, so when you hear it again later, pretend it was the first time."

Zoe laughed, the strain on her face falling away as the music inside the sanctuary shifted, and Rawley began the sweet strains of "Marry Me" on his guitar.

Zoe sucked in a breath as Ruby reached for the door. "All right, ladies, everybody ready?"

"Let's do this," Josephine said.

Daisy gave Zoe a smile. "You're about to make Cruz the happiest man in the room."

"Aw, thanks, Daisy."

Hope gave Zoe's hand a squeeze, then ushered little Gracie to her place in line. She smoothed her own blush-colored dress as Ruby opened the door with a *whoosh.*

It was finally time. They'd been so busy this week with last-minute wedding arrangements. The rehearsal last night had gone smoothly and had been followed by a lovely dinner at the Blue Moon Grill.

Hope advanced in line as Josephine made her way down the aisle. Ruby handed Gracie her miniature bouquet.

Hope drew a breath in and breathed it out, letting the day's stresses flow away. She'd been on matron-of-honor detail since first thing this morning. She hadn't even seen Brady today, but she couldn't wait to see him now in his tux. Little had they known when Zoe and Cruz had asked them to serve as maid of honor and best man that they'd be married themselves when the big day arrived. Crazy.

But crazy good. A smile curled her lips as she eased forward, thinking back to the other night. To the way his lips had felt on her neck. On her mouth. At some point those passionate kisses would continue on into the bedroom. Some point soon, she thought.

She moved into the doorway and, at Ruby's signal, began the slow walk down the aisle. She looked to the front, her eyes seeking and finding her husband. He stood at Cruz's side, his eyes homing in on her. His eyes smiled a split second before his lips turned up.

As the quiet strains of "Marry Me" shifted to

the chorus, Hope couldn't take her eyes off him. He was gorgeous, her man. She was sure he'd looked this good at their own wedding, but she must've been too distracted to pay much mind. She was noticing now. So were her thumping heart and her laboring lungs and her wobbly knees.

⇥‡⇤

Good heavens, she's beautiful.

Brady's heart stuttered at the sight of Hope. Dressed in the palest of pinks, her dress was the same color as the bridesmaids' but a different style. He'd seen it on the hanger at home, but . . . yowza.

The gauzy skirt hit just above her knees, making her legs go on forever, and a shiny ribbon encircled her waist. The lacy top was cut in at the shoulders, narrowing to a ribbon that tied low around her neck. The sides of her hair were pulled back, and the rest spilled in glossy waves over her shoulders.

As she neared, he winked at her, and her lips curled into a smile just for him. Her green eyes sparkled with warmth under the chandeliers. For a moment he pitied Zoe, having to follow this gorgeous creature. He couldn't take his eyes off her even when she made the turn at the altar and joined the rest of the wedding party on the stage.

Only when the crowd began murmuring did he

turn his attention to where Gracie was proceeding down the aisle—probably faster than she'd been instructed. With her red curls and ivory skin, she was Zoe's mini-me.

He cast a sideways look at Cruz, who wore his proud-daddy smile. The groom gestured his daughter toward the other side of the stage where Hope was discreetly waving her over. There was a collective sigh of relief as Gracie took her proper place.

A moment later Rawley finished the melodic notes, ending the processional, and the organist began the first notes of the "Wedding March." A loud rustling ensued as the crowd rose to their feet and turned toward the doorway where Zoe appeared.

He felt the moment her eyes locked on Cruz's. Sensed his friend's tension just falling away. Zoe's lips turned up, and the look of sheer joy on her face was enough to make Brady's throat constrict a little.

A sideways glance at his friend told him Cruz was having a harder time keeping a check on his emotions. The corners of his eyes tightened as tears filled them, and his Adam's apple dipped with a swallow.

When Zoe reached them, Cruz took her hand and brought her to his side, seemingly blind to everyone else in the sanctuary.

A movement beyond the bride and groom

caught his eye. He looked over in time to see Hope brush a tear from her cheek. As he caught her eye, his stomach did a flip. And he knew.

He was so in love with his wife.

She'd become his best friend. The person he wanted to share his day with. The one he wanted to share his nights with. He held her gaze for a long, poignant moment, his love for her all but bubbling from within.

Somehow she'd wiggled her way right into his heart with her devotedness and her soft heart and her quirky little ways. Real love had happened.

His mind snagged on the thought. On the minor inaccuracy of the statement. It had happened for *him*. He had no idea if it had happened for her. And if he recalled, she hadn't seemed too keen on the idea of real love back before they'd married.

His breath hitched. A prickle of fear poked hard. What if it never happened for her? What if he became trapped in a marriage of unrequited love?

⁂

Zoe's backyard had been transformed into a dreamland. Stars twinkled brightly over the moonlit landscape, and the scents of pine and honeysuckle lingered in the air. Beyond the peach orchard, the Blue Ridge Mountains stood tall and dark against the night sky.

Hope took a seat at the oblong wedding party table facing the crowd as Zoe and Cruz worked their way toward the makeshift dance floor. Last Chance started the moving melody of "Amazed," and Cruz drew his bride into his arms.

Hope watched the newlyweds, her elbows propped on the table, her hands clasped against her cheek. The two moved together as one, joy and relief obvious in the width of their smiles and the relaxed lines of their shoulders.

"I just love this song." Josephine was sitting to her immediate right. "It's so romantic."

"It's perfect for them." Daisy sighed from the other side of Josephine. "He can't take his eyes off her. That's just so . . . dreamy. Gives a girl a little hope."

Hope glanced at Daisy. It couldn't be easy being the only remaining single woman of their friend group. "Your day will come, Daisy. Try to enjoy the journey."

"In the meantime, I'll be corralled onto the floor later with the other old maids, dodging an airborne bouquet."

Hope laughed. "You're what—twenty-four? Twenty-five? In whose universe is that an old maid?"

"My mother's, that's whose. Everybody my age is getting married and having babies, and Mama reminds me of it every time she calls."

"Believe me, I know how you feel," Hope said. "But God will bring someone around in His own time."

"Maybe you'll meet someone tonight," Josephine said.

Daisy gave her a look. "While the air is heavy with the scent of wedding flowers and desperation?"

"That's what the whole bouquet toss is really about," Josephine said with a wink. "Lets all the single guys know who's available."

"Oh, is that what it's for? I thought it was the bride's last chance to humiliate all her single friends."

"No, that's what the bridesmaid dresses are for—*usually*," Hope added quickly. "I have to admit Zoe was very kind to us."

"Judging by the look on Brady's face when you came down the aisle, he completely agreed," Josephine teased.

"I'll definitely be wearing this dress again," Daisy said. Her eyes lit up. "Or maybe I'll donate it to the dress drive."

Each year the girls did their part to make the Spring Fling the highlight of the year for the girls at the local orphanage. Josephine provided hairdos and makeup, Hope ran the dress drive, and Daisy donated boutonnières for the girls' dates.

"That's a great idea," Hope said. "I might do that too. I don't have many occasions for a fancy dress anyway."

The music swelled as the band shifted into

the chorus, and on the dance floor Cruz brushed Zoe's hair behind her ear.

Hope's gaze drifted down the table to Brady, and she caught him looking at her. Heat rose to her face as she smiled, feeling suddenly shy under the intensity of his gaze.

"Look at her, flirting with her husband," Josephine said. "You go, girl."

Hope pulled her gaze from Brady. "Who, me?"

"You two are so cute," Daisy said, turning back to the dance floor. "Oh, look."

Gracie had escaped her grandma's arms and scurried onto the dance floor to join her parents. Cruz waved off his mom and scooped his daughter into his arms. There was a collective sigh, and not a dry eye in the house, as the three continued the dance.

Hope was so happy for her friend. For a while there, none of them had been sure Cruz was going to let go of the past. Look at them now. Look what happened when grace was freely given.

The photographer circled them, taking pictures. Those were going to be some keeper shots.

A few beautiful minutes later the dance came to an end, and the crowd applauded. Hope went back into matron of honor mode as she made her toast. Brady followed, his words sentimental and charming.

As the evening progressed, Hope made sure Zoe had everything she needed. She helped keep Gracie occupied, fetched drinks, answered catering questions, and took candid shots of the couple with friends as they mingled.

Time seemed to fly by, and before she knew it the bouquet had been tossed and the cake cut. The band started a set of songs guaranteed to get people moving.

A while later the band struck up a slow song, and couples began making their way to the dance floor. Hope approached the bride, who'd been cornered by the overly talkative Ida Mae Simmons.

"Excuse me," Hope said. "I hate to interrupt, Zoe, but I do believe your husband wants to claim a dance with his bride."

Zoe took Ida Mae's hand. "We'll have to catch up later then, Ida Mae. It was so nice of you to come." Zoe tossed Hope a grateful smile as she went in search of Cruz.

Hope took the older woman's arm. "Ida Mae, Pearl Hawkins was just asking after your son. I was so tempted to share your wonderful news, but I thought you might like to do that yourself."

Ida Mae's finely-drawn eyebrows shot up under her fringe of brown bangs. "Oh my, yes, I would. Thank you, Hope." She scuttled off on her matronly heels, and Hope felt a pinch of guilt for turning Ida Mae loose on Pearl.

"Very diplomatic." Brady had suddenly appeared at her side. "But it's time for Hope to have a little fun too—on the dance floor with her husband."

Hope took a quick look around to make sure all was going smoothly. "Well, I guess I can—"

But Brady was already tugging her toward the dance floor. They joined the throng, and he turned to take her in his arms. Her eyes found Zoe and Cruz, turning in a slow circle in the center of the floor. Zoe tilted her head back, laughing at something he said.

"Relax," Brady said. "Your only job now is to be a wedding guest, and that entails lots of fun, lots of smiling, and lots of dancing."

Hope's eyes swung to his. He was right. Zoe was having a wonderful time, and everything was under control. She blew out a breath, letting her shoulder muscles relax. She closed her eyes for a quick minute, drawing in the fresh scent of mountain air. The temperature was mild for an October night, perhaps midseventies. They'd worried about the weather for nothing.

She shuffled in Brady's arms, their legs brushing close. "I didn't realize how much my feet hurt until this very minute. Ouch."

"Pinched toes?"

"Like ten little hog-tied piggies."

"Kick them off. Nobody'll care."

Tempting. "Maybe in a bit, after the crowd dwindles down."

"You're just afraid I'll step on your toes."

"The thought did cross my mind." But in truth, Brady was all masculine grace on the dance floor.

"You must be exhausted," he said. "You've been running since sunup."

"And we still have to tear down all this." She looked around at all the tables and chairs and the twinkle lights strung over the stage.

"It'll go fast. There'll be plenty of help."

He tugged her closer, and she laid her head on his shoulder, slipping her arms around him. Contentment rolled over her. She liked having Brady for a husband, and it was nice to take a few minutes and soak it all in. He'd been pretty distracted this week with preparation for the final hearing. He was worried. Anyone could see that. But none of that tonight.

She played with the ends of his hair instead, marveling in the softness. "You look very handsome tonight, in case you couldn't read my mind earlier."

"Thank you. You're absolutely stunning. I had this moment when you were walking down the aisle—I actually felt a little sorry for Zoe." His lips moved against her temple as he spoke, his voice low and husky.

"Why's that?"

His hand moved in a circle over her lower back. "No bride should have to follow that kind of beauty. You took my breath away, Hope."

Hope's heart turned over in her chest as she

huffed a laugh. "Clearly you're a little biased. Zoe can hold her own any day of the week, and today she's gorgeous."

He drew back and tilted up her chin. She gazed into his soulful eyes and felt her legs wobble.

"So are you," he said. "Inside and out. I'm one lucky son of a gun."

She didn't know what to say. Sometimes he made her speechless, and some might call that a miracle. He leaned down and swept a gentle kiss over her lips before drawing her back into his arms.

Oh yeah. She liked being married to Brady. If only things could stay just like this forever. But the hearing was Monday, and though she hadn't said it aloud, something deep inside warned her that a major shift was coming. A foreboding tingling in her chest. A relentless tightening in the spaces around her heart.

Determined to enjoy the present, she pushed the feelings aside and snuggled more deeply into her husband's embrace.

CHAPTER TWENTY-FIVE

The moonlight filtered through the filmy drapes in the nursery, casting a dim glow on Sam's sleepy face. The rocking chair creaked beneath Hope with each lulling roll. The baby worked his pacifier intermittently. His dark eyelashes were a feathery shadow against the soft curve of his cheek.

It was just after two in the morning, and he'd awakened twenty minutes ago, fussing. That darn tooth was giving him fits, poor little guy. She'd rubbed some numbing gel on his gums and given him some Tylenol, and he was finally sleeping again, although fitfully.

Hope smothered a yawn. It had been such a long day. They hadn't gotten home from the reception until almost one.

She wanted Brady to get a good night's rest. Monday was the court date, and he'd had to deal with the fallout from the Parkers' visit this week as well as the wedding stuff. He'd also asked April to keep her distance until the hearing was over.

Witnesses were lined up. Zoe and Cruz had delayed their honeymoon by two days to accommodate the hearing. Brady had plenty of people who could vouch for him, but no one closer than those two.

Hope caught up on her prayers, thinking ahead to the upcoming week. Not only the hearing but also the job in Atlanta, which, if she got it, started in only a week and a half. Diana had called this week, apologizing profusely for not having an answer yet. This guy from Chicago—his schedule had been the holdup, but he'd finally visited the station and interviewed yesterday. Hope put in some prayers about that too.

By the time she'd finished praying, Sam had gone limp in her arms, so she stood and carefully laid him in the crib. He stirred as she covered him with a lightweight blanket, but he settled quickly.

She tiptoed from the room. The nightlight glowed from the bathroom down the hall, and the furnace kicked on, chasing away the early October chill. She was pulling the nursery door closed when she heard the floorboards creaking behind her.

"Everything okay?" Brady whispered as he emerged from his room across the hall.

"Yeah. Poor baby's teeth are just bothering the daylights out of him."

His hands came around her from behind. "Sorry I didn't hear him. Was he up long?"

Hope's heart thumped as she leaned back into his chest. "No, I just gave him some medicine and rocked him back to sleep."

She wrapped her arms around his, her fingertips running over the springy hairs on his forearms.

She held back a yawn, reveling in the solid, masculine feel of him at her back. When he nuzzled her hair, a shiver rippled down her arms.

"You smell so good," he said, his voice low and throaty.

She smiled. "The fresh fragrance of baby?"

"More like the sweet scent of Hope."

"I see what you did there . . ." She sucked in a breath as he pressed a delicious kiss on the side of her neck. "The little play on words."

"You have no idea how long I've been dreaming about doing that."

"Kissing my neck?" Her whisper was all air, little substance.

He strung a trail of kisses back toward her ear. "It's a very sexy neck."

"Well . . ." She tilted her head, giving him access. "Far be it from me to impede your dreams. As you might know, I'm a big believer in aspirations and goals and making a plan to—"

"Hope . . . ," he said.

"Mmm?"

"Shhhhh . . ."

But she ran out of words anyway as he nipped her earlobe with his teeth, giving a gentle tug.

Her heart pummeled her ribs. Hard to believe she'd been yawning less than a minute ago. She couldn't fall asleep now if her life depended on it.

She turned in his arms and found him close. But not close enough. His eyes glittered darkly

269

and were laser-focused on hers. His hair was sticking up at odd angles—that cowlick—only making him more appealing somehow.

He gave her lips a soft brush that made her heart tug. She leaned into his kiss, her hands working up to his shoulders. She loved the feel of him, all warm, soft flesh over taut muscles. Loved the scrape of his bristly jaw against her palm. His hands moved over her back, restless, as he deepened the kiss.

She was out of breath when he drew away just enough to speak. "That big bed getting lonely yet?" he whispered against her lips.

Her mind spun with thoughts that went unfinished as his lips swept over hers again. Helpless to do anything but get lost again, she returned his kiss with equal fervor.

A moment later he pulled away. Someone whimpered as his lips left hers. Possibly her.

His eyes flickered with something—hesitation? Concern? His thumb brushed her face. "Hope . . . I—"

Behind the nursery door, Sammy let out a sharp cry.

Brady set his forehead against hers. Their breaths mingled in the space between them as they held perfectly still, waiting to see if Sam would settle down on his own.

She couldn't seem to get her breathing under control. Or her heart.

"Maybe he'll go back to sleep," Brady said a moment later.

As if the baby had heard his hopeful tone, his fussing shifted to a full-out cry.

She gave a reluctant smile. "Guess not." Not wanting to let go just yet, she dragged a thumb along his jaw. The scrape was barely a whisper in the wake of Sam's escalating cries.

"I'll get him," she said.

Brady exhaled a long, regretful sigh. "No, I will."

"I don't mind." She wasn't going to sleep anytime soon anyway.

"Go on back to bed and get some sleep." He eased away from her, reaching for the door handle. "I'll see you in the morning."

"All right. Don't forget I already gave him Tylenol."

"Okay." He pressed a quick, soft kiss to her mouth. "Night, Hope."

"Good night."

CHAPTER TWENTY-SIX

Brady's hands shook as he tied his tie. He'd spent twenty minutes dithering over which one to wear. Which one would make him look like a stable, loving father who deserved custody of a child who wasn't biologically his?

He'd settled on the blue stripes.

He frowned at his reflection in the bureau mirror. His eyelids were swollen, he had dark circles under his eyes, and his cowlick was out of control. Heartbroken derelict. Not exactly the look he was going for.

He'd been up half the night, praying. Begging, more like. His eyes stung even as his heart took flight in his chest again. He swallowed against the lump swelling in his throat. What if he lost Sam? What if today was the last time he ever saw him?

There was a tapping on the doorframe of his room. In the mirror he watched Hope approach, a sympathetic smile on her face. She looked like the embodiment of motherhood in her simple lavender dress. The front of her hair pulled back, she looked soft and natural and approachable. He was so grateful she'd be by his side today.

"Ruby's here to watch Sam, so we can leave anytime you want."

"I'd like to get there a little early. Go over things one last time with Calvin."

She wrapped her arms around him from behind and met his eyes in the mirror. "Take a deep breath. It's going to be fine. We've got everyone praying."

"I just wish that last visit hadn't happened." April had better not have messed this up for him. He didn't know how he'd ever forgive her if she had.

"Calvin will handle it. He knows what he's doing. And you have so much support. We're going to overwhelm that judge with hearty endorsements."

"I hope you're right." His eyes drifted back to the mirror, and he scowled at his reflection. "The tie's all wrong, isn't it?"

"The tie is perfect. You look like a committed, loving father who's ready to do battle for his son."

His eyes met hers in the mirror. He tried to grab onto the strength and faith he saw there, but his heart wasn't buying in.

She gave him a squeeze. "There's bacon and eggs downstairs. You should grab a bite to eat."

His stomach felt like a lead brick. He was afraid food might actually come back up. "Thanks, but I couldn't eat a thing right now."

"All right." She stepped back, grabbing his navy suit coat from the bedpost and holding it for him to slip on.

She smoothed the lapel. "You look great. Now let's go get custody of our boy."

That was the only thing on his mind over an hour later as he sat behind the defense table with Calvin. Hope sat behind the bar since she wasn't named in the case. The courtroom was imposing, with its high ceilings and aura of hushed silence. The stale air held hints of floor cleaner, perspiration, and fear.

Judge Alders didn't look any happier than he had at the temporary hearing. He sat atop his bench, flanked by two American flags, his eyeglasses perched on the end of his nose.

At the plaintiff's table the Parkers, dressed in dark suits, looked somber and determined.

The courtroom was filled with witnesses for Brady. As Calvin had predicted, when the judge saw the size of the crowd, he'd limited the witnesses to four each. The tactic still left a favorable impression—half the town had come out to support Brady.

The attorneys had given their opening statements, and it was time for the Parkers' attorney to call the first witness.

"The plaintiff calls Brady Collins to the stand."

Brady stood and approached the witness stand. Calvin had warned him this might happen as a result of last Friday's encounter. He seated himself and was sworn in.

As the attorney approached the stand, Brady

forced a pleasant expression and resisted the urge to wipe his sweaty palms down the length of his pants. Calvin had hammered on the importance of keeping his composure and, above all, showing no anger. To that end, Brady kept his gaze from straying to Audrey's parents.

"Mr. Collins," the attorney said, "is it true that when the Parkers picked up their grandson on September twenty-eighth, your mother, April Russell, was at your residence?"

"Yes but only for a few minutes."

"Is it also true that your mother is a known drug addict?"

"I believe that's still the case. But she—"

"And you allowed a known drug addict into your home, with your child?"

"I wasn't home when she got there. I arrived after the Parkers." He barely stopped the wince. His eyes flickered to Hope in apology.

"And who was at home with your son at that time?"

"Hope."

"Hope Collins, your new wife?"

"Yes."

"Do you believe your mother was on drugs at the time of her visit?"

"I couldn't tell you."

"Didn't you notice her bloodshot eyes and dilated pupils?"

"No."

"How long has your mother been addicted to drugs, Mr. Collins?"

Brady pressed his lips together. "Since I was a child."

"That's twenty years or more?"

"Yes."

"Wouldn't it have been fair to assume she was on drugs at the time of her visit?"

"I suppose so, but—"

"How long have you been married, Mr. Collins?"

The abrupt change of topic threw him for a moment. He knew where this was going, and he shoved down a sense of dread.

He cleared his throat. "About a month and a half."

"The timing is awfully convenient, isn't it?"

Brady held the attorney's gaze. "I don't understand the question."

"Let me be clearer then. Did you marry Hope Daniels for the direct purpose of getting custody of Sam?"

Heat surged into his neck. "It's Hope Collins now. And I married her out of love. I love my wife."

He could state that with absolute truth now, with every meaning of the word. His face heated at the admission, and he avoided looking Hope's way for fear she'd see the truth on his face. This wasn't the way he wanted her to find out his feelings had grown into something more.

"Are you saying it's a coincidence that the wedding fell at such a convenient time for this case?"

He lifted his shoulder. "Coincidence, luck, blessing . . . Call it what you will."

"When did you get engaged?"

Brady shifted, forcing himself to maintain eye contact. "The end of June."

"And what was the date of the temporary hearing on this case?"

"I don't recall the exact date."

The attorney smirked. "Does June 28 sound about right?"

"Yes."

"Do you expect us to believe that the temporary hearing, which coincided with your engagement, had no bearing on your decision to get married?"

"I've known and loved Hope a long time. We didn't see a reason to wait any longer."

The attorney held his gaze for a long, uncomfortable moment.

Brady's muscles twitched and his heart palpitated.

❊

Hope resisted the urge to squirm on the wooden bench as Brady left the stand and took his seat at the defense table. It didn't take a lawyer to see that it hadn't gone well.

The other attorney called Mr. Parker, and Hope relaxed into her seat as he was questioned. There was nothing new or surprising here. Calvin passed on the opportunity to cross-examine. Elaine Parker was called next, and she made her sister sound like the very definition of love and charity.

Mrs. Parker was last. The questions and answers seemed to move the woman into Grandmother of the Year status. But Calvin took the opportunity to cross-examine and highlighted her lack of involvement in Sam's life prior to Audrey's death. A point in their favor.

Then he brought up the heart problems she'd been plagued with the past several years. It was something, but it didn't seem to quite balance the scales. To Hope, it felt as if the deficit was on their side. She hoped she was wrong.

Several minutes later Calvin was finished with redirect. The Parkers had finished calling their witnesses, and it was their turn now.

"The defense calls Hope Collins to the stand," Calvin said.

Hope stood and made her way to the witness stand. She took the oath and answered Calvin's questions just as she'd been prepped. She began to settle a few minutes in, her determination to show Brady as the wonderful father he was winning out over nerves.

By the time Brady's attorney finished with her,

she was confident and ready to face the Parkers' attorney. They were going to be thorough about last Friday's event. She prayed she'd be able to remain unemotional. It would be hard with the Parkers sitting right in front of her.

"Mrs. Collins . . ." The attorney looked at her over his black readers. "You're currently the child's primary caregiver, is that correct?"

"Yes."

"How long has that been the case?"

"I've cared for Sam often since his mother passed away, but I didn't become his full-time caregiver until my temporary job ended."

"And when was that?"

"The end of June."

His brows hitched up. "That's also when you became engaged to Mr. Collins, was it not?"

"Yes."

"And about the same time as the temporary hearing?"

She fought the urge to fidget. "Yes."

"Were you home alone with the child on September twenty-eighth when Mr. Collins' mother, April Russell, visited?"

"Yes."

"Were you aware of her drug addiction at the time of her visit?"

"Yes."

"And isn't it true that you allowed April Collins into your home?"

280

"No. The visit was unexpected, and she simply came inside of her own free will while I was tending to Sam."

"She just showed up and entered your home without knocking?"

"No. She knocked, and I answered the door. But while we were talking Sam needed me, and when I went to help him April came inside."

"And how did Ms. Russell come to be holding Sam?" The attorney raised a superior brow.

Heat surged up Hope's neck as she worked hard to keep the discomfort from her face. "She asked to hold him."

"She asked to hold the child, and you just handed him over?"

"I was standing right there."

"But wasn't Ms. Russell, in fact, inside the home, alone with the child, when the Parkers arrived?"

Hope's heart kicked her ribs. "Only for a moment. When I heard the car pull up, I went to the porch. I thought it was Brady."

"At any point did you notice that Ms. Russell showed signs of being on drugs?"

Her stomach dropped. "Not until Mr. Parker pointed it out."

The attorney's eyes shifted to the judge. "No further questions."

As Hope got up, fear spiked her adrenaline. That hadn't gone well. She'd looked careless. She *had* been careless. Her breakfast congealed in her stomach. As she passed the defense table she traded a worried look with Brady. If she cost him his son, she'd never be able to live with herself.

CHAPTER TWENTY-SEVEN

Brady's hands shook, and his palms sweated. He'd never been so scared in all his life. He barely noticed when his phone vibrated in his pocket with an incoming text. He was supposed to have left it in the car, but he'd forgotten.

His attorney was nearly done questioning Zoe. She was doing a great job. Making him sound like Superfather. But he knew the Parkers' attorney would come along and cast doubt, just as he had with their other witnesses.

Sure enough, moments later the attorney began picking apart everything Zoe had said. A terrible dread was building deep inside Brady. He tried to objectively weigh everything he'd heard today. The Parkers' attorney had repeatedly brought up his drug-addicted mom as well as the convenient timing of his and Hope's wedding.

Brady didn't like their odds right now. His phone vibrated, announcing another text. He didn't know who it could be—practically everyone he knew was sitting in the courtroom.

Pastor Jack would be their last witness. He sure hoped his friend's words would pack a wallop. But he didn't know what the man could say that hadn't already been said.

Brady swallowed hard, felt the muscles in his

shoulders bunching up. He wished Hope were beside him right now. He needed her to squeeze his hand and tell him everything would be fine.

As the plaintiff's attorney questioned Zoe, Brady's gaze drifted to his attorney, trying to read his expression. There had been no comforting smiles or slight nods as there had been at the first hearing. Right now the man wore his poker face. He jotted notes but otherwise appeared relaxed and calm.

But it wasn't Calvin's son on the line. Wasn't his future. He wouldn't be the one saying good-bye to his boy and never seeing him again.

Brady's heart squeezed, and the backs of his eyes burned. *Please, God. I'll do anything. Please. I can't bear the thought of losing him. I can't bear the thought of the Parkers stealing that sparkle from his eyes.* He blinked against the rush of emotion, against the feeling of his breath trapped in his lungs.

His phone vibrated again. Someone was being persistent. He thought of Sam, at home with Miss Ruby. What if something had happened? He had to check.

Slipping his hand into his pocket, he discreetly pulled it out and opened the text app. Three texts from Heather. What could Audrey's sister want? She was sitting right here in the courtroom somewhere. He'd seen her when she'd entered.

Her most recent text was a series of question marks. The one before it was just his name. Then he reached the first one.

Tell your lawyer to call me.

Brady frowned at his phone. Call her? They were in the middle of the hearing. Another text vibrated in.

As a witness.

He gaped at the screen as a shiver ran down his spine. He turned, looking over his shoulder, searching for her in the crowd. There she was. In the first row, immediately behind the Parkers, staring back at him somberly.

Heather had made no secret that she didn't approve of the way her mother and father had parented. Or that she felt Sam was better off with Brady. But as far as he knew, the Parkers weren't aware she felt that way. Heather was all about keeping the peace—she was the unofficial mediator of the family. But, he realized suddenly, maybe the Parkers knew more than he thought they did. After all, they hadn't called Heather as a witness.

He gave her a look. *Are you sure?*

She nodded discreetly. He held her gaze for a long moment. She seemed determined. And having her on his side would carry a lot of weight—if that's what she intended to do.

Brady turned back around, wrote on the scratch pad in front of him, and slid it in front of Calvin.

His attorney read it, his eyebrows popping. He looked at Brady, his eyes searching.

You sure? Calvin scrawled a moment later.

Yes, Brady wrote, underlining the word twice.

Calvin gave a nod.

Brady wrote down a few pertinent questions for Calvin to ask Heather. Then Zoe was being dismissed from the witness stand. His sister gave him a wan smile as she passed the table on the way back to the gallery.

Beside him, Calvin rose to his feet. "The defendant calls Heather Greer to the stand."

A gasp sounded, and Brady didn't have to look to know it had come from Patricia. A quiet murmuring filled the courtroom as Calvin approached the witness stand. Heather was sworn in.

"Mrs. Greer, can you tell us how you're related to the plaintiffs?"

"They're my parents."

"So the child's mother, Audrey Collins, was your sister."

"That is correct."

"How would you characterize your relationship with your parents?"

"We're on good terms."

"And with your late sister?"

Heather's eyes filled, and she blinked back the tears stoically. "We were very close. Not that we didn't have our little tiffs, but she confided in me more than anyone else."

"Did she ever talk to you about her ex-husband, Mr. Collins?"

"Oh, yes. All the time."

"According to Audrey's disclosures, how did their relationship come about?"

"Objection," the Parkers' attorney called. "That would be hearsay."

"Your Honor, if I may," Calvin said. "Georgia evidence laws changed in 2013, stating that the judge has discretion to hear such testimony in extraordinary cases—and I would argue that this is, indeed, an extraordinary case."

Judge Alders pursed his lips, reflecting a moment. "I'll allow it. Proceed, Counsel."

"Again, Mrs. Greer," Calvin said. "Can you tell the court how Audrey came to be in a relationship with Mr. Collins?"

Heather looked down at her lap, then back up. "Audrey was pregnant and scared because she was alone. She said the baby's father wasn't father material, though she never told me who he was. Audrey was a little . . . wild, I guess you'd say. She set her sights on Brady because she knew he'd marry her if he thought he'd gotten her pregnant."

"Set her sights on him?"

Heather squirmed. "She decided she was going to trick him into thinking he was the father of the baby."

"Looks like her plan succeeded. Did you know Mr. Collins at this point?"

"No. If I had I would've warned him. I tried to talk Audrey out of it, but once she got something in her mind there was no changing it."

"Why did Audrey choose Mr. Collins?"

"They went to the same high school, though they were a couple years apart. She talked about what a great, upstanding guy he was. That he was a man of his word. That he was kind and patient. Father material, she called him."

"If he was so wonderful, why did she divorce him shortly after they married?"

"All the things that made Brady a great father also made him completely wrong for Audrey. My sister craved excitement. She called Brady . . ." Heather cast him an apologetic look. "She thought he was a little boring."

Calvin paced toward the stand and tilted his head. "Mrs. Greer . . . Did your sister ever tell you verbally whom she'd want to raise Sam if anything happened to her?"

"Objection!" the opposing counsel called.

Judge Alders gave the attorney a look over the rim of his glasses. "Asked and answered, Counsel." He gave Calvin a nod. "Proceed."

Brady's short nails bit into his palm. He leaned forward in his seat, breathless.

"Mrs. Greer . . ." Calvin stepped toward the bench. "Did your sister ever tell you whom she'd want to raise Sam in the event of her death?"

Heather's gaze flickered over Calvin's shoulder to her parents, then back. Her Adam's apple bobbed. "Yes, she did. She told me she'd want Brady to raise Sam."

A stunned silence fell over the gallery. Then a murmuring arose.

Calvin gave Heather a modest smile, then addressed the judge. "The defense rests."

The Parkers' attorney had finished questioning Heather on redirect, but nothing could outweigh Heather's assertion that Audrey had wanted Brady to raise her son.

Heather offered Brady a tired smile on her way back to the gallery. Beside Brady, an energy vibrated from Calvin, and a new spark in his eyes fed Brady's hope.

All that remained was the judge's decision. Brady's eyes cut to Judge Alders, who was looking down at either documents or notes. His glasses had slid down his nose, and the court lights gleamed off the dome of his head.

Brady couldn't pull his eyes from the bench where the judge was either about to break his heart or offer him the best gift he'd ever received. His heart was ready to leap from his chest. He pressed his palm against it.

Finally the judge looked up and cleared his throat. He pushed his glasses back with his index finger.

Come on, Brady thought. *I'm dying here.*

"I want to begin by thanking the parties for being here today and thank the witnesses who have testified," the judge said in a rehearsed tone. "After careful consideration of the evidence and testimony and arguments made by counsel, it is the court's order that sole custody of the minor child be awarded to the defendant."

Defendant. That was him. Brady's breath tumbled from his lungs in one unsteady rush. His eyes closed in a long blink.

"However," Judge Alders continued, "the court has heard testimony from the plaintiffs as to their relationship with the minor child. Georgia has long recognized grandparents' rights to visit with a minor child should the child be harmed absent such visitation. Therefore, the court does order that the plaintiffs, the grandparents of the minor child, have visitation on the first weekend of each month. Plaintiffs' counsel will be responsible for preparing a written order reflecting my oral order today. If there is no further business before the court, we are adjourned."

Calvin stood. "Your Honor, that concludes my business with the court today. May I be excused, along with my client?"

The judge agreed, and Brady stood as the rumble of chatter sounded behind him. *Thank You, God!* All the emotion he'd stuffed down for the last hour could be held back no longer. A knot swelled in his throat, and his eyes leaked tears of gratitude.

"We did it!" Hope burst through the gate and grabbed him around the waist, squeezing tight, all but jumping for joy. "Oh, Brady, he's ours. He's ours!"

Brady tightened his arms around her, and he lifted her off the floor. He buried his face in her hair. "Thank You, God!" He'd never been so relieved in all his life. He attempted a prayer of gratitude but couldn't get past, *Thank You, thank You, thank You!*

He felt Calvin's hearty clap on his back. "Congratulations, you two."

Brady set down Hope and pulled his attorney into an awkward hug. "Thank you so much, Calvin. Seriously. Thank you."

Calvin chuckled as he pulled away, straightening his suit. "All in a day's work, Brady. You enjoy that baby now, you hear?"

"Oh, I will. You can count on that."

Brady grabbed Hope's hand as their eyes locked. Hers were teary but so happy. Having her in his corner today had meant everything. Sharing a smile, he pulled his hand to her lips and brushed her knuckles with a kiss.

Then everyone was upon them. Zoe, Cruz, Pastor Jack, his dad, and on and on they came, offering congratulatory hugs and teary smiles. These were his people. His family. He felt a rush of gratitude for the people God had put into his life. It was enough to make his eyes burn all over again.

A quick glance around showed the Parkers had vacated the room. He couldn't blame them. He even felt a sharp pinch of pity for them.

A text came in. Miss Ruby sent her hearty congratulations. Zoe must've texted her. He would respond, but first there was something else he had to do.

He squeezed Hope's hand. "I'll be right back."

He made his way through the throng and out the back of the courtroom. The halls were empty and quiet. He was probably too late. But when he rounded the corner he caught Heather emerging from the restroom. She came to a stop when she saw him approaching.

Her eyes were bloodshot, but she managed a strained smile. "Congratulations, Brady. It worked out just the way it was supposed to."

"Heather . . . I don't even know how to say thank you."

She blinked rapidly. "Just raise that little guy up right. And let me see him sometimes?"

"Of course. I want him to know his auntie." He shook his head, staring at her with disbelief. "I can't believe you did that for me, Heather."

"I did it for Sam," she said, not unkindly. "And for my sister. Audrey wouldn't have wanted Mom and Dad raising her son. She went to a lot of trouble to make you Sam's daddy, and for once she chose well."

He swallowed hard. He'd never be able to pay Heather back for what she'd done today. "Thank you."

"It was the right thing to do."

"Your mom and dad . . ." They were grudge holders. They'd see this as the ultimate betrayal, and they were going to rake her over the coals for this.

"They're not going to be talking to me for a while, but they'll come around eventually. I hope. But I don't regret what I did. I feel at peace about it."

"I'm glad." He wondered anew how she'd turned out so great. Audrey had never been very kind to Heather, and still her sister only wanted to abide by her wishes. "Audrey was blessed to have you for a sister."

"Thanks, Brady. You take care of that boy." She turned to go.

"Call me anytime you want to spend some time with Sam."

Heather tossed a smile over her shoulder. "I'll take you up on that."

Ten minutes later, Brady's seat belt was the only thing keeping him from floating right into the sky. The adrenaline still coursed through his veins, and Hope, fidgeting with her seat belt and talking a mile a minute, seemed to be experiencing the same thing.

Their troop of supporters had wanted to go out and celebrate, and Brady had hated to turn them down. But right now he only wanted one thing: to go home and scoop his son into his arms.

CHAPTER TWENTY-EIGHT

Later that night weariness fell over Brady as he went downstairs. He'd rocked Sam to sleep tonight, an indulgence he didn't allow very often. But he just couldn't seem to soak in enough of his son today.

His son.

A feeling of pride washed over him, and he couldn't stop the smile that curled his lips. When he reached the first floor his phone was buzzing from the coffee table, but he ignored it. As his son slept peacefully in his crib, all he wanted right now was his wife.

Finding the living room and kitchen empty, he peeked out the back door and found Hope leaning against the deck railing, staring out into the dark night. The twinkle lights she'd added weeks ago glittered around her, adding to the light from the lamps.

He slid open the door and slipped outside. The cool evening air brushed his skin, and a chorus of cicadas and crickets greeted him. The earthy smells of decaying leaves mingled with the crisp October air. Fall had eased into the valley, and he'd been so preoccupied he'd hardly even noticed.

Hope turned and offered him that wide, trademark smile of hers. Her eyes sparkled as she leaned back against the deck railing. "Sammy down for the night?"

"Out like a light. I just wanted to enjoy him for a few minutes."

"What a great day, huh?"

"The best." He went straight to her and drew her into his arms. He wanted nothing more than to hold her close.

She accommodated, slipping her arms around his waist. "I'm glad it worked out so well. And I'm so relieved."

"Not going to lie . . . I was worried there for a while."

"You and me both. That other lawyer was kind of vicious."

"Thank God for Heather. I think she really swayed the judge, don't you?"

"She saved the day." Hope pulled back, still in the circle of his arms. "What'd she say to you?"

He thought back to Heather's bloodshot eyes and felt a little prick of guilt. "That she did it for Sam, and for Audrey. That it's what her sister would've wanted."

"That was a big sacrifice for Heather to make. I can't imagine it's going to be a happy holiday at the Parkers' this year."

"I hope they'll forgive her in time. She's their only living child, and she has their other grandchildren, so maybe that'll speed up the process a little."

"You'd think. She wouldn't have risked the relationship if she weren't sure she was right about you."

He tipped up her chin, gazing into eyes that were warm and inviting. "I don't want to talk about the Parkers anymore."

"Yeah?" she said softly, flirtation flickering in her eyes. "What do you want to talk about, Collins?"

His thumb brushed her cheek. So soft. "I don't want to talk at all."

Her sweet mouth didn't even have a chance to curl upward. He took her in a kiss like he'd been wanting to since the other night. But now was even better, without the final hearing hanging over their heads. Now was perfect.

She gave back with equal abandon, stirring all the desire he'd been feeling for months. Had it only been months? It seemed like he'd wanted her forever. More than anything he wanted to finish what they'd started Saturday night. But was it a good idea? Would she be this happy if she knew how deeply he'd fallen for her?

But maybe this was exactly what they needed. Maybe she'd forget all her reservations about love and fall for him too. Then they'd be on even footing.

She made a little mewling sound that had him hauling her up against him. She was perfect, all soft curves and warm, heavenly woman. He could kiss her like this all night long. For the rest of his life.

Yes, please.

He pulled back, needing to see her. Needing to connect on a deeper level, look into those soulful, green eyes. Their gaze locked, her eyes at half-mast, and all the feelings he'd had at Zoe's wedding rushed over him again. He really loved this woman. The feeling swelled inside until he thought he'd bust with it.

"Hope . . . I . . ."

She claimed his lips in a bold move that was seductive, though the timing gave him pause. But with her lips on his, desire fogged his brain, and the qualm was soon forgotten. If he wasn't going to tell her how he felt . . . he'd just have to show her.

⊰∦⊱

Hope couldn't catch her breath. Wasn't sure she wanted to. Brady had brought every cell to life until she was humming with raw energy.

There was no denying the intensity of his kiss or where he hoped it would lead. They'd made it this far Saturday night and had only turned back because of Sammy's cries. Tonight there would likely be no interruptions. He'd courted her slowly, patiently, and he'd done his job so well. Hope was ready to take things further.

Boy howdy, was she ready.

Something tweaked her conscience, something vague and indistinguishable. Something easy enough to forget with the way his mouth and his hands moved on her.

"Thank you," he murmured against her lips a long, delicious moment later. "Thank you for everything you've done for me, Hope. For us."

That tweaking returned to Hope—and with it some clarity. The kiss was perfect. It was the timing that gave her pause. He'd just won custody of his son and was feeling grateful.

She wanted this. They'd been building up to it for months, but . . .

When he leaned in to kiss her again, she palmed his face and pulled back, looking him square in the eye. Those eyes. They smoldered, sucking her in until she'd almost forgotten what she was going to say.

"What?" he asked softly.

It was hard to breathe. Hard to think with him looking at her like that. But the tweaking had become a full-fledged pinch, and she needed to be sure.

"Brady . . . I don't want to do this just because you're feeling grateful."

A dozen emotions shuffled across his face, too quickly to follow them. Then his lips turned up and something flashed in his eyes. Something that unsettled her a little with its intensity.

He took her hands from his face and kissed

both of them slowly before meeting her gaze again. "There are a hundred reasons why I want to make love to you, Hope. Grateful is way down the list."

She couldn't look away from the sincerity in his eyes. He looked like he wanted to say more, but suddenly she didn't want to talk anymore.

She leaned in and brushed her lips across his.

"Okay?" he whispered, his voice as thick as honey, as if he needed to be sure.

"Okay," she said.

CHAPTER TWENTY-NINE

The frenzied thumping of Hope's heart had diminished a long while ago. Her breath whispered against the fine hairs on Brady's forearm. She lay snuggled against him, warm and cozy and content.

He'd drifted off a long time ago—she could tell by his deep, steady breathing and the lovely weight of his arm across her shoulder.

The lights were out, and the moonlight filtered through the curtains. Despite the long and emotional day, she was wide-awake. Because during the last hour she'd realized that something had happened. Something had changed.

She'd gone and fallen in love with her husband.

Until this very moment she'd put the thought on hold. Refused to acknowledge it, much less dissect what it might mean. But now she gathered up a bit of courage and brought the realization out into the open, as if holding it in her hands, examining it in detail.

It was true. Her heart gave a shudder as the realization sank in. Somehow she'd been so caught up in the day-to-day, so focused on the final hearing, on Zoe's wedding, on Brady's mom, and on attaining her dream job that she hadn't noticed what was happening.

That the feelings of friendship had shifted into

something more. Something much more. And given the way he'd looked at her tonight, she didn't think she was alone in this.

The realization should've been cause for celebration. The ultimate blessing for their union. But she'd only been in love once before, and she couldn't help but remember how that had ended. Couldn't help but recall the pain she'd suffered. The wreck she'd become.

As the memories took root, the breaths that had been flowing so easily became shallow and thready. A trembling, like an earthquake, started rumbling inside.

She tried to push it all down. Tried to get a grip on herself. Tried to tell herself that Brady wasn't Aaron. He surely didn't have a rare heart defect, waiting to go off like a bomb. He wouldn't drop dead out of the blue.

Her fear was illogical. Unreasonable. She knew better. If she could help other people handle their feelings, surely she could control her own. If she could dole out advice, surely she could take it.

But the fear wouldn't go away. Instead, it sucked the moisture from her mouth. Flooded her system with adrenaline and planted a seed of dread in the soil of her heart.

⟨⟩

Brady came awake slowly, yesterday coming back in bits and pieces. His eyes still closed, a smile tugged at the corners of his lips. He was quite fond of yesterday. It had been a banner day all the way around.

Last night sifted through his mind like the best kind of dream. He rolled over, reaching out, his hands seeking the warmth of his wife but finding only cold bedsheet.

He blinked his eyes open. The other side of the bed was empty, the pillow still bearing the impression of Hope's head. Maybe Sam had awakened early. Dawn already filtered through the drapes, and a quick glance at his phone told him it was time to get up anyway.

He rose and showered, dressing in work clothes. He wished he could take the day off and spend it with Hope and Sam. But he had a customer needing a new clutch on his Maserati Coupe by tonight and a tight schedule the rest of the week.

The smell of bacon greeted him as he left his bedroom. He stopped by the nursery on his way downstairs. Sam was still sleeping in his crib, his diapered bottom pooched in the air, his hands tucked under him.

He pulled the door closed and found Hope downstairs in the kitchen, standing over a skillet of sizzling bacon. She wore pajamas, and her hair was pulled into a messy bun. He scoped out his favorite spot on her neck and made a beeline for her.

"Good morning," he said.

Her gaze bounced off him as she scooped the last strips of bacon from the skillet and dropped them on a paper towel–covered plate. "Morning."

Not exactly the warm reception he'd hoped for. "How'd you sleep?"

"Just fine. You?"

"Like the dead."

"Yesterday was a big day."

"And a big night," he added.

Her cheeks colored as he wrapped his arms around her from behind, pulling her against him.

She turned off the stove and moved the skillet off the burner. "That it was."

She'd tensed up, but he didn't let that stop him from planting a kiss in the curve between her neck and shoulder.

He heard her breath catch and smiled against her fragrant skin. "We're not going to be all awkward about last night, are we?"

" 'Course not. We're man and woman. Husband and wife. Nothing to be concerned about."

He turned her in his arms, searching her eyes.

She smiled back at him, maybe a little blandly. She wore no makeup, and yet she was still beautiful. Those almond-shaped green eyes, the long sweep of her lashes. Those barely-there freckles on her nose.

He brushed a stray hair behind her ear. "I didn't say concerned. I said awkward."

"Right." She nodded. "Nothing to be awkward about."

"Or concerned?"

"Of course not." But she wasn't quite meeting his eyes. She toyed with the sleeves of his T-shirt, biting her lip.

He'd never thought of her as shy, but maybe she was, just a little. Given the right circumstances. He tipped up her chin.

Her gaze climbed slowly to his, something softening in those green depths. He wondered if her thoughts were going back to the night before. To the connection they'd shared: emotional, physical, spiritual. He'd never experienced anything like it.

"I like having you in my life, Hope. In my arms. In my bed." *In my heart.* He wanted to add that last bit, but he was still afraid she wasn't ready to hear it yet.

"Me too," she whispered.

He felt a sudden lightness at her admission. A tornado could've swept through the valley, and it couldn't have stopped him from pulling her close. From brushing her lips with his. He'd never get enough of her.

Her arms roped around him, and she sank into his chest. Her response was gratifying and heady. It filled him with wonder and awe and gratitude. He might just be the happiest man alive right now. Hope had made him that way.

He was about to scoop her up into his arms when he heard Sam's morning babbling coming through the monitor. Maybe his son would be content for a little while. He was usually pretty happy in the morning.

But apparently Hope wasn't on the same page. She'd already pulled back, a hand sliding down to push against his chest. "I'd better go get our boy."

He took solace in the fact that she was out of breath, that her cheeks were flushed with want as she pushed away. She was as affected as he.

"Maybe we can . . . ," he began.

But Hope was already slipping from the room.

CHAPTER THIRTY

Hope gave Sam a little push in the baby swing, tickling his bare feet as he swung forward. He chuckled, his blue eyes sparkling with laughter, his chubby cheeks bunching up.

"Gonna getcha!" She went for his tummy this time and got a belly laugh in reply. The sound was so infectious she couldn't keep from laughing.

It had turned into a gorgeous fall day. The temperature was a pleasant seventy or so, the sun shining bright through the colorful canopy of leaves. The crisp air was heavy with the earthy scents of pine and decaying vegetation. It wouldn't be long before winter arrived and then the holidays. Unsettled at the notion, she pushed away thoughts of the future.

Children's laughter rang from the other side of Murphy's Park, and the metal chain bearing Sammy's weight creaked rhythmically with each *whoosh* of the swing.

"Ba-da-ba-ba!" Sammy cried, soliciting her attention.

"You want to go higher?" She gave him a gentle push, and he squealed in approval. "You're going to be an adrenaline junkie, aren't you? You're going to start climbing up on everything and scaring Daddy and me half to death with all your antics!"

Sammy laughed at her silly face.

Taking him to the park had been a last-minute decision. Since the somewhat awkward scene in the kitchen this morning, she'd needed a distraction. She'd run some quick errands in town and decided to treat her little guy to some park time. He'd been so patient in the car. His front tooth had finally poked through his gums on Sunday, and he'd been in a much better frame of mind ever since.

"Only nineteen more teeth to go . . ." She grabbed the bucket seat and held on, bringing him to a sudden stop.

His eyes lit up, and he made a happy, guttural sound.

"Think we can make it? I think we can. Yes, I do." She suddenly let go of the swing, and he laughed in surprise as he completed the backward arc.

Her phone vibrated in her pocket, and she checked the screen. Her breath caught at the sight of Diana's name. The oldies station. Oh, sweet heaven. They'd finally made their decision. She just knew it. The official start date was just one week away, and she'd all but given up hope.

"Oh, God, please let it be good news."

She answered the call, her hands suddenly unsteady. Diana greeted her, and they exchanged pleasantries while bile climbed the back of Hope's throat. She pressed her palm against her chest where her heart was threatening to explode. She wondered if it would be rude to beg the woman to cut to the chase.

As it turned out, that wasn't necessary.

"Listen, Hope, I'm sorry this interview process has been so drawn out. The jock from Chicago, his schedule was so hairy, and he insisted on coming down to Atlanta to check out the station."

"No problem, Diana." *Just my career hanging in the balance is all.* "I totally understand."

"Well, after much deliberation with Darren . . . I'm very pleased to offer you the position. We both feel you're a better fit for the station."

Hope's breath escaped. She closed her eyes for a long moment and had to work to keep her voice calm and professional. "That's wonderful news, Diana. I'm so glad to hear it."

"I can take that to mean you're accepting the position?"

As if she'd turn it down! "Absolutely. I can hardly wait to get started."

"I'm so glad. Well, as you know, Dirk's last day is Friday, so your start date would be next Monday. However, I can get someone to fill in if you need to make arrangements. We've dragged this out so long, we understand if you're not quite ready to make the transition."

"That's all right. I'll be good to go next Monday." They'd talked to Miss Ruby about watching Sam, just in case. She was already taking care of Zoe and Cruz's daughter and seemed more than happy to add Sam to the mix.

"Terrific." Diana confirmed the details of the position, including salary and benefits, and stated that she'd be sending the offer via e-mail shortly.

By the time Hope finished the call, she was shaking. She let out a whoop. "Oh my gosh. Oh my gosh."

"Ga-ga-ga-ga!" Sam called. He'd almost swung to a halt and was kicking his feet impatiently.

"I got the job!" she told Sam. "Can you believe it, Sammy? I got the job!"

"Da-da-da-da!"

She laughed. "You're so right. We should go tell Daddy right away!"

She held her arms out to him, and he reached up for her so sweetly. "Let's go see Daddy!"

Her heart pounding a mile a minute, she made her way to the car, suddenly so eager to see Brady she could hardly stand it. It was all she could do to keep herself from calling him. Only the desire to see his face when she told him the news held her back.

The drive home seemed interminable. When she got there she pulled right up to his garage. She was going so fast she had to brake a little hard. By the time she shut off the engine, Brady was striding toward her, concern on his face.

He met her at her car door, wiping his hands on an old rag. "What's wrong? Everything okay?"

"Everything's fine." She stepped out and hurried to get Sam, who wasn't appreciating the monotony of the car ride after the fun at the park.

"You tore down the drive like you were being chased by a grizzly bear. And I didn't expect you back for a while."

She tossed a smile over her shoulder as she pulled the baby from his car seat. "Well, as it happens, while we were at the park I got a bit of good news."

"Yeah . . . ?" Expectation lined his face.

She turned to face him, holding eye contact for a long, poignant moment. "I got the job, Brady. I got the job!"

His eyes lit up a second before a smile spread across his face. "Hey! That's great news, Hope. The best." He pulled her into a hug, Sam squished between them. "Congratulations, honey. I knew you'd get it."

"Thanks. I was definitely losing hope there. I mean, the job starts next Monday. I thought for sure they'd given it to the other guy."

"They'd have been crazy to turn you down." He pecked her on the cheek as they parted. "I'm so happy for you."

"And just a little relieved?" she teased.

His smile said, *You caught me.* "All of this has gone so well for me. I wanted things to go well for you too."

"Well, they did." She still couldn't quite believe

it. Her pulse raced, making her breathless. Keyed up.

"Is this really happening?" She laughed in wonder. "Maybe you'd better pinch me."

He gave a flirty little smile, and she noted the streak of grease running across his chin. "If you're giving me options I'd rather kiss you."

She swept her thumb across the bristly surface of his chin, only managing to smear the grease. She suddenly forgot all the reservations she'd had last night. This morning. For the moment she felt high on life and blessed beyond measure.

"I like the way you think, Mr. Collins."

CHAPTER THIRTY-ONE

Hope couldn't breathe. The scene in the gym came to a halt around her as she bolted across the floor. Her feet were heavy, as if she were slogging through air as thick as mud. She had to get to him. To where he lay as still as death on the wood floor.

Help him, God!

But the harder she tried, the slower she moved. She whimpered at her helplessness. When she finally drew near, a group of people was there, forming a blockade around him. Diana . . . Judge Alders . . . the Parkers . . . What were they doing here?

Her heart beat into her throat. "Let me through!" she screamed through a throat tightened by fear.

But they didn't seem to hear her.

"Hope," someone said from far away.

It went quiet. The people blocking her were dressed up, she saw now, and she suddenly realized they weren't in a gym any longer, but in a courthouse. She found a break in the barricade and busted through, falling onto the polished tile at Aaron's side. But it wasn't Aaron who lay on the courthouse floor.

It was Brady.

His eyes were closed, his body still. He wore a suit, a blue striped tie, and his hands were folded across his body as if he were laid out in a casket. His hair was carefully combed, and his dark lashes lay lifeless against his pale skin. The only imperfection was a smudge of blood that streaked across his chin.

No, please, God. Not Brady! Please!

Her breath was trapped in her lungs. Her heart tightened painfully, her chest collapsing in on her.

"Hope."

Someone was there, shaking her, but she batted the hands away. She couldn't leave Brady!

She grabbed his arm, but he was as stiff and unyielding as iron. "Brady! Brady, wake up! Don't leave me. Please don't leave me! Oh, God, please don't take him!"

He was gone! He wasn't coming back. Terror built in her throat, releasing in a guttural scream. "Noooo!"

• • • • • • • • • • • • • • • • • •

"Hope!"

Her eyes popped open to darkness. Ragged breaths filled the room. Hers, she realized an endless second later.

The faint light of dawn crept through the curtains. Her heart pounded like a jackhammer, the bed feeling like it was shaking with the force of her heart beating. Brady's bed. She was in Brady's bed. At home.

He was leaning over her, alive and beautiful. Oh, so beautiful! He brushed a thumb across her damp face. "Shhh . . . Don't cry, honey."

Her dream—her nightmare—rushed back, making more tears flow. Making her heart rate accelerate. She gasped for air until dizziness swept over her.

"It's okay now," he said. "You're safe. It was just a dream."

She closed her eyes, wishing the nightmare away. But it was there in the darkness, reaching for her. Clinging to her with its long tentacles.

He murmured to her softly while he mopped up her tears. When she finally got herself under control he said, "You all right?"

She nodded, her throat choking off anything she might've said.

Anything she might've said. What had she said? What had she called out while she'd been in the throes of her nightmare?

"Must've been some dream," he said. "What was it about?"

She wiped the remnant of her tears and sniffed. She couldn't breathe through her nose anymore.

He got up and disappeared into the bathroom.

A moment later he returned with tissues, the bed sinking under his weight.

"Thanks." She sat up and blew her nose. More tears leaked out, and she hid her face, not wanting him to see she was still broken up over it.

Get a grip, Hope. For heaven's sake, it was a dream. Just a dream.

He lay down beside her and reached out to her.

She crawled into his embrace, burying her face in his chest. Soaking him up. He was warm. Strong. Alive. She clung to him, listening to the beating of his heart. Maybe if she held tightly enough she could make the nightmare go away. Convince herself it wasn't reality. That she hadn't lost him just as she'd lost Aaron.

The tears were starting again, and she blinked hard, fighting to shake the nightmare.

"What was it about?" he asked again.

She shook her head.

"You don't remember?"

She didn't want to remember. "No. Did . . . did I say anything?"

He brushed back the damp hair at her temples and continued sifting her hair with his fingers. "You just whimpered and moaned mostly. You said no."

She tightened her arms around him. "Hmm."

"Does that happen often? Bad dreams?"

"No . . . No. I haven't had one in years." And man, oh man. She never wanted another one.

"Good. I don't like seeing you so upset. You wouldn't wake up. It was scary." He tightened his arms around her. "The timing's weird, huh? We've had two great days—banner days."

"Yeah . . . Go figure."

"You okay now?"

"Yeah . . . Just tired."

"Well, let's get a little more sleep. We have an hour or so before our little alarm clock goes off." He kissed her on the top of the head. "And no more bad dreams."

She closed her eyes, her mind. No more bad dreams.

CHAPTER THIRTY-TWO

Brady gave April a strained smile. He'd agreed to meet his mother at the diner for breakfast, but he'd hated leaving Hope and Sam. He'd gotten used to spending those lazy Saturday mornings together, wearing their pajamas until noon if they wanted.

But April had called four times, asking. It seemed she wanted to make an effort to get to know him, and he wasn't going to be cruel. He was trying to show her some grace. Trying to work on that forgiveness thing.

She was trying to get back on the right track. She'd come to church twice since she'd been in town, sitting in the back, holding herself a little apart from everyone else.

This morning there were no dilated pupils or frenzied behavior. But he'd caught a faint whiff of marijuana when he first joined her. And he'd called her on it.

She'd given him a wan smile. "I'm trying to give up the other stuff, Brady. But I need a little something, you know?"

When he said nothing, she took his hand across the table. "Be patient with me, all right? I'm trying. I really am."

That was something, he supposed.

She'd changed the subject then, asking about

the court hearing. She seemed thrilled that he'd gotten custody of Sam. She apologized again for getting in the way when the Parkers came to pick up his son. That had been her wake-up call, she said. She couldn't bear the thought that she'd almost cost Brady his son.

They'd finished breakfast and were lingering over coffee. She was telling him a story about a trip to Disney that ended with a bout of food poisoning and an unfortunate incident that left her vomiting on Goofy's floppy shoes.

She laughed. "It's only funny now. Believe me, at the time I wanted to die a thousand deaths. All those poor kiddos watching . . ."

He couldn't help but wonder if she'd really been suffering from food poisoning. "Not to mention Goofy."

"Oh, yes . . . I'm sure I traumatized him—or her. Hard to tell who was under that getup."

April wore no makeup and looked a little older in the morning sunlight streaming through the plate glass windows. There were laugh lines and hollow places under her eyes. The ever-present braid spilled over her shoulder.

"I've been thinking of moving back, you know," she said out of the blue.

His eyes cut to her. News to him. "To Copper Creek?"

"Of course, silly. I have a son and grandson here. I'm looking for a job, so if you get wind of anything, let me know. I'm kind of hurting for cash. I've done all kinds of things over the years—waitressing, bartending, sales. I even worked on a farm, if you can imagine that."

"I'll keep an eye out for you," he said. But everyone in town knew about April's long history with drugs. He wasn't sure anyone would give her a chance.

"I appreciate that. I need to get back on my feet. I've already put my application in at a few places. Can't mooch off my friends forever, and funds are running low, you know?"

"Sure." He was starting to feel baited, but he didn't bite.

She took a sip of coffee and set it back on the saucer. "So, tell me more about you. Your business . . . your wife . . . anything you want to talk about."

He didn't want to talk about Hope. As great as the week had started out, things had gotten a little . . . strained. He'd hoped once they'd made love they'd only grow closer. Instead, he sensed a distance in her that he didn't understand.

A little awkwardness the morning after, but more so in recent days. He'd asked if anything was wrong, but she just smiled and said, "Of course not." In truth, he was afraid to press her too hard. Maybe she was just nervous about her new job. Or concerned about how they'd manage a long-distance marriage. It would be a big change. He'd miss her a lot through the week.

Or maybe she sensed that his feelings had grown, and hers hadn't quite caught up. Maybe she just needed more time. He wouldn't push her. He could wait. She was worth waiting for.

"Brady?"

He blinked away the thoughts and began telling April about his business. About how he'd started it and how it had grown. How God had blessed his efforts. He left out the inheritance from his grandma—April's mother—and the way it had afforded him his much-needed garage. Granny hadn't left April anything, and he didn't see the need to rub her nose in it.

By the time he hugged her good-bye, he'd almost put his worries about Hope to the back of his mind.

⌖

"Where are you going, little man?"

Sam had followed Hope into the kitchen, his hands and knees working quickly. He reached for the slice of peach peel that had fallen onto the floor.

"Oh, no, you don't. That's yucky."

As she scooped him off the floor, his face wrinkled up in his pre-cry expression.

She slid a bit of juicy peach between his lips. "There you go. How's that? A lot better than that ol' peel."

He immediately forgot his disappointment,

322

vocalizing his approval of the sweet flavor.

Once he swallowed, she held up another bit. "Want more?"

He opened his mouth like a baby birdie, and Hope accommodated. She glanced at the clock. Brady would be home soon. He'd met his mom for breakfast, and for some reason that made Hope nervous.

She was feeling nervous a lot lately. The nightmare she'd had Monday night hadn't been her last. Fortunately she'd not awakened Brady again. But she'd awakened herself and lay in the dark, sweat drying on her brow. Her heart pounding like a bass drum. Thinking about her fear. Her life. Her future. Watching Brady sleep peacefully, his chest rising and falling.

She told herself the nightmares weren't real. But her fear was real enough. Brought on by a terrible event that had left her with major scars. The fear always dissipated with the morning light, but it never went completely away.

Sam complained, reaching for the next bit of peach, and she fed it to him automatically.

Her heart suddenly began to race, and her breaths grew short. An overwhelming sense of terror swept over her.

Oh, no. Please, God, no. Not this again.

She hadn't had a panic attack in years, but she knew this feeling. It bloomed inside, spreading into the tips of her fingers, making them tingle.

She was helpless against the rising tide of panic. Against the complete loss of control. She tried to slow her breathing, but it seemed impossible to keep up with her body's demands.

Sam reached for more peach and nearly toppled from her arms. She grabbed a slice, placed it in his mouth, then set him down on the living room floor before she dropped him.

She was shaking with terror. It felt as if someone else were inside her body, looking out her eyes. Needing an outlet for the nervous energy building inside, she paced the living room floor, making quick work of the space. Waiting, waiting for it to pass.

You're fine. You're not in any danger. It only feels like it. This will pass. Soon you'll feel normal again. The coping skills came right back to her.

Coping skills. What a joke. This didn't feel like coping. It felt as though she were fighting for her life and losing. And she was already dreading the next attack. There'd be another one coming, she knew.

A long moment later—it felt like an hour—her heart rate began to slow. Her breathing followed suit.

A choking noise drew her attention, and she turned to see Sam staring at her, wide-eyed. His face was red, his mouth open in a silent scream.

"Oh, dear God!" Hope rushed to him. He wasn't coughing or crying. He was choking!

"Sam!" She set him on her lap, facing away. She only knew how to do the Heimlich maneuver on adults. But she clasped her hands together and used her fists to thrust in and up.

Please, God!

She thrust twice, three times. Was she doing it too hard? Or not hard enough? The fourth time something came up. Sammy made a garbled sound, then began to scream.

Thank you, God! She turned him around and pulled him against her. He clung to her, wailing. Her eyes fell on the piece of fruit on the rug. It was much too big for him. She'd given him a slice she hadn't finished cutting. What had she been thinking?

Her heart was out of control again, but the panic attack had subsided. The terror she was feeling now was based in reality. Sammy had been unable to breathe, and it was all her fault.

"What's wrong?" Brady was rushing into the house.

She hadn't even heard him pull up. Sam was wailing in her ear, and she was crying, she realized, as Brady swept his son into his arms.

"Hope? What's wrong? What happened?"

She stood on shaky legs, moving to cover the piece of peach on the rug. "He's fine. He . . . he choked. On a piece of peach. I did the Heimlich maneuver, and it came back up. It just happened. Oh my gosh."

Hope ran a hand over her heated cheeks, the close call making her break out into a cold sweat.

Brady looked his son over. "Are you all right, buddy?"

Sammy's wails had slowed to a mere cry. He clung to Brady for life.

Hope brushed the back of the baby's head. *I'm so sorry, honey. I'm so sorry.* "He wasn't breathing. Not at all. His face turned all red, and he just looked at me like . . . We should get him checked just to be sure he's okay."

"All right."

Brady reached out to her, brushing her cheek with his thumb. "Are you okay? You look really shaken."

The dampness at the back of her neck sent a chill down her spine. "It was . . . It was terrifying."

He pulled Hope into a hug. His warm breath feathered her skin. "But he's going to be all right. Thanks to you."

Yeah, she thought, closing her eyes against Brady's shoulder. *Thanks to me.*

CHAPTER THIRTY-THREE

The following Saturday found Hope at the Rusty Nail with the full group. The table was rowdier than usual, having wedding stories to rehash and celebrating Hope's job, which was starting in just two days.

Brady was up at the bar getting them refills, Sam resting against his shoulder. She watched Brady a minute, admiring the straight line of his shoulders and the firm curves of his biceps. He wore fatherhood like a second skin. She was sure going to miss him while she was in Atlanta.

Her eyes drifted across the restaurant to Zoe and Cruz on the dance floor, fresh from their honeymoon, looking flush with love and happiness. They danced now in the middle of the throng, staring at each other like the lovebirds they were.

As she watched, little claws of envy scratched at her from the inside. They made it look so easy, love and marriage. So simple. Zoe wasn't having nightmares and panic attacks. She wasn't scared to death of losing everything she had. But then, she was blissfully unaware of the devastating pain such a loss could bring. Hope could claim no such ignorance.

She forced the thoughts away, fearing another

panic attack. She'd had three more this week, and out of desperation she'd made an emergency appointment with a colleague in Ellijay yesterday. Brianna was a friend and a psychiatrist she met with occasionally for lunch.

Hope had unloaded on her in the quiet of her office, and in the end, Brianna had given her a prescription for Zoloft. But it would take a few weeks for the medication to be fully effective. So far she'd only experienced the side effects. Drowsiness and nausea. She'd slept last night, whether she'd wanted to or not, and of course, the nightmare had followed.

She hadn't told Brady about any of it, and she felt guilty about that. But how would she explain what was happening to her? Even despite her education on the matters of mental health, she couldn't help but feel a little crazy. What if he thought she was off her rocker? He hadn't exactly signed on for this.

She counseled people, for pity's sake. She was supposed to have her own life under control.

Physician, heal thyself.

She rolled her eyes. Well . . . she supposed that's what the drugs were for. If only they'd start working. Preferably before Brady noticed something was terribly wrong with his wife. Or before she had a panic attack on the air. Or before she put Sam in harm's way again . . .

She looked around at the table full of friends,

all talking and having a good time, somehow feeling isolated from them. Her gaze roamed back to Zoe and Cruz on the dance floor. She wished she could talk to her friend. Zoe had been there when Aaron died. She understood the deep hole Hope had clawed her way out of.

But she was also Brady's sister. Hope wasn't sure Zoe could be objective about this, and anyway, it wouldn't be fair to put her in the middle. No, she'd work through this on her own. The medication would kick in eventually, and she'd be fine. They'd all be fine. In the meantime, she had a job to mentally prepare for.

❖❖❖

The next evening, Brady walked Hope out to her car, carrying her bag in one hand and toting Sam in the other. He couldn't believe the day had arrived. She was officially leaving for her new job.

Hope opened the passenger door, taking her duffel bag and dropping it in the seat. She was all set. He'd gassed up her car yesterday, changed the oil, and made sure the tire pressure was optimal.

Man, he was going to miss her. Friday already seemed like a month away. He'd get a lot of work done, of course. And he'd made plans to meet his mother at the park with Sam tomorrow evening. Best he just stayed busy.

He let his eyes drift over Hope's womanly

curves and felt the urge to pull her into his arms and drag her back into the house. He loved the way she sank into his embrace at night. The way she clung to him. The way she looked at him in the darkness, her eyes saying things her lips never did.

He'd nearly told her he loved her at least a dozen times this week. But he sensed she still wasn't ready for the words. While they had those close, intimate moments like he'd never experienced before, they also had other moments. Moments when she didn't quite meet his eyes. Moments when she pulled away from his embrace too quickly. When she made a joke or became flippant rather than let the mood grow too serious.

Her gaze met his now, the waning sunlight making her eyes vivid green, giving her skin a rosy glow. Before he could sink too deeply into those twin pools of heaven, her eyes cut to Sam, and she reached for him.

Then there was that—the way she used Sammy as a shield whenever Brady got too close or too serious. Or maybe he was just imagining that.

But he wasn't imagining the stacks of her clothing still in the spare-room drawers. Or the row of dresses still hanging in the spare-room closet. He hadn't brought it up. She'd move into his room when she felt comfortable with the idea. He didn't want to rush her.

But now she was leaving for the week, and he couldn't help but wish there wasn't already a distance between them that had nothing to do with miles.

She was giving Sammy a dozen kisses, all over his cheeks and neck. The baby grabbed onto her hair with both hands, giving a belly laugh.

"Gonna miss you, sugar. Be good for your daddy." After nuzzling the baby's cheek, she drew back, covered a great big yawn. "I'd better get on the road and make it an early night."

He thought of teasing her about keeping her up too late last night. They'd always been that way, teasing and flirting, even when they'd only been friends. But she never brought up their lovemaking in the light of day, so he held back the comment.

She handed Sam over and leaned in, brushing Brady's lips with a sweet kiss. "I got his bag packed up for Ruby. It's on the table. And there are a couple meals in the freezer if you don't feel like cooking. Oh! I forgot the Tylenol and teething gel. You'd better add that to the bag just in case."

"We'll be fine. It wasn't that long ago I was a bachelor, you know." He put his arm around her, threading his fingers through her hair. Inhaling the scent of her and wondering if he'd find it on her pillow. "I'll miss you."

"Me too." She pulled away too soon, gave him

a final peck, and made her way around the car. "Take care."

"Good luck tomorrow. You're going to do great."

"Thanks." She flashed him a smile before getting into the car.

"Call me after the show?"

"It'll be late," she warned.

"I'll be up listening. Say bye-bye to Mommy," he said to Sam.

The baby did a backward wave—his new trick.

Hope laughed, waving back. "Bye-bye, sweet thing. See you soon." Then she was in the car and starting the engine.

As the little red Civic made its way down the drive, an emptiness swept through him. And somewhere deep inside, that old familiar ache kicked up.

Sammy was still waving even as Hope reached the road, his brows pulled together. "Ma-ma-ma-ma!"

"She'll be back, little buddy. She'll be back." Brady wasn't sure which of them he was trying to reassure.

CHAPTER THIRTY-FOUR

Hope's first shift at her new job was almost over. She'd had some preshow jitters, but they'd disappeared quickly as she'd gotten back into the swing of things. She'd been anticipating her call-in show—the last segment of the night. And the hour was flying by.

She adjusted her headphones—they'd given her a headache—and leaned into the mic, pressing the call button.

"You're on the air with Hope. Go ahead, Mary."

"Hello . . . ?" a woman said after a brief pause.

"You're on the air, Mary."

"Hi, uh, thanks for taking my call, Hope."

"You're welcome. How can I help you tonight?"

Mary turned out to be a middle-aged woman who was frustrated with her workaholic husband. He didn't seem to notice her anymore, and she wanted advice on how to get his attention.

Hope delved into their history a bit and offered some advice. A quick glance at the digital clock warned this was her last caller of the night, so she took her time, engaging in a subject she knew many women could relate to. Leo, the nighttime jock, entered the studio during the call, and she gave him a nod as he took the other seat.

"Thank you so much, Hope," Mary said. "That

was most helpful. I'm going to take your advice and run with it."

"Glad I could help. Keep in touch, Mary." Hope disconnected the call and queued up her show's outro music. "And that's it for tonight. Thanks for joining me in my first live broadcast of *Living with Hope* from WKPC. Join me, Hope Collins, again tomorrow night at ten, when the lines will be open for your calls. Leo the Lion is coming up next."

She played the top of the hour ID and removed the headphones.

"Nice job," Leo said. He was in his early twenties, just getting started—and thus stuck with the all-night shift. He had thick strawberry-blond hair and a wild beard that had prompted his radio name.

"I was listening on the way in," he said. "That Carla sounded a little creepy."

Hope unplugged her headphones. "Turns out there's a fine line between pursuing and stalking."

"No doubt. I think you helped her see that—very gently." He settled in front of his computer and took a gulp from his travel mug—the engineers would probably have a fit if they drank from open containers around the expensive equipment.

By the time Hope emerged from the building, the adrenaline had dissipated, and she was wilting with fatigue. She crossed her arms against the October chill and made her way to the corner, then across the deserted street toward the parking lot. She was renting a garage apartment from the station's news director. It was a one-room studio not far from the station, cheap and perfect for her needs.

Her mind was spinning, rehashing the call-in show. It was the part of her job that kept her coming back—that she might be helping people live happier, healthier lives. As strange as it felt to be living in a city, above someone's garage, and as much as she already missed Brady and Sam, it felt good to be doing her thing again.

A few minutes later she pulled into the short drive and followed the porch light she'd left on at the top of the staircase. The apartment's stale air hit her as she entered. She was turning up the heat when her cell phone rang.

"How's it feel to be Atlanta's new favorite jock?" Brady asked.

She laughed. "I don't know about that, but it felt pretty darn good to be back on the air again."

"You're amazing, Hope. The way you handled that Carla chick. And the advice you gave Mary . . . All of it. You're so good at what you do."

His kindness was like salve on a wound. "Thanks, Brady. That means a lot to me. Did you listen to my whole shift?"

"Yep, since three. Sammy too, since we got home from Zoe's. Though I'll admit he conked out before *Living with Hope* started—the little fuddy-dud."

"Was he impressed?"

"He recognized your voice," Brady said excitedly. "You should've seen his face when he heard you. He went all still, and his eyes got wide. He started looking around the living room for you."

Her heart gave a punch. "Aw . . . That's so sweet. Did he get upset when he couldn't find me?"

"A little. I had to distract him with Cheerios. I want him to get used to hearing your voice on the radio, though."

They talked for a few more minutes about his and Sam's day, and on Hope's third yawn Brady called it quits.

Hope disconnected the call and readied for bed. She thought she might fall asleep before her head hit the pillow. The bed was a little lumpy, but she had high hopes for a good night's sleep since she hadn't had any bad dreams last night.

And that's when she realized . . . she hadn't had a panic attack since she'd left Copper Creek yesterday. She rinsed her toothbrush and studied herself in the mirror. Was it possible the meds had kicked in so quickly? She didn't think so.

But she didn't want to think about any of that right now. She didn't want to be the mental health patient with problems beyond her control. She wanted to be the host of *Living with Hope*—calm and controlled, the woman with all the answers.

CHAPTER THIRTY-FIVE

The week flew by, and by Friday Hope was fully into the swing of her new job. Diana and Darren seemed very pleased with her start. The other folks at the station had welcomed her back, and the listeners seemed to have taken to her program. Tonight there'd been call after call—no dead air to fill at all.

She made the long drive home, yawning every few minutes and working to stay awake. Not so much because she wasn't well-rested, but because of that darn medication. At least the nausea was gone now.

She was sleepy as she pulled up to the darkened house. She hadn't expected Brady to still be up. But when she reached the stoop, he opened the door and pulled her into a hug before she could drop her duffel bag on the floor.

"I missed you," he said against her temple, his voice as thick as honey.

Ah, it was so good to be missed. "I missed you too."

Good to be in his arms again also. She inhaled the familiar scent of him and dropped her bag so she could get both arms around him. Talking on the phone just wasn't the same as being with him.

He put the exclamation mark on that thought

as he drew her into a kiss that quickly deepened. Their hands grew urgent in a matter of seconds, seeking skin, grappling for buttons. A minute later he was carrying her up the stairs where she would show him just how much she'd missed him.

⊰⊹⊱

The nightmare returned in the middle of the night. This time Brady collapsed in his garage and a crowd gathered to witness the horrific event. April blocked Hope's path to him, while her friend Brianna nodded sympathetically and told her the medication would kick in soon. So bizarre. Yet so real.

At least she hadn't awakened her husband. Her heartbeats shook her until she worried the movement alone would awaken him. She lay there for hours afterward, afraid to close her eyes again.

Finally she slipped out of their warm bed and checked on Sam. He was sleeping peacefully on his back, his arms angled at his sides like field goalposts, his hands curled into fists.

The next morning she still felt a little off, and Brady noticed. She waved away his concern. But as she stood on the deck while he grilled hamburgers that evening, the panic returned. It flooded over her like a tsunami, threatening to take her under.

"Be right back," she said, slipping into the house and heading to the bathroom in case he came after her. It took five endless minutes for the attack to subside. And by the time it did, her forehead was covered with a sheen of perspiration, and her optimism had faded like the waning daylight.

"Hope," Brady called from the other side of the door. "The burgers are ready."

She swallowed down the last of the panic. "Be right there."

She dabbed her forehead and the back of her neck with a cool washcloth. Shook off the vestiges of fear and gently smacked some blood back into her pale cheeks.

"Get it together," she whispered to her reflection in the mirror.

If Brady noticed anything amiss when she rejoined him and Sam on the patio, he said nothing. And when they turned in that night, she went into his arms as if nothing had changed.

But deep inside she knew it had.

❖

Brady talked her into staying until Monday morning. There would be time enough to make the drive and arrive to work on schedule. Hope hated the thought of another sleepless night and more potential panic attacks, but she couldn't think of a good reason to say no.

After church, Brady went home with his dad, who was having issues with his Mercedes. Hope grabbed a quick lunch, then strapped Sammy into his car seat and took him to the park to wait until Brady needed to be picked up.

She gave Sam a gentle push on the swing. He was getting sleepy—it was time for his nap. Hope smothered a yawn of her own. She'd only slept a few hours last night. She'd have to take a nap today. As long as she didn't get into deep sleep she'd be fine.

A few minutes later a text came in from Brady. Hope collected a sleepy Sammy from the baby swing and smiled as he went limp against her.

"Is my baby tuckered out?" She pressed a kiss to his temple, breathing in his wonderful baby scent. He didn't even complain as she put him in his car seat.

It was a fifteen-minute drive to Mr. Collins's house. He lived in the country in a beautiful ranch house, surrounded by rolling green hills and a white split-rail fence.

She was glad Brady had gotten to spend some time with him. They got along just fine, though their relationship was a little superficial. Zoe would've been thrilled with that much effort from their father, but Mr. Collins had always been harder on her than he was on Brady. No doubt his expectations were higher for his "real" child.

The highway stretched before her, long and

straight, past flat farmland and long, gravel driveways. A semi *whooshed* past, going the other direction, shaking her little Civic with its force. She yawned, already looking forward to that afternoon nap. In the back seat Sam's eyes had drifted shut, getting an early start on his own nap. She hoped she'd be able to get him to his crib without waking him.

Relaxing into the seat, her eyes fixed on a distant mountain and began drifting shut. She gave a few hard blinks and flipped on the radio. The oldies station was playing a little REO Speedwagon. At the top of the hour they cut to the station ID, then segued straight into the news.

She'd hardly even seen Zoe this weekend, just at church. It seemed Brady had wanted to keep Hope to himself, and she couldn't help but like that notion. It was obvious he'd missed her. Her mind went back to the night before. And the night before that. She pushed aside all her troubles and just remembered the way he'd looked at her. The way he'd touched her. So sweet. So reverent . . .

A horn sounded and she jerked awake. Her eyes fastened on the silver grill of a truck. She gasped and swerved. Her car fishtailed, the back slipping off the shoulder. She turned the other way, and the back slung the other direction. She braked hard, not even thinking to check behind her.

An endless moment later she brought the car under control as it slowed. She came to a stop on

341

the side of the road and shoved the car into park. Her whole body shook, and she gasped for air. She turned in her seat to find Sam still sleeping peacefully, working his pacifier. His head was tilted to the side, and a frown puckered his brow.

"Oh, dear God. Oh, thank You. Thank You!" She envisioned that semi's grill again. So close! She'd fallen asleep while driving—with Sammy in the car! She shuddered to think what would've happened had she awakened just a split second later. If that semi hadn't honked his horn. A head-on collision. Sam would probably be dead right now. She couldn't bear the thought.

Thank You, God!

She choked back great gulps of air, her eyes burning, adrenaline flooding through her system. She was awake now, all right. And she couldn't go on like this. Even if the medication eventually kicked in and stopped making her so drowsy, it was unlikely it would stop the nightmares.

The nightmares, brought on by her fear of losing Brady. Because she'd gone and fallen in love with him. What a mess. She was a wreck. And she'd risked Sam's life—twice now! She was fixing to bring about her own worst fear. She covered her face, catching her breath. She'd never forgive herself if something happened to him. And neither would Brady. Who could blame him?

She thought of her apartment in Atlanta. Yeah,

it was a little lonely there, but at least when she was gone, those she loved were safe. And she was in a better frame of mind. She knew she needed therapy. Probably months of it, but the thought of digging up all that pain . . . of going back to the time that had left her in a helpless puddle . . . It was so daunting. Overwhelming. Impossible.

She needed to put some distance between them. She needed room to breathe and time to think about how to handle this. Brady already had a wreck for a mother. He didn't need one for a wife as well. He and Sam were both better off without her if this was the best she could do. Clearly.

She thought of Brady and the way he might feel if he lost her. She hated to cause him pain when he'd been nothing but good to her. She hated the thought of losing him at all. A vise tightened around her heart at the very idea. But she didn't know what else to do.

She just didn't know what else to do.

CHAPTER THIRTY-SIX

Brady found Hope in the kitchen the next morning, quietly unloading the dishwasher. She was already dressed and ready for her trip back to Atlanta. The welcome aroma of coffee filled the air, and a crisp morning breeze drifted through the kitchen window.

"Good morning." He brushed her hair aside and pressed a kiss to that place on her neck that his lips craved.

"Morning."

He drew in a breath of her sweet scent. Mmm. "You're up early. Didn't sleep well?"

"I've got work on my mind, I guess."

She'd had something on her mind all weekend. She'd seemed especially quiet since she'd picked him up from his dad's house yesterday. His gut was telling him it wasn't work, however. But maybe he was just imagining things. Or maybe she really was distracted by her new job. He let go of her so she could continue her task and went for the coffee.

"I thought I'd drop Sam at Zoe's on the way out of town," she said. "It's right on my way."

"What time are you leaving?"

"Soon as he's up and fed. I have some commercials to produce at the station, and I'd like to stop in and chat with Diana before the week starts."

He'd hoped to spend a little time with her this morning. He poured a mug of coffee and took a sip. "Sounds like you have a big week ahead."

"I do. In fact . . . I'm not even sure I'm going to make it back at all next weekend," she said offhandedly.

He blinked. "You're not coming home Friday?"

She turned to put away a mug. "I have a lot of extra stuff to do this week, and it has to be done at the station."

He frowned at her back, worry niggling in the recesses of his mind. Maybe he hadn't misread her after all. He watched her closely, careful to keep his tone casual. "How about if Sam and I come down then? We can hang out at the apartment while you're at work or go to the park or something."

She reached for the silverware basket, not quite meeting his eyes. "I don't know, Brady. The bed's uncomfortable—it's so lumpy—and it's only one room. We'd be pretty crowded. And it's not childproofed."

"We can fix that. And I don't mind cramped quarters."

"I'll be working all the time anyway. We'd hardly even see each other."

His gaze sharpened on her. On the mottled pink washing over her cheeks. On her bottom lip, clamped by her teeth. And suddenly he had a hard time drawing a breath. He forced himself to ask the question that had been buzzing in his mind all weekend. "What's really going on, Hope?"

The spoons clanked as she nested them in the island drawer.

"Nothing, I just—I have a lot of work to do, what with just starting and all . . . and I want to make a good impression. This job's important to me."

"I know it is. But I'm getting the sense it's more than that. Something's different between us."

Her eyes flickered up. "I don't know what you mean."

"You seem a little distant lately and . . . I don't know. Quiet. Did I do something wrong? Are you mad at me?"

"Of course not."

"Then what is it? What's going on?"

"I don't know. I just . . ." She gave her head a shake. She was finally out of silverware. And out of words, apparently.

"Come on, honey. Talk to me. We've always been honest with each other."

"I just . . ." She ran a hand over her neck, looking everywhere but at him. "Maybe I need a little bit of a break, that's all."

Ouch. "A break? From me?"

"It's not like that—"

"Then what's it like?" He hadn't meant to raise his voice.

His breaths were coming too fast, and his stomach was churning with dread. He had a terrible feeling something worse was coming. Though his wife asking for a break was bad enough.

"Just calm down a minute, okay?"

But he was in no mood to be placated. He thought of their nights together, of all the tender moments they'd shared, and felt a terrible dread that she'd been faking it all. That the feelings were all on his side, and he'd been too big of a moron to notice.

The pity in her soulful eyes made a fist tighten in his chest. "I don't want to hurt you, Brady. That's the very last thing I want."

Oh, God, is it true then?

Had he been fooling himself? Had he pushed her into a physical relationship she hadn't wanted or been ready for? But no, she'd been so responsive. She'd even initiated things on more than one occasion.

She needed a break from him? They'd only been married two months! And they'd just been apart for five days last week. What the heck did she need a break from?

He was sure his feelings were all over his face right now, but he was helpless to conceal them. "Are you kidding me right now? We're married, Hope—and just barely, at that. We're not supposed to be craving breaks from each other."

She covered his hand, which was fisted on the countertop. "I just think . . . a little distance right now might be for the best."

"Best for who, Hope? I don't want more distance, I want less."

Her eyes grew glassy, and darn it, he didn't want to soften toward her. He didn't want to feel bad for her when he was feeling so bad himself. When she was doing this to them. But he watched her struggle to hold back the tears. Watched the genuine strain on her face.

Audrey had put a lot of doubts in his mind. Doubts about his own instincts. He'd been second-guessing himself lately where Hope was concerned. But despite this unexpected turn of events, he knew she cared about him. Maybe even more than that.

He didn't understand what she was going through right now, but he hadn't exactly been forthright about his own feelings either. His instincts had held him back, but maybe it was just what she needed to hear.

He drew a deep breath and turned his hand over, lacing his fingers through hers. His eyes bored into hers with all the intensity he was feeling. "I should've said this earlier. I don't know why I didn't, but, Hope, you should know . . . I've fallen in love with you."

She flinched. "Don't say that."

He reared back as if she'd slapped him. It

would've been far less painful. In fact, she couldn't have surprised him more if she'd delivered a sucker punch to his gut.

"It's true whether I say it or not," he said gruffly.

He pulled his hand away and took a step back as if the bit of distance could protect his fragile heart. His mind spun with her hurtful response. He tried to clear the smoke of pain and see deeper. See what he might be missing here.

The recent weeks flashed through his mind like a flipbook. The way she'd touched him and kissed him and made love to him. He hadn't imagined the look in her eyes. He hadn't misread her intent. He wasn't that big of an idiot. And she wasn't that good of an actress.

He swallowed against the knot in his throat. "I hate to be the one to tell you this, Hope. But I think you might be in love with me too."

Her eyes hardened. "I don't want to be in love. That wasn't part of the deal."

He remembered this conversation, of course, before they'd set out. *It was hard, losing Aaron. I don't ever want to go through that again . . . I push men away. I'm starting to see that.*

Yeah, well, that was becoming real obvious to him now. But he hadn't exactly seen this coming. And he'd been too focused on getting custody of Sam to consider her words at the time or take them seriously. And now it was too late. She'd already worked her way past his defenses and stolen his heart.

He took in her stiff posture, the flicker of fear in her eyes. The way her arms were crossed over her chest like a shield. "I think maybe you're just scared, Hope."

"You think I don't know that? I studied psychology, you know. But identifying the problem isn't enough." Her shoulders rose and fell on shallow breaths.

He felt a prick of sympathy. He didn't know what it was like to suffer the death of your soul mate, but he knew what it was like to have your heart broken in two. The feeling was becoming more familiar with each passing second.

Sounds came from the living room monitor. Sam was up and babbling animatedly.

He took a step closer to her. "What you went through with Aaron was painful, Hope. I get that. What I went through with Audrey was painful too. But love always requires risk. And in the end it's worth it."

She thrust her chin up, her eyes shooting sparks. "Is it? How do you know that, Brady, huh? How do you know? Because you read it in a book somewhere?"

Oh, she had that wall up high. He wondered if he had the tools to get through it. His heart felt as if it might explode from his chest. "I guess you just have to take it on faith."

She studied him, defeat slowly dimming the sparks in her eyes. "Well . . . maybe I don't have that kind of faith anymore, Brady."

"I don't believe that for a minute."

Sam's babbling was growing more insistent.

Hope grabbed the empty silverware basket, placed it in the dishwasher, and pushed the door shut. "I should go get him. I need to get on the road."

He gently took her arm. "We need to talk, Hope. I don't want you leaving like this."

She straightened, looking at him, her eyes shiny. "Like what, Brady? We're just on different pages here. I don't like it any more than you do, but talking about it isn't going to change anything."

"And time apart will?" He had the sudden thought that she could go to Atlanta today and never come back. Could she just leave him like that? Leave *them?* Maybe that's what she'd been planning while she'd been staring off into space all weekend. Fear lifted the hairs on his arms.

She reached out, fingering the sleeve of his T-shirt. She swallowed as she met his eyes. "I'm not trying to hurt you, Brady. Honest, I'm not." Her voice was raspy with tears, and she was looking at him with regret. Remorse.

He swallowed hard. "It turns out you don't really have to try."

CHAPTER THIRTY-SEVEN

By the time Hope arrived in Atlanta she was a wreck. She'd cried all the way there and couldn't get it together in time to go in early as she'd planned. It had been all she could do to collect herself in time for her shift.

Losing herself in her work, she found, helped. So she stayed late that night and each night that week. She worked until she was too exhausted to do anything but fall into a sound—and nightmare-free—sleep.

Brady texted her some that week. They even talked on the phone twice. He kept the conversation light, carefully avoided anything serious. He caught her up on the goings on in Copper Creek and filled her in on Sam's escapades.

Oh, how she missed them both! She swallowed back lumps in her throat as he talked. His voice was deflated, like a balloon someone had let the air out of. And she was that someone, she knew.

It was easier when she didn't have to talk to him. So sometimes she let his calls go through. He didn't leave voicemails.

Zoe tried to call on the weekend, but she let that go through too. From her voicemail it was obvious Brady had mentioned their problems to her. Zoe didn't sound too happy with her, which didn't exactly make Hope eager to return the call.

Instead, Hope texted that she'd get back with her soon. But it was easy to fall back into a busy workweek and "forget" to return Zoe's call.

On the next Thursday, Hope answered Brady's call, part of her missing him so much she wanted nothing more than to hear his voice. Another part feeling like she was just a glutton for punishment.

"Are you coming home this weekend?" he asked after they'd chatted a few minutes.

Her heart squeezed tight. "I don't think so, Brady. Not yet."

His profession of love had replayed over and over the last week. After Audrey's callousness, she knew it had taken courage for him to own up to his feelings, and she regretted her impulsive response. *Don't say that.* The memory of the way he'd flinched made her chest ache.

"Hope . . . We can't just keep on like this. We're married. We made a commitment to each other." She heard his frustration in his tone.

"I know. I know." She did know. She didn't have a plan. She only knew she felt better when she was in Atlanta. She wasn't plagued by panic and nightmares here. She wasn't endangering Sam. And the distance somehow made the risk her heart had taken seem more manageable.

But she missed Brady. She missed her boy. When they got off the phone, she cried herself to sleep and awakened the next morning swollen-eyed and miserable.

She'd planned to visit a new church this weekend, but sadness seemed to weight her to the bed like a cement block. She turned off her alarm and sank back into oblivion.

She woke sometime later to a pounding at her door.

Frowning at the intrusion, she reluctantly threw back the covers. It was probably Candice, the woman who owned the garage apartment. She dropped by every now and then to let her know the landscaper was coming to get the leaves or that they were having friends over and would she mind parking on the street?

Hope finger-combed her hair and wished she hadn't been so lazy this morning. It was obvious she'd only just rolled out of bed, and it was well after noon.

She pulled open the door, and her eyes widened. Zoe stood there, arms crossed. Her green eyes were tightened at the corners, and her lips formed a taut line.

Zoe's eyes fell over Hope's disheveled appearance, the T-shirt and yoga pants, the messy hair. She probably sported pillow creases on her face too. There might've been a little compassion in Zoe's expression. Possibly some waves of anger radiating off her.

"You sleeping the day away?" she asked.

"Trying to." Hope very briefly considered shutting the door. She didn't want to face this yet. She was barely awake. But she stepped back and let her friend pass. There was no avoiding her now.

She became aware that her apartment smelled vaguely of the dirty dishes in the sink and the takeout from the night before. The Styrofoam container was still open on the tiny table.

"Have a seat." Hope gestured toward the table, the only place that seated two. She closed the container and pitched it into the trash, then sat across from Zoe, who was ramrod straight in the chair. "I wasn't expecting you, obviously."

Zoe scowled at her. "What did you think would happen when you ran away from home, refused my calls, and ignored my texts?"

"I'm not a teenager, Zoe. I didn't run away from home." Though Zoe would know all about that. But Hope wasn't going to throw her past in her face.

"Well, you took off on Brady, so I don't know what else to call it. Desertion? Abandonment?"

Okay, definitely mad. "It's only been two weeks." But, man, did it feel longer than that. "I was going to ask if you were here as my best friend or as Brady's sister, but that's becoming obvious."

"I can't really separate the two, Hope. But yes, right now the Brady's sister side is more prevalent. But maybe that's just because I've only heard his side."

"So you're here for my side of things, is that it?"

"I'm here because I want the best for both of you."

"What did Brady tell you?"

Zoe tucked her auburn hair behind her ear and gave her a look. "He kept it pretty vague."

"Told you it was none of your business, did he?"

Zoe leaned in, her eyes shooting sparks. "Do you know how hurt he is, Hope? You're breaking his heart. I can't stand to see him like this." She smacked the table. "Darn it, this is exactly what I was afraid would happen. I sat right there in the Mellow Mug and warned you both, but would you listen?"

"Fine, you were right. Is that what you want to hear?"

"No, that's not what I want to hear. I want to hear that you're going to go home and work this out with your husband. Your *husband,* Hope. You made a commitment to him and to Sam."

"Well, maybe they're better off without me."

"Baloney! You're just afraid. You're bailing on them because you're in love with Brady after all, and you're too chicken to follow through on your feelings."

"Wow, thanks for the compassion. No offense,

Zoe, but I think I'm going to go with Brady's response here and tell you to butt out."

Her breaths had drawn shallow, and heat flushed her cheeks. Or maybe it was shame. Zoe would never know how much she hated hurting Brady. Or how badly she wished she could just be normal. But the fear was too overwhelming, and she didn't have the courage to go through this again. She just didn't.

"This isn't just a fear issue, you know. It's a faith issue."

Hope gave her a withering look.

"Glare at me all you want, but you know I'm right. When you truly trust God with your future, there's no room for fear. You know He's got your back. You know He's going to get you through, no matter what happens."

Zoe's words pierced her heart like an arrow on a bull's-eye. "That all sounds real nice until you're paralyzed by fear."

Zoe gave her a sympathetic look. "I didn't say it was easy. I'm just asking you to take a step of faith here."

Hope's eyes stung, and she blinked against the rise of tears. Gah! She was so tired of crying. She swallowed against the knot in her throat and picked at a thread on her T-shirt.

Zoe placed her hand over Hope's. When Hope met her eyes, there was sympathy shining there. That only made her feel worse. A tear tumbled down Hope's face, and she brushed it away impatiently.

"You're not going to lose Brady the way you lost Aaron, honey."

"You don't know that."

"Well, the odds are definitely in your favor. He's a healthy twenty-seven-year-old man."

Hope shook her head. "It's not just Brady, it's Sam too. This is just . . . more than I bargained for, Zoe. It's too much. I don't want it."

"Hope . . . Deep down everybody wants to love and be loved. You know that."

"Not me."

"Well," Zoe said gently. "You sure liked being in love with Aaron, best I recall. You were very happy with him. It was losing him that was so hard. And I get that. I do. I was there. I remember."

Hope's back stiffened. "No, you don't know. Watching it isn't the same as experiencing it. It was horrific, and I never want to experience that again."

Zoe studied her for an uncomfortable moment. "So you're just going to live without love for the rest of your life? What kind of life is that?"

"I'm no good to Brady this way. Or Sam. You'll have to trust me on that."

Zoe sighed, giving her a long, steady look.

Hope went back to the thread on her shirt. The clock wall ticked in the quiet. She looked at her bed longingly. She wanted to climb back under the covers and stay there for the rest of the day. The rest of the week. When would it get better? When would she stop missing him? Stop loving him?

As if reading her mind, Zoe said, "Why don't you go get a shower? I'll take you out for breakfast—or I guess it's lunch at this point."

"I was kind of wanting to hang around here today."

"Sulking and suffering under a fog of depression? No way." Zoe stood, pulling Hope to her feet. "If you shower, I'll do your dishes. And for gosh sakes, wash your hair. You look like a hobo."

"It's the weekend," Hope grumbled.

"You didn't even go to church."

She lifted a shoulder. "I overslept."

Hope made her way to the shower. It had been a couple days.

After she was clean and in fresh clothes she felt minutely better. She took Zoe to a diner down the street, and they talked about everything but Brady and Sam.

An hour later they were saying good-bye in her driveway.

Zoe hugged her. "I love you, you know."

Hope's heart squeezed tight. "I love you too."

"Please answer me when I call, or I'll be forced to drag you out of bed again. And think about what I said, okay?"

"I will." A moment later she gave Zoe a wave as she pulled from the drive.

Hope couldn't seem to help thinking about Brady and Sam. She just couldn't work out a solution she could live with.

CHAPTER THIRTY-EIGHT

Brady put Sam down in his crib and pulled the nursery door closed. Saturdays were the longest days, and he was glad this one was almost over. It was his third weekend without Hope.

Without hope.

He huffed as he took the stairs. Was there ever a more accurate play on words? She'd taken most of her clothes with her. Yes, he'd checked her closet. Her drawers were almost empty too. Was it because she wasn't coming back at all?

He'd never seen things going this direction. He'd been right about her pillow, however. It did smell like her. Despite his best intentions he found himself pulling it close at night, inhaling her. Pathetic.

The long night stretched ahead like a barren desert. He'd been working crazy hours, leaving Sam with Ruby too much. He had to stop that. His boy needed him. He had to find a better way to cope. He just wasn't sure what that was.

Instead of joining the gang at the Rusty Nail, he'd caught a meal at the diner with Jack. Brady couldn't tolerate the thought of all his besotted friends tonight. Jack, being as lovelorn as Brady, made a better companion these days. Misery loved company and all that.

A knock sounded on the door, and foolish hope bloomed inside. Just as quickly he stuffed it down. *Hope wouldn't knock, you idiot.*

Even so, he welcomed the distraction. Anything was better than a block of time with nothing to do but ache.

He pulled open the door to find his mother standing on the stoop under the puddle of the porch light. Okay, not his first choice. He felt a prick of guilt at the thought. She was trying to make amends, and he was trying to accept the olive branch. It's just he felt he had to prop her up sometimes, and he didn't have the energy for that tonight.

She toyed with the braid hanging over her shoulder. "Hi, honey."

Brady dredged up a smile as he opened the door wider. "Hey there." He avoided addressing her in any particular way. He already had a mom—she was gone—but calling her April seemed hurtful somehow.

"Sorry to drop by," she said as she stepped inside. "Is now a good time to chat?"

"Good as any." Part of him was glad he'd already put Sam down. He felt so on guard when she held his boy. But the baby was also a nice distraction from their awkward conversations. From their stilted and strange relationship.

"Can I get you something?" he asked. "Soda or iced tea?"

"Some tea would be great. Thanks."

He went to fetch it from the fridge.

"Where's my little guy?" she called from the living room.

"Just put him down for the night. He was pretty tuckered."

"Too bad. I was itching to play with him."

A minute later he found her in front of the bookshelves, looking at the photos and knick-knacks. His grandma's antique mantel clock. His array of fiction and Hope's hefty tomes on psychology and social issues.

"Thanks," she said, taking a sip of iced tea. "Where's Hope?"

"She took a job in Atlanta. She's commuting." If April had heard any differently in town she didn't dispute it. He sure wasn't baring his soul to her.

"This is a good picture." She pointed at a selfie he and Hope had taken on their honeymoon.

Hope had enlarged it to a five by seven and mounted it in a wedding gift frame. The sunrise was in the background, and there was so much happiness and affection shining from her eyes it made his chest ache.

He turned away and sank into his armchair. "Have a seat. I'd offer you a snack or something, but we're a little down on groceries at the moment."

"I'm not hungry anyway. I just had a sandwich."

She sat on the sofa end closest to him and settled her big satchel of a purse at her side. "Listen, Brady, this is so awkward, but I'm just going to cut to the chase. You know I've been trying to get my act together. I got that job at the Laundromat this week, and I just found a place, an apartment, that I think I'll be able to afford."

"That's great." He sensed there was more coming, and wariness washed over him.

"Thanks. I'm very optimistic about my future. But . . ." She gave him a wan smile. "I don't have the money to put down the first month's rent and security deposit. And at the wage I'm making it'll take a good long time to come up with it. My friend's about had it with sharing her place."

First month's rent and deposit. That wasn't too much. They had it. He'd have to talk to Hope . . .

"And then there're things in my past I can't quite get away from, you know? I've racked up some debt that's kinda got me in a bit of a fix. I'd never ask if I had another option, and of course I'd pay you back. Monthly installments or whatever."

"How much?"

"The debt's a little overwhelming, I admit. It'd take about ten to get me paid off in full."

He blinked. "Ten *thousand?*"

She had the grace to look a little sheepish. "It goes back a long ways, and I'm afraid my creditors are getting a little impatient with me."

Creditors. Probably more like dealers. He wondered if she was in physical jeopardy.

"I know it's a lot, and I wish I had someone else to ask. I hate to be a burden."

"April . . ." He shook his head. "I don't have that kind of money sitting around."

"Well, okay, but you can get your hands on it, right? Cash in some CDs or stocks or something? I'd never ask if it wasn't an emergency."

CDs? Stocks? He looked closely at her, wondering what kind of emergency she was talking about. It was then he noticed the way her fingers trembled as she twisted her purse straps. There was a sheen of perspiration on her forehead despite the coolness of the night.

"I'm sorry." He really was, but not for the reasons she might think. "We just paid for a wedding and an attorney. I don't have that kind of money right now."

A shadow flickered in her jaw, and she entreated him with desperate eyes. "Come on, Brady . . . You're my last hope here. I know I haven't been much of a mom to you, but you have to know I love you. You're my baby boy. I'd do 'bout anything for you, and I know you're a real good man. I'm so proud of the way you turned out."

He steeled himself against her approval. A man never completely outgrew the need to make his parents proud. "I wish I could help you, but we don't have that kind of money."

April leaned forward, all traces of affection draining from her face. Her eyes darkened, and the lines around her mouth showed as her lips twisted. The shift in her countenance was jarring.

"You think I don't know about that inheritance you got? She was *my* mama, and she left me nothing! That money should've been mine—all of it—and I'm just asking for half."

He shook his head in disbelief. "That . . . that money's long gone. I spent it on my business—on that great big barn out there. It took the inheritance and then some."

Her nostrils flared. "You're lying. That money was *my* birthright."

"She couldn't leave you the money, April. She didn't even know where you were, and you would've snorted it all up your nose anyway."

April shot to her feet. "How dare you judge me! That money is mine, and I want it!"

Her eyes were bloodshot and crazy now. She was coming down, he realized, and needing another fix. And he was the one standing in her way.

He got to his feet, planting himself between her and the stairs. "I think you'd better go now, April. You're not going to get what you came here for."

"You can't treat me this way—I'm your mama! And you owe me." She darted around him, and he dodged to block the stairs.

But she didn't head that way. She headed to

the bookcase. She swiped his grandma's antique clock from the shelf and dropped it into her satchel. Next went his first-edition copy of *The Lost Road* and a '53 Chevy truck model his mom—his real mom—had given him for his sixteenth birthday.

He watched wordlessly as she snatched up his valuables in a frenzy. He could've stopped her easily enough. She was only going to sell the stuff and get high off it. But it was just stuff. She could take what she wanted as long as she left his boy alone.

When she'd shopped her fill, she buzzed past him, all righteous indignation. She didn't even bother to look at him in her rush to get her next high. Objects poked from the top of her purse like so many toys from Santa's bag. Without a word she stormed out. The door slammed behind her.

Only then did the breath fall from his body. His shoulders sank under the weight of her betrayal, and that familiar hollow ache spread across his chest.

Brady dribbled the ball across the deserted basketball court at Murphy's Park. The sky was cloudy, threatening drizzle—a gloomy but balmy November day.

He went in for a layup, and it banked off the backboard, falling through the net with a *swish*. He caught the ball and headed back to half-court, not bothering to stop and catch his breath. The ball smacked the cement, and his feet ground against the grit and pebbles as he went.

His gaze swung to the sidelines, where Sam napped in his carrier. He'd fallen asleep on the drive over. Brady couldn't bear the thought of another Sunday afternoon in that quiet house. He could've gone to lunch with his friends, but that would've been almost worse. The pitying looks, the subtle questions . . . He'd sooner jump off a cliff than subject himself to that today.

He drove toward the basket and missed. He worked on some dribbling drills and found he'd lost some agility since he'd last played. No problem. Gave him something to focus on.

"Wow, someone's working up a sweat."

He finished a between-the-legs dribble and caught the ball, panting hard.

Zoe approached from the sidelines, holding out her hands for the ball. He passed it to her. She dribbled for a minute, then tried for a three-pointer, but it bounced off the rim. She wasn't a bad athlete. Growing up they'd played plenty of one-on-one, until Cruz came along and offered him more competition.

"How'd you know I was here?" he asked.

"Just had a feeling. You took off out of church fast enough."

"Didn't feel like eating with the gang today."

She passed the ball back to him. "Fair enough."

He drove toward the basket, and she made an effort to block him. But he pulled up short and sank the shot.

They played wordlessly for five or ten minutes until Zoe was breathing hard too. She twisted the band off her wrist and pulled her hair into a messy bun. Her gaze drifted over to Sammy, still sleeping peacefully.

"I'm out of shape," she said. "And I've lost my touch."

"You never had the touch," he taunted. In truth, she used to have a three-pointer that had threatened his male ego a time or two. But he'd never admit it to her.

She rolled her eyes and sank a jump shot, probably just to spite him.

"Lucky shot," he said.

She laughed and passed him the ball. "You're full of it, you know that? After all the times I let you win, you owe me."

He dribbled back to half-court to catch his breath, leaving Zoe near the free-throw line.

You owe me. Those had been April's last words, and her face immediately popped into his mind. That angry, harsh look she'd given him just before she'd swiped his things and taken off. Man. She'd been like Jekyll and Hyde.

He should probably warn Zoe. April might come after her niece for money next, since she obviously felt she'd been gypped out of her inheritance. Though Zoe could hardly liquidate the orchard.

He turned with the ball, dribbling toward her. "You should probably know . . . April might come around asking you for a loan. If she does, don't give her anything."

Zoe gave him a thoughtful frown as she crouched to guard him. "I know better than that. She try to get some money from you?"

"She came by my place last night and tried to talk me out of the money Granny left me."

Zoe gave up her guarding stance. "What?"

Brady held his ground several feet away, dribbling. "When she found out there was nothing left she got pretty mad. Made off with all the valuables she could stuff into her purse."

"Oh, Brady. I'm so sorry. You could've stopped her. She's only going to sell those things."

"Think I don't know that?" He lifted a shoulder. "They're just things. I just thought I'd warn you in case she was still hanging around. She's probably already hightailed it out of town, though. Seems she only came for one reason." And it sure wasn't to get to know her son better.

"Wow, bro. You're sure having a bad month."

"You think?" Suddenly feeling the weight of the last few weeks, he slammed the ball down, pounding it repeatedly against the concrete.

He'd sat in church this morning, squirming with anger. He didn't understand why all this was happening. Why were women always leaving him? His mom, Audrey, Hope . . . A man could get a complex.

Zoe reached out for the ball, snatching it before he could smack it down yet again.

But he needed to take his anger out on something. "Had enough punishment for one day, have you?"

She tucked the ball under her arm and tilted a look at him. "You want to talk about Hope?"

"Not with her best friend."

"I'm your sister too, you know." Her eyes softened on his as she studied him for a long moment. "I love you, Brady, and I hate seeing you like this."

He walked toward the sidelines. "Yeah, well, talk to Hope about that. She's the one who took off. Seems to be a recurring theme in my life."

Guess he really was a bad husband after all. He'd tried to warn her. Or maybe it was like Audrey had told her sister—he was just too boring. Maybe he bored women to death.

On the grass now, he grabbed a burp cloth from the diaper bag and wiped the back of his neck.

Hope joined him on the sidelines. "She's just afraid, you know."

"I wouldn't know. She won't talk to me. A few texts . . . but she won't answer my calls anymore. And she's obviously not coming home these days."

"Don't give up on her. She's just overwhelmed and afraid. Give her some time to figure things out."

"It's been three weeks, Zoe." And he could feel her slipping away. His heart gave a heavy punch. "What's all this distance accomplishing anyway? She doesn't want me anymore; time's not going to fix that."

"That's not true."

He gave her a withering look.

"It's not," she said insistently.

His eyes sharpened on her. On the confident tilt of her chin. On the sheepish look that had come over her face. "You've talked to her."

"I went to see her last Sunday."

"And you didn't tell me?" he growled.

"Give me a break. I'm kind of in the middle here. But I want what's best for both of you. And I can tell you this . . . She loves you, Brady. She really loves you."

Hope sprang like an infernal weed, tangled around his hurting heart, and gave a tight squeeze. He searched her eyes with a desperation that overcame all pride. "Did she say that?"

Zoe shifted, uncertainty flickering in her eyes before she looked away. "Not in so many words, maybe."

He scowled. "Yeah. What I thought."

"But I know her, Brady. She's just running scared. The last time she was in love she went through an awful lot, you know. She's not sure she can handle that again."

"Yeah, well, I'm not planning on dropping dead any time soon, Zoe." He knew he was being insensitive, but he couldn't bring himself to care.

"Don't give up on her. Go see her. Talk to her."

'Cause that should be on him, right? Because he was the one who left. No. He was so tired of trying to convince other people he was worthy of their love. Tired of being forced on people who didn't even want him.

His whole birth had been an accident—April hadn't even wanted him. His aunt and uncle had gotten stuck with him. He'd worked his whole life to make sure they'd never regretted the decision, and he had no idea if he'd succeeded or not.

Audrey hadn't wanted him either. She'd only been pregnant, backed into a corner. She'd left him the second he'd served her purposes.

And Hope. She hadn't wanted him, really. She'd just wanted a husband and a family. Apparently they hadn't lived up to her expectations.

It was enough to make a man punch a wall.

Zoe grabbed his arm, her blue eyes piercing his. "Come on, Brady . . . Don't give up. Go after your wife."

He jerked away. "You know what, Zoe? Hope's not the only one with wounds. Maybe this just makes me selfish, but . . ." He swallowed back the knot of emotion clogging his throat. "For once in my life I want someone to choose *me*. Not drugs. Not freedom. And not some stupid fantasy. *Me*."

Her face fell, her eyes glossed over. "Oh, Brady."

He jerked his gaze from the pity in her eyes and shouldered the diaper bag. The backs of his eyes burned, and a boulder was lodged in his throat. He was finished talking about this.

"I gotta go." He grabbed the baby carrier and took the ball from Zoe. He made it all the way to his car before she took his arm, stopping him.

He drilled her with a look. "What now?"

But she didn't back down. Not Zoe. She waited a long minute, making sure she had his full attention. "I think she's going through something, Brady. More than she's ready to admit to. I'm worried about her mental health."

"Phfft. She's practically a mental health professional."

"Right?" Zoe took the ball and diaper bag from him, set them in his passenger seat, then closed the door. "Well, you know what they say about doctors, Brady . . . They always make the worst patients."

He was still thinking about Zoe's parting words as he made his way back to his quiet house.

CHAPTER THIRTY-NINE

Hope adjusted her headphones and addressed Laura, a recently divorced middle-aged woman with an abusive past. "It sounds as if you're learning to stand on your own, Laura, so that's good."

"But it's been two years since my divorce," the caller said. "And I keep finding myself with the wrong kind of men. I get in too deep, too fast, only to discover they're just like my ex-husband. What's wrong with me?"

Hope could hear the tears in her voice, and her heart went out to the woman.

"There's nothing wrong with you, Laura. You're in a place so many women find themselves. In fact, you're helping other women right now just by speaking out. You're their voice. Sometimes issues from childhood are so deep they require a little digging. A little unpacking. Some good counseling can help you get to the bottom of issues and keep you from making the same mistakes over again. This is not a hopeless situation." She glanced at the clock.

"Can you stay on the line, Laura? I'd like to give you a couple of resources. And if you're listening, you'll find those resources on our website. The lines are still open, and we have time for one more call. We'll be right back after this break." Hope cut to a commercial and spoke privately with Laura, giving her the numbers.

When she got off the phone she took a sip of her coffee, thinking about the woman. It didn't escape Hope that she'd just recommended something she wasn't even willing to do herself. How could she convince others to be brave enough to face their pasts when she didn't have the courage to do it herself?

Living with Hope. What a joke. She was such a hypocrite.

The realization only depressed her further. It was Friday, and she had nothing to look forward to. Just another long, lonely weekend. She hadn't heard from Brady since last Friday, and who could blame him? She'd been unresponsive every time he'd called or texted.

Sammy had turned eleven months last week, and she had no idea if he'd starting cruising the furniture or if he'd said his first word. Did he miss her? Cry for her? She missed him so much. Sometimes her arms ached for the solid weight of him. She longed to rub her cheek against his and inhale his sweet baby scent. She shut down the thoughts before tears could form.

Was she just supposed to live with this aching loss? The thought of it was like a brick on her chest. So heavy, so hopeless. At least the nightmares and panic attacks were gone. It was probably the medication, but she had no way of knowing for sure since she hadn't been back home to test the theory. She wasn't drowsy anymore. But that also meant she'd lost her favorite escape; she could no longer sleep away her weekends.

The studio door opened and Leo entered. His thick hair was plastered to his head, and his button-down clung to his skinny frame. He wiped a hand over his bushy beard. "Cats and dogs out there, man."

"Thanks for the warning." Hope handed him some napkins so he didn't drip all over the equipment.

"Good show tonight," he said after he'd settled in front of his computer. "I don't know how you come up with all that stuff. I can't even get my own life together half the time."

If only he knew. "Thanks."

The last commercial came to an end, and Hope shook off her lingering sadness. She leaned into the mic and injected some energy into her voice. "You're listening to *Living with Hope*, and we have time for one more quick call." She pushed a button. "Hi there, you're on the air with Hope . . ."

The line was open but nobody spoke.

"Go ahead, caller," she said. "You're on the air."

"Um . . . I'm here. Hi."

Something about that voice.

Hope's eyes narrowed on the screen in front of

her. "Hi there. Thanks for calling in. Tell us your first name please."

Another pause, then, "This is Brady."

Her breath caught in her lungs. She blinked. What was he doing? What could he want? Her heart hammered in her chest so loud she feared the mic would pick it up. She felt Leo's eyes on her and realized several seconds of dead air had passed.

"Go ahead with your question, Brady." Her voice was somehow strong and steady.

"I was wondering if you could . . ." The scrape of his voice made a shiver pass down her arms.

When he didn't finish, she prompted him. "You were wondering if I could . . ."

He cleared his throat. She could imagine him right now, standing in their living room, pacing the floor, his phone to his ear. Sammy sleeping peacefully upstairs.

"I want to know . . . How can I get my wife back?"

His question drove the air from her lungs. Made her heart squeeze tight. She closed her eyes against the pain. "I-I guess that depends on why she left."

He gave a wry laugh that made her picture his rueful smile. "I'm pretty sure that had something to do with me. I seem to have a way of chasing off women. I'm not too good at this marriage stuff, I guess."

380

She pressed her palm against the ache in her chest. "I'm sure that's not true, Brady."

"She's everything I ever wanted. I love her, and I want her back. I'll do anything. Just tell me what to do."

She blinked against the sting in her eyes. She couldn't breathe. Words failed her. For once she didn't know what to say. Dead air filled the studio, and still she had nothing.

Leo nudged her.

"Um, maybe . . . maybe she just needs a little time. A little space." She palmed the back of her neck, suddenly unsure if that was even what she wanted anymore.

"So . . . you think there's still hope, then?" He sounded so sad. So dejected. And she'd done that to him.

Leo pointed to the clock, ticking off seconds. She was running out of time.

"There's always hope, Brady," she said huskily. She swallowed against the lump in her throat and tried to project a strength she didn't feel. "I'm afraid that's all we have time for tonight. Thanks for listening to *Living with Hope*." She queued the program's outro music. "Leo the Lion is up next."

When the outro finished, she queued the top-of-the-hour ID. Her hands shook as she removed her headphones and unplugged them.

Oh my gosh. He'd actually called into her

show. He'd all but begged her to come back to him, live, on the air. His voice rang in her ears. *She's everything I ever wanted. I love her, and I want her back. I'll do anything.*

The burn built behind her eyes, and the knot in her throat swelled. She had to go. She stood and started gathering her things.

"Hey, you okay?" Leo said, frowning at her hand.

She realized she'd just picked up his travel mug instead of hers. "Yeah. Sorry." She traded mugs. "I'll see you tomorrow."

"Now up," Leo said into the mic, still watching her. "A little Stevie Nicks, followed by Chicago."

Hope's legs shook as she fled the studio. The halls were empty, the offices dark. She couldn't hold it back any longer. A sob rose in her throat, and tears flowed down her face.

She thought of her little empty apartment and knew she couldn't go back there tonight. Oh, how she wanted to see him. How she wanted to fall into his arms right now. She was so stupid. She'd given him up because she was afraid of losing him. And she was losing him by turning her back on him. She was miserable, and the misery was self-inflicted.

Worse, she'd hurt Brady too. Just the defeated sound of his voice had broken her heart. To say nothing of the way he blamed himself. None of this was his fault. None of it.

Well, she was finally done fighting. She couldn't live without him anymore. She was a hopeless mess. What else could she do but take her own advice? All she needed was a little courage. She'd dig through those memories and come to grips with her fear.

If he could put his heart on the line like that, surely she could find the strength to face her issues. Maybe medication could alleviate her symptoms, but the root of her problem was still there. It wouldn't go away on its own. She had to face this once and for all.

She had to trust God with this. With her future. It might not be easy. But even if hard times came, God would get her through them just as He had when she'd lost Aaron.

Now that she'd made up her mind, she couldn't get home soon enough. She bypassed the sluggish elevator in favor of the stairwell. Her footsteps echoed in the enclosed space, her flats squeaking on the clean, polished floor. She'd been wrong. She'd been a coward. But she'd make it up to him if only he'd have her back.

At the bottom of the stairs she burst through the doors and out into the rain. She ducked her head against the onslaught and didn't look up until she reached the corner. She was looking both ways when she saw him.

He was standing across the way, under a street-lamp. He stared back at her, his hands tucked into his front pockets, his shoulders hunched against the rain.

Brady. Her heart gave a heavy sigh.

Of their own volition, her feet moved toward him. She couldn't tear her eyes from the intensity on his face. She was halfway across the street when she broke into a run.

He held his arms out to her, and she fell into him. He wrapped her up in his arms, good and tight, lifting her off the ground.

"Oh, Brady." Everything broke loose. She sobbed against his chest. "I'm sorry. I'm so sorry. It's not you. You're perfect. You're wonderful. It's all me. I'm a mess."

"Shhh . . . ," he said against her temple. "It's okay, baby. It's okay."

But it wasn't. She couldn't get hold of herself. She'd been hurting so bad, but she'd hurt him too, and that was so much worse. She couldn't forget the pain in his voice as he'd sought her help on the air. He'd done nothing to deserve this. Only loved her.

Rain fell down her face, mingling with her tears. He gently stroked her back, murmuring words of comfort. But that only made her ache worse. How could he be so tender with her after she'd been so careless with his heart?

"Enough," he said softly a while later. He set her back on her feet, took her face in his palms, and brushed the dampness with his thumbs.

"That's enough, honey. No more sadness. No more tears. I love you. We're going to get through this."

She grabbed his wrists, her vision going blurry. "Oh, Brady, I'm such a mess. You don't even know." It was deep inside where nobody could see.

He looked at her with those soulful eyes, his lashes spiky with rain or tears. "Then talk to me. Tell me everything. I'm a bit of a mess too, you know, but we're in this together, Hope. I'm not going anywhere."

It was time to come clean. Time to admit her weaknesses. He would love her regardless. She knew it with a surety that bolstered her strength.

"Come on," he said. "Let's get you out of the rain."

Inside the car he turned the engine over and cranked up the heat. He wrapped her in a baby blanket he found behind the seat and settled her in the warmth of his arms.

The rain pounded the roof, and rivulets of water trickled down the windshield. Once she started talking she couldn't seem to stop. She told him about the fear. The nightmares, the panic attacks. The medication and side effects.

She tried to explain how desperately afraid she'd become of losing him the way she'd lost Aaron. She admitted her close calls with Sam, and her overwhelming fear that she'd cause him harm—how that had only compounded her panic.

"Oh, baby." He listened. He held her. He murmured sympathetically and dried an unending stream of tears. He didn't patronize her with advice or suggestions, and she loved him for that. Most of all . . . she just loved him.

She suddenly realized she'd never even said the words. She was finally warm, and the shivering had stopped. He'd been holding her quietly for several minutes, waiting patiently for her to continue. But there was only one thing left to say.

She pulled from his embrace and looked up into eyes that promised her forever. "I love you, Brady. I love you so much. I don't ever want to lose you."

"I'm right here, honey. And I love you too. So much." He brushed her lips with his, once. Twice. Then he deepened the kiss, warming her from the inside out.

She leaned into him, never wanting it to end. Oh, how she'd missed this. Missed him. There were hard times ahead for sure, but he'd be there. That's who Brady was. Strong and steady.

They'd started with only friendship, but a true and abiding love had grown from there. *Friendship on fire.* She'd heard the phrase but had never really understood it until now.

A short while later the windows were steamed over, and a pit stop at her apartment was tempting. But no. She wanted her boy. She wanted them all together under the same roof. The way it was supposed to be.

"Let's go home," she said against his lips.

He drew back, his eyes searching hers. "Are you sure? I can stay—I'm sure Zoe will keep Sam for the weekend."

Hope huffed a laugh. "Oh, no way am I waiting another day to get my hands on my little punkin. I've missed him so much."

His mouth curved into a grin. And she could just about drown in the soulful eyes that stared back at her. Oh yeah. She could see herself looking into those eyes for many years to come. Could see herself seeking and finding security in the strength of his embrace. Could see another little punkin or princess in their future if Brady was game. She hoped he was game.

He brushed his thumb over her cheek. His eyes pierced hers, making her heart roll over.

"Let's go home," he said.

EPILOGUE

Hope braked at the stoplight in the heart of Copper Creek. She was supposed to be heading toward Atlanta right now, but she had to see Brady. She couldn't wait to share her news.

She pulled a tissue from her purse and gave a hearty blow. It had been another rough counseling session with her therapist, a colleague her friend Brianna had recommended. There was nothing easy about digging up your most painful memories, but Hope was making headway, having breakthroughs.

Today she'd had a breakthrough of a different sort. The light turned green, and she accelerated past the brick storefronts and colorful canopies jutting out over the sidewalks.

January had brought colder temperatures and a bit of snow. But the morning sun had already melted it away. She and Brady had made it through the rushed holidays and Sam's first birthday. Their little guy was walking now and into everything. Climbing on furniture, putting everything into his mouth, and generally scaring the daylights out of both of them. His first word was neither *Mama* nor *Dada*, but *no*. He used it on every occasion.

Hope was still working at WKPC through the

week and traveling home on the weekends. It was getting to be a little much. She missed her little family during the week—especially when Sam had visitation with the Parkers on the weekend. Or when she missed a milestone. She'd been in Atlanta when he took his first steps.

They'd had long discussions about her job at the station, but Brady didn't want her to give up something she loved so much. He was amazing that way.

A few minutes later she turned down the lane that led to his garage, gravel popping under her tires. Her heart thudded in excitement. In anticipation of seeing him. She had to leave soon for Atlanta, but they had a bit of time.

When she reached the barn she braked, and he emerged from the structure, wiping his greasy hands on a dirty rag. A frown pulled his brows low over his eyes as she got out of her car.

"What's wrong?" he asked. When they'd parted this morning, he hadn't expected to see her until late Friday night.

"Not a single thing."

"Why'd you come back?" His gaze sharpened on her, and his frown deepened. "You've been crying."

He usually didn't have to witness the aftermath of her Monday-morning appointments. For that she was grateful. Right now he looked like he wanted to shake her counselor.

She waved away his concern. "It's just your normal therapy tears. You got a minute?"

"Of course." When she reached him he put his arms around her. "All the time you need. You want to go in the house? Have a cup of coffee?"

"No, I can't stay that long." She leaned back in his arms, grasping his biceps, seeking his eyes. "Brady . . . I know what I want to do. I want to counsel people—like my therapist does. Not in one-hour radio segments. Not five or ten minutes with an anonymous caller. I want to counsel all day long. Give people real help. Real hope."

His eyes smiled just before the corners of his lips ticked up. "Sweetheart. That's wonderful."

She gave her head a fervent shake. "Before you jump on board, you should know . . . It'll mean more school. I'll need my doctorate, and after that comes a bunch of supervised hours of practice and an exam that'll probably have me on the crazy train for months."

He gave a mirthful smile, his eyes glinting with amusement. "I say, all aboard."

"I don't know if you know what you're signing up for here. This could take a long time, Brady. We need to give it some thought. It'll have a big impact on all of us."

He gave her a long, steady look. "I don't need to think about it. You'll make a wonderful counselor, Hope. You have such a big heart. And who knows better than you the kind of courage it takes to seek help?"

A shiver ran through her at his insight. She loved him for thinking of that.

"My only concern is, how are you going to fit that into your already busy schedule? Have you considered that?"

"Well . . . yes. That's another thing. I could take classes in Atlanta during the week. It would take a while to get through them with a full-time job, though. Or . . ." She bit her lip, giving him a sheepish look.

He searched her eyes, hope gleaming there. "Or . . ."

"Do you think we could make it on one income again, Brady? If I quit the station I could get my degree a lot faster. I could always go back to working at the Rusty Nail on weekends—and I'd promise to keep my shoe fetish under control."

A wide grin split his face, and he tightened his arms around her. "You don't need to work weekends if you don't want to. We'll do just fine. I'm all for having you home again. I miss you when you're gone, Hope."

"Are you sure? Because going down to one income, giving up my paycheck will be a huge—"

He placed a finger over her mouth and gave her a pointed look. "Blessing."

She tilted her head and studied him. He was

a beautiful man, inside and out. He was so supportive. He'd hardly complained about all her traveling even though she knew it placed a big burden on him.

She grabbed his finger, kissing it. "You're pretty wonderful, you know that?"

His countenance grew serious. "I only have one serious reservation about this new plan of yours."

If it wasn't the money, she had no idea what the holdback was. She shook her head. "What is it?"

His eyes tightened in a wince. "Am I going to have to call you Dr. Collins? Because I'm not sure I could do that."

She quirked a saucy brow. "Of course not. Dr. Hope will do just fine."

A chuckle broke loose, low and delicious, and his gaze roved over her face like he loved her or something. "I think I can manage that."

"Oh yeah?" She pressed closer, delighting at how quickly all amusement slid from his face. When she had his full attention she laid a long, slow kiss on him.

By the time Hope pulled away her lungs were empty, but her heart was full to the brim. She took him in, reveling in his adoring gaze, in the sweet fall of his breath on her lips. She didn't know what she'd done to deserve his love, but she was going to make sure he didn't regret giving it.

"You know what, Collins?" she whispered, her eyes piercing his. "You've gone and made all my dreams come true."

His eyes softened, his lips turning up just an instant before he claimed her mouth again, his kiss filled with promises she knew he would keep.

DISCUSSION QUESTIONS

1. Who was your favorite character? Why?
2. What was your favorite scene in the book? Why?
3. How did Hope's loss of her high school sweetheart affect her ability to love again? Do you think such a reaction is realistic? Have you ever been afraid to love someone?
4. Back in high school Hope planned her own future around Aaron's. How were you feeling when she agreed to marry Brady, even though she thought she'd have to give up her dream job? Have you ever made such a choice?
5. Discuss the role of faith when dealing with issues of fear. Do you struggle with fear? How have you overcome it?
6. When Hope realized she'd fallen in love with Brady, she began to deal with severe anxiety. She knew she needed therapy but was reluctant to dig up her painful past. Have you ever known you needed help and lacked the courage to seek it? What advice would you give someone in that situation?
7. Do you think Brady treated April, his biological mother, fairly? Do you think he should've been more or less accepting of her when she returned to town?

8. Brady never quite felt like he belonged in the family that adopted him. Why do you think that is? Do you think his adoptive family contributed to that? Do you think his biological mom's disruption in his life played a role? Have you ever felt as if you didn't quite belong?

9. Brady felt as if he'd been deserted by all the women in his life. Have you ever felt abandoned? How did it affect you?

10. If you could call in to Hope's radio program, Living with Hope, what question would you ask her? If you could host your own radio program, what would the subject be and what would you call it?

Acknowledgments

Writing a book is a team effort, and I'm so grateful for the fabulous team at HarperCollins Christian Fiction, led by publisher Amanda Bostic: Jocelyn Bailey, Matt Bray, Kimberly Carlton, Allison Carter, Paul Fisher, Kristen Golden, Kayleigh Hines, Jodi Hughes, Karli Jackson, Becky Monds, and Kristen Ingebretson.

Thanks especially to my editor, Karli Jackson, for her insight and inspiration. I'm infinitely grateful to editor LB Norton, who saves me from countless errors and always makes me look so much better than I am.

I owe a huge debt of gratitude to Christopher A. Flowers, Esq., of Smith and Flowers Law, P.C. He generously answered my numerous—and I do mean numerous—questions about family law in Georgia and was kind enough to read the court scenes for accuracy. Thank you also to Mandy Fehman and DJ Melissa Montana of Star 88.3 for all your help with the radio aspects of the story. Any errors that made it to print are mine alone.

Author Colleen Coble is my first reader. Thank you, friend! Writing wouldn't be nearly as much fun without you!

I'm grateful to my agent, Karen Solem, who's able to somehow make sense of the legal garble of contracts and, even more amazing, help me understand it.

Kevin, my husband of twenty-nine years, has been a wonderful support. Thank you, honey! I'm so glad to be doing life with you. To my kiddos, Justin, Hannah, Chad, and Trevor: You make life an adventure! It's so fun watching you step boldly into adulthood. Love you all!

Lastly, thank you, friend, for letting me share this story with you. I wouldn't be doing this without you! I enjoy connecting with friends on my Facebook page, www.facebook.com/author denisehunter. Please pop over and say hello. Visit my website at the link www.DeniseHunterBooks. com or just drop me a note at Deniseahunter@ comcast.net. I'd love to hear from you!

ABOUT THE AUTHOR

Denise Hunter is the internationally published bestselling author of more than thirty books, including *A December Bride* and *The Convenient Groom*, which have been adapted into original Hallmark Channel movies. She has won The Holt Medallion Award, The Reader's Choice Award, The Carol Award, and the The Foreword Book of the Year Award and is a RITA finalist. When Denise isn't orchestrating love lives on the written page, she enjoys traveling with her family, drinking green tea, and playing drums. Denise makes her home in Indiana, where she and her husband are currently enjoying an empty nest.

DeniseHunterBooks.com
Facebook: authordenisehunter
Twitter: @DeniseAHunter

Books are
produced in the
United States
using U.S.-based
materials

Books are printed
using a revolutionary
new process called
THINKtech™ that
lowers energy usage
by 70% and increases
overall quality

Books are
durable and
flexible
because of
Smyth-sewing

Paper is
sourced using
environmentally
responsible
foresting methods
and the
paper is acid-free

Center Point Large Print
600 Brooks Road / PO Box 1
Thorndike, ME 04986-0001 USA

(207) 568-3717

US & Canada:
1 800 929-9108
www.centerpointlargeprint.com